A Deadly

Feast

Also available by Lucy Burdette

Key West Food Critic Mysteries

The Key Lime Crime

A Deadly Feast

Death on the Menu

An Appetite for Murder

Death in Four Courses

Topped Chef

Murder with Ganache

Death with All the Trimmings

Fatal Reservations

Killer Takeout

A Deadly Feast

A KEY WEST FOOD CRITIC MYSTERY

Lucy Burdette

CROOKED LANE

NEW YORK

Copyright © 2019 by Roberta Isleib

All rights reserved.

Published in the United States by Crooked Lane Books, an imprint of The Quick Brown Fox & Company LLC.

Crooked Lane Books and its logo are trademarks of The Quick Brown Fox & Company LLC.

Library of Congress Catalog-in-Publication data available upon request.

ISBN (mass market): 978-1-64385-352-9
ISBN (hardcover): 978-1-68331-969-6
ISBN (ePub): 978-1-68331-970-2
ISBN (ePDF): 978-1-68331-971-9

Cover illustration by Griesbach/Martucci
Book design by Jennifer Canzone

Printed in the United States.

www.crookedlanebooks.com

Crooked Lane Books
34 West 27th St., 10th Floor
New York, NY 10001

Mass market Edition: October 2020
Hardcover Edition: May 2019

10 9 8 7 6 5 4 3 2 1

For my grandmother,
Mary Lucille Burdette

Chapter One

Pounding your table cloths on a rock in the river isn't going to make it a better restaurant, you know? Get a linen service and call it a day.
—Michelle Wildgen, *Bread and Butter*

Sometimes it's useful and, I might even say, absolutely necessary to be a control freak. But sometimes letting go of your death grip on life can result in a beautiful outcome. I was learning the truth of that second maxim during the period I'd been engaged to marry the love of my life, Detective Nathan Bransford. He, after all, had been the one to buy the houseboat next to my roommate Miss Gloria's place. And this wasn't because he loved the idea of living in a floating trailer—he hates Houseboat Row, but he loves me, Hayley Snow. And he could see how much it mattered that I stay close to eighty-plus-year-old Miss Gloria, so she could remain in Key West without her sons wigging out. This was a gesture so extravagant, thoughtful, and downright sweet that it brought me and my women friends and relations to tears.

Exhibit 1: Nathan releasing death grip = beautiful outcome.

The houseboat renovation had started out just fine, with the contractor ripping out the appliances in the old kitchen and the fixtures in the bathroom, and a definite schedule in place to begin work on the rest of the demolition. But then Hurricane Irma blasted through in mid-September, and all bets were off. Every working stiff on the Keys and more from Miami and even further up the mainland were instantly absorbed in hurricane cleanup.

Each time Nathan and I showed up for consultations and progress reports, the contractor canceled, and the tension between us escalated. And finally last Wednesday, it had all blown up into the biggest fight of our relationship. Afterward, I couldn't have said exactly what the fight was about, though I was definitely stressed by my to-do list: my work as the food critic for the Key West style magazine, *Key Zest*, those ill-fated plans for the renovation of the houseboat next door, and the last-minute details of my marriage to Nathan. Truth be told, my life felt a bit like a stew made by a novice chef who'd strayed from the master recipe and begun throwing in random ingredients.

Miss Gloria, with a long and happy marriage under her belt, suggested the argument might have been fed by a wellspring of anxiety about our upcoming wedding. Not the details so much as the whole idea of "'til death do us part." Every bridal couple promises that, but only half of them make it to the finish line. I didn't want to be one of the losers.

The fight started out innocently enough, with me soliciting his opinion.

Hayley: "Do you think we should put the double ovens against the far wall so the sink and counter will be open to the living area?"

Although, looking back, this was a rhetorical question. Of course the ovens should go against the wall so they didn't block the view or trap the chef. Truth of it was, I wanted him to feel involved, but I also wanted him to agree with what I'd already silently decided.

Nathan, with a small frown: "Will you actually use two ovens, or is that a fad?"

Hayley: "How long have you known me? And how many of my baked goods have you eaten?"

After that exchange, to be brutally honest, things slid downhill fast and ugly. We stormed off to our respective corners and sulked for a day until I realized I'd started it and apologized by text. He was quick to accept half the blame.

Enlisting my mother's help to meet with the contractor to talk over my houseboat-to-be's kitchen renovation had been Nathan's brilliant idea. She and I had an appointment this afternoon at three PM, to be followed by Nathan's and my final marriage counseling appointment at five. Neither of us wanted to show up at that second appointment so fresh from a second fight that the officiant counseled us to split up.

Exhibit 2: Releasing death grip again = everybody happy.

Meanwhile, the seafood walking tour I was taking, which had started at 10:30, was edging into the third hour. (I know, who eats shrimp at 10:30 in the morning? But my clever friend and our tour guide, Analise Smith, had maneuvered around this awkward pairing by scheduling the dessert stop first. And what soul wouldn't be tempted by key lime pie in the morning?) My energy was starting to wane a bit, but maybe the beer tasting at the final stop would give me a boost. Though frankly, when had a glass of beer increased anyone's energy? Never. More likely it would point me directly in the direction of a nap. Which I tried to convince myself would give my brain a chance to catch up with my stomach.

The truth was, I couldn't afford to take the time. I needed to do my sleeping at night in an orderly way, during the hours I'd allotted. And leaving the tour early wasn't an option either. A piece on the venues we were visiting was my major contribution to this week's issue of *Key Zest*.

Right after my appointment with the contractor, Nathan and I were meeting at five with my good friend and his colleague at the police department, Steve Torrence, who would be officiating at our wedding. Torrence had been an ordained minister before attending the police academy and now had a thriving wedding officiant business on the side. That meeting absolutely couldn't be delegated to my mother.

Along with the four other foodie tourists, I followed our guide Analise into the Waterfront

Brewery, which overlooked the historic Key West seaport. We had already made five stops, enjoying the authentic key lime pie in a small mason jar from Chef Martha at Isle Cook Key West, jalapeño- and cilantro-sprinkled fish tacos prepared in Garbo's Grill's adorable Airstream trailer, the richest lobster macaroni I'd ever tasted from Bagatelle, conch salad and smoked fish dip—island standards and always favorites at Lagerhead's Beach Grill—and seawater-fresh Key West pink shrimp at the Eaton Street Seafood Market.

Analise got us settled on wooden stools at a high round table and then thanked the group for coming on the tour. "My brother is getting married tonight and my to-do list is a mile long." She winked at me. "Seems to be a big season for weddings. So I'll excuse myself here. Thanks again for joining us. If you had a great time, please consider leaving a review on TripAdvisor." She shook hands with each of them, gave me a quick hug, and headed out through the wide-open doors to the docks.

Once I'd finished writing down my thoughts and filling in some notes from the other stops on the tour, I scrolled through all those scribbles, trying to settle on what my angle would be for this piece. When nothing brilliant came to mind, I relaxed for a couple of minutes, observing my fellow diners.

The group consisted of one couple, plus another man and woman who hadn't said much to each other or the rest of us, so I assumed they were unrelated. Or if they had come together, maybe things had gone super-sour between them and now they weren't speaking to each other. That was my nervous bride-mind talking. Based on their tans and casual cloth-ing, I guessed them to be local residents.

The couple did not pass the test my roommate and I had used to amuse ourselves back in college: do these two people "go together," and how did they meet? Both perhaps in their late forties, the woman was dressed in slightly upscale tourist attire, linen capris and a flowing white shirt, while the man wore a black leather vest, chains on his belt, boots with multiple zippers, and well-worn jeans with holes at the knees that any stylish teen might have drooled over. He had a dark beard and sunglasses. Physically, they were not a match. But I guessed from the wed-ding rings that they were married, and from the way they held hands and shared food that they were devoted to each other. Maybe her more than him. And that brought my next thought—was it better to be the adored, or the adoring? These kinds of obser-vations were especially interesting to me these days, with my marriage to Nathan approaching quickly.

"You all live here, right?" asked the wife of the couple to the rest of us. "Where would you go if you had one night left to eat out?"

"Audrey," said her husband, a little shortly, "they don't want to talk about food right now. We're all stuffed to the gills."

To be kind, I said, "If you look on the back of the food tour brochure, they have a nice list of local restaurants. All of my favorites are there."

"But which is your true favorite?" she asked. "I never know whether to trust promotional material. I worked for the Minnesota Development Council, and we would have touted anything local as delicious. If they paid their dues, they were delicious."

The other woman—I thought she had introduced herself as Jean or Jan—piped up: "Partly it depends on what you're in the mood for. And how hungry you are. You can order Key West pink shrimp anywhere on this island, and it's almost always good. And how important is a view, and do you want a quiet, romantic atmosphere, or are you a little tired of each other and happy to join the party?"

The two men laughed. I zoned out a little on the conversation because she had just given me an idea for my article's opening. I would tell readers that sometimes you don't have enough days to sample every restaurant on your list. Food tours are a good way to get an overview of island food, exactly the way I'd recommended that first-time visitors take the conch train tour around the island. OK, the idea was rough and not completely compelling, but I would polish it before I turned it in.

Audrey's voice was getting a little louder, and her face grew flushed as she leaned toward the second man and began to grill him. "Are you local here? Where would you go to dinner? Do you have a favorite restaurant?"

He angled himself away from her like a hermit crab retreating; she was definitely starting to get on his nerves. She pressed him harder, pelting him with questions until he finally answered.

"You can't tell much by the restaurant's name, because the chef—and probably he's the only one in the place with a creative spark—could have quit the day before and then everything changes. It's not the restaurant that matters, it's who's working in the kitchen."

"But do you read Yelp reviews? Or OpenTable? Often they're up-to-date, so you get to hear if anyone had a bad meal lately. I hate not knowing what to choose. We have only one night left and it's already freezing in Minneapolis, so I don't want to waste a minute."

Thankfully, a cheerful waitress broke the woman's escalating interrogation by delivering a flight of beer glasses to each of us. "These three will provide you tastes of the beer we brew right here on the premises."

I took sips of each and scribbled my preferences and reactions in my phone. I especially enjoyed the Crazy Lady blonde ale made with local honey, while the others preferred the more hoppy Lazy Way toasted IPA and the Island Life lager. Several televisions hung above the bar, blaring footage of sports events—hockey, basketball, and football—none of which I particularly cared about. My anxiety about my own to-do list was gathering steam. Time to nip into the restroom, then say good-bye to the group. I was unlikely to see any of them again, so I didn't have to worry about seeming rude.

After I'd washed my hands and reapplied lip gloss in the ladies' room, I wended my way through the tall tables back to where the group sat. When I was only yards away, Audrey slumped. In slow motion, she slid down the rungs of her stool and collapsed in a heap, clutching her head.

"What's wrong? What happened?" I asked, running up to her.

She let out a low moan.

The man wearing the chains and the ratty jeans dropped to the floor next to his wife. "Audrey, Audrey can you hear me?" He shook her shoulder, and her head lolled over to the right and hit the wood floor with a disturbing *thunk*.

"Is she ill?" the other woman asked.

"Have you ever seen this before?" I asked her husband, hoping vaguely that she had low blood sugar or some other easily fixed ailment. I'd had a diabetic girlfriend in college who carried honey sticks in case of an emergency. Though how could anyone have low blood sugar after what we'd eaten?

"Never!" the man said.

"Then we need an ambulance." I had my phone out and my thumb hitting 911 before I finished the sentence.

Chapter Two

Good baking, I've been told, comes from love, and treacly as that sounds, I find some truth in it. Good baking means being able to roll with setbacks and mistakes and ovens that for some reason run twenty degrees hot but only on Sundays, a metaphor so aligned with loving someone that it feels almost too obvious.

—Geraldine DeRuiter, "I Made the Pizza Cinnamon Rolls From Mario Batali's Sexual Misconduct Apology Letter," Everywhereist.com

After the paramedics—who double as firefighters in this town—had attended to Audrey, taking her vital signs and placing an oxygen mask over her mouth and nose, they loaded her onto a stretcher and rolled her out to a waiting ambulance. I trotted the two blocks over to Southard Street, retrieved my scooter from behind the *Key Zest* office, and started home. What a dreadful way to end a beautiful day. I hoped she would have a speedy recovery. I texted Analise to let her know that one of her customers had taken ill and suggest that she might want to call the hospital later to see if they'd give her any information.

I was relieved not to be responsible for follow-up, though the relief was mixed with guilt. When I'd mentioned to Nathan that I'd been feeling paranoid lately about all the bad luck that seemed to be happening around me, he'd suggested that I have a tendency to troll for trouble. He was smiling when he said it, but the comment still stung. This time, it was hard to see how the disturbing incident could be pinned on me.

When I reached our houseboat on Tarpon Pier, I found the cats, my gray tiger Evinrude and Miss Gloria's black Sparky, stalking a small lizard on the deck. Miss Gloria was on the telephone. She waved at me and smiled, pointing at her phone to indicate an important conversation in progress. I glanced over at the houseboat next door—Nathan's boat now—ever hopeful that the latest in a series of contractors might have made an appearance and maybe actually gotten something done. But no such luck. The lights were out, and piles of mildewed shag carpet and random pieces of termite-infested wood remained on the deck. I dropped my backpack next to my lounge chair and headed inside to grab a glass of water.

Miss Gloria had been clucking and exclaiming during the whole phone conversation. It was hard to tell who was in trouble and in what way, but I'd hear soon enough.

Miss Gloria hung up and ran her fingers through her white hair until it stood up in little whipped-cream peaks. "You're not going to believe this one," she said.

"Do tell." I grinned. She'd tell me anyway, even if I didn't ask.

"You know how I'm supposed to cover the nine thirty–to–eleven thirty shift tomorrow at the Friends of the Library book sale, right?" The Friends of the Library organization raises funds to support the Key West Library, and Miss Gloria is a stalwart volunteer.

"Right," I said. "You and Mrs. Dubisson sit at the front table near the bake sale and sample all the cookies. You've got the winning record for selling canvas Friends' totes and hard-cover mysteries to customers who thought they were done shopping."

She looked delighted. She loves when people pay attention to what she's told them—and honestly, who doesn't? "That's it. But now, Marsha—she's the president of the Friends' board of directors—called, and they're desperate for help setting up at seven thirty AM because the stomach flu appears to have felled half our volunteer force." She shook her head. "Old folks. Sometimes they are just too fragile to rely on."

I looked up from my phone to see if she was kidding. People who don't know my roommate well tend to dismiss her as a frail elderly woman. Before Miss Gloria roared into my life with more energy than most of my peers, I would have thought that too. Now she was positively vibrating and grinning like a monkey.

"It's not only the stomach flu—some of the committee members are fighting about shifts. No one wants to get up early enough to take the crack-of-dawn assignment. So I told her I would get there early, of course." A guilty look crept over her face. "And I told her you would come too and that you were young and strong, and not afraid to work alongside the prisoners."

Trusted inmates at the Stock Island jail, called trusties, were allowed to assist in community service projects such as the book sale setup. I had absolutely no problem with that. At this point, I wasn't really listening to the details of who was nervous or mad at whom; I was studying my tortured list and trying to figure out how I could say no to my darling roommate rather than fill the only empty slot in tomorrow's calendar. The slot during which I was planning two extra hours of luxurious and desperately needed sleep.

I glanced up at her hopeful face again. The *no* forming in my head stood no chance.

"How about an hour; will that help?"

She heaved a great sigh of relief and nodded vigorously. "So if we buzz up to the library at seven thirty, you'll be finished by eight thirty, and then you can get on with your day."

My phone sang out and Analise's name popped up on the screen. I suspected this meant trouble, because it wasn't a text. None of my friends call anymore, because everyone in my generation knows that nobody wants to talk on the phone.

"I just got back from the hospital," she said, her voice grim. "My customer isn't doing well, to put it mildly. Her pulse and blood pressure shot sky-high, and now she seems to be in major organ failure. The family's been called in."

"That is absolutely horrible," I said. "Devastating in every way. I'm so sorry. And I'm especially sad for her husband. They seemed devoted to each other, didn't they?" As a bride-to-be, the idea of losing one's spouse hit me hard, especially because it hadn't been easy to find the right guy in the first place. "Did they find out what's wrong?"

"Well, it's bad news all the way around. They think she had a stroke, but they haven't ruled out the possibility that it's related to some type of food poisoning. If she dies, not only does that ruin that poor woman's life—and her family's—it decimates my business, and it could ruin the reputation of every restaurant we visited."

"Don't panic until they find out what actually happened," I said, my own stomach churning sour at the very mention of food poisoning. "Maybe she had a food allergy she didn't tell you about, or a bee stung her—there are lots of reasonable possibilities that would have nothing to do with you." Although why those would cause a stroke, I had no idea. I was just trying to make my friend feel better at this point. "And maybe she'll recover, right? Hope is always a good option."

"I'm not feeling hopeful," she said. "In fact, I'm on the way to the police station right now so they can ask me questions about where we were and what we ate and everything else under the sun. Apparently one of the possibilities is food tampering. Though everyone assures me that's unlikely." She paused. "I hate to ask, I know you're so busy . . ."

I assumed she was wondering if I minded contacting one of my cop friends. Or Nathan. Which I didn't really want to do, because it would appear meddlesome and probably not glean any more information than what she would get during her visit.

"Would you mind terribly checking in with Nathan? He might tell you something they'd never tell me."

I gnawed on my lower lip. She would certainly help me out if I was the one in trouble.

"Call me when you finish with your interview. Maybe it'll all be sorted out by then, fingers crossed." I held up my hand with the digits crossed, and Miss Gloria held her arthritic fingers up, too. "If you get the sense they're not telling you anything but they seem to suspect something serious, I'll do a little poking around. Best case of all, this poor woman rallies and it can all be laid to rest."

Chapter Three

My ex wife ruined blondes for me—like getting food poisoning after eating shrimp. You never want shellfish again.
—Roberta Isleib, *Deadly Advice*

Nathan texted me right before my mother was scheduled to arrive at our boat.

So sorry. There's a situation. Probably be up all night. Have to reschedule, lunch tomorrow at noon? I'll let Torrence know.

Once married to him, I knew I'd have to get used to these mysterious cancellations, but I still felt worried—and a tiny bit annoyed. Shouldn't he be able to trust me with more details than saying it was a "situation"? Last time he'd told me they were expecting a "situation," a gruesome murder occurred.

I quickly decided it was better to tackle that complaint in person rather than by text. After a few messages back and forth, we agreed that he would pick me up outside *Key Zest* just before noon and drive us over to Camille's together.

"Hello!" my mother's lilting voice called from the deck outside. I hurried out to greet her and we hugged, then I held her at arm's length to look her over. Her Key West life seemed to totally agree with her—today she looked almost like a teenager, in body-hugging jeans, a ball cap with a ponytail of auburn hair sticking out the back, and a spray of sun-enhanced freckles across her nose.

"Want a cup of coffee while we wait? And maybe a mojito cookie?" I grinned. All the Snow women have a sweet tooth. And besides, I had decided that part of my role as wife would be to always have something delicious on hand for Nathan. Even to my ears, that sounded like something a retro housewife from the fifties might have endorsed. Still, it felt like one concrete way to show him how crazy I was about him. My mother had taught me well that food is love. Good food, that is.

"I'm trying them out for Christmas and would love your opinion." I ducked into the kitchen for mugs of coffee and a small plate of pale-green cookies studded with flecks of mint and lime. "Let me know if they taste too summery, or if you think they'd be better without the frosting."

She bit into one. "Mmmm. These are perfect exactly as they are. Especially on a platter paired with some more traditional choices—maybe the sugar cookies with the candy-cane frosting? I think you need the sweetness of the icing, because the cookie itself is slightly tart." She swallowed and sipped her coffee. "How's it going with the wording for the ceremony? You guys are scaring me a little bit, waiting until the last moment to finish the details."

I just laughed. "We have seven whole days before the wedding. This isn't the last moment. You should've seen me turning in papers during college. *That* was a little harrowing." I pushed my shoulders down—honestly, I would have felt better having all of this stuff done way in advance, but I didn't want to complain to my mother. Some things were better kept between me and my guy. "Nathan's been so darn busy. We were supposed to meet right after we finish here, but he thinks he'll be up all night with a 'situation.'"

"Isn't this supposed to be the quiet season on this island?"

I shrugged. "You know if it gets too quiet, the Tourist Development Commission invents a new event to bring people down to the Keys. Don't worry, we're having lunch with Steve Torrence tomorrow and I'm sure we'll get it squared away. Which is more than I can say for this reconstruction project." I pointed to the pile of trash next door.

I couldn't help sounding glum. We had hoped to have the newly purchased houseboat in move-in condition by early December. I understood there were many more pressing problems than my houseboat renovation. Two and a half months post-Irma, people only miles up the Keys from us were still living in tents and motels in the areas where the hurricane's eye had crossed over the string of islands and flattened their homes. And plenty of others had lost their personal belongings when the storm surge backed up and swept through their property.

Still, I felt a little sad about the fact that we had planned our wedding date based on the contractor's estimate for the completion of the renovation. We wanted to be able to move in together as soon as we were married, as long as the work was far enough along to make the space livable. Right now, livable it was not.

I glanced at my watch. "We should probably head over there so we can be waiting for him when he arrives." We hopped off Miss Gloria's houseboat and walked the few yards to what was soon to be our home.

"Watch your step on the rubble," I said.

She picked her way past the pile of paneling and insulation that Nathan and I had stripped out of the boat last weekend. We figured we could save the contractor some hours by chipping away at the grunt work. Inside the place, with the kitchen counter and appliances gone and some of the walls stripped down to studs, it looked as though this might have been hurricane ground zero.

My mother put her hands on her hips and twirled slowly, taking in the full picture. She finally turned to look at me. "Honey, I hate to be a downer, but I don't believe this will be finished in nine days or even nineteen. Have you thought about where else you might live? You're welcome to the upstairs bedroom at our place."

"You're sweet," I said. "But I'm not sure Nathan could handle starting married life living with my mom." I snickered. Just the idea of it felt like a terrible karmic joke. "Though he'd have a lot to learn from Sam."

Sam was my mother's second husband and a sweetheart of a man. He totally supported her desire to own a catering business, even to the point of giving up his law practice in New Jersey to move south and serve as her sous-chef. Without any training or experience, he was like a sponge, fascinated by how ingredients melded together to make something more delicious than any individual item on its own. And he had a way of calming my mother down when she approached hysterics, which was bound to happen from time to time in the catering business.

"And me from you," I added quickly with a big grin. I opened up the two webbed lawn chairs Nathan and I used occasionally at cocktail hour, role-playing living our dreams.

"How was the seafood tour?" my mother asked.

"I totally forgot to tell you." I described how the woman had fallen ill during the last stop of Analise's tour.

"Could it have been a heart attack?" my mother asked. "People don't take care of themselves and then they're surprised when they get sick. Although to be fair, bad things can still happen even if you do all the right stuff."

"Unfortunately, on the one hand they're saying she might have had a stroke. But Analise got the impression that they might be suspecting foul play."

"Oh no," my mother said. "Not again. Did you see this happen? Or notice anything unusual before she took ill?"

"I didn't see what happened before the woman keeled over, but as I was coming back from the ladies' room, she slid to the floor, clutching her head and moaning. I called 911, and then the fire department showed up and took her away. Up until then, she seemed perfectly perky and healthy. Maybe even too perky."

"Awful," she said. "Life can be so harsh sometimes." She glanced at her watch. "Are you sure this contractor is coming? He's twenty minutes late already. I don't mean to rush you, but Sam is starting to panic a little about Thanksgiving. You're coming by tomorrow to review the menu, right?"

My mother had insisted that the two of them would prepare the main part of the dinner if I could handle dessert. All that by itself was really no problem. I had been helping her with a lot of big events as her business took off, including catering a major weekend of meetings between Havana and Key West last winter. We billed ourselves as catering professionals, quite capable of handling most events.

The problem came with the guest list, which included my father—Mom's ex—my stepmother, Allison, and my stepbrother, Rory. They'd decided to fly in early and enjoy the island for a few days instead of rushing down at the last minute for the wedding.

Hearing that, my mother had insisted they be invited for Thanksgiving dinner. My parents could manage a civil conversation for a couple of hours, or even a couple of days. But Sam hadn't met my dad, nor had Nathan. Even if the day went perfectly, the room would be pulsing with stress. I texted the contractor for an update. The reply whooshed back in.

Sorry. Emergency. Same time tomorrow?

Chapter Four

My boss's appearance, while not entirely unhandsome, evoked an icebox crowned by a cauliflower.

—Kathleen Rooney, *Lillian Boxfish Takes a Walk*

Miss Gloria's co-conspirator, Mrs. Dubisson, met us at the parking lot at quarter after seven. Since there were three of us, we decided that I would drive Miss Gloria's old Buick to the book sale. And when I was finished "volunteering," I would walk to the office, which was close enough to the library that it would be a pleasant stroll. Nathan would pick me up at the office right before lunch. All of that would leave me a few quiet hours to work.

Mrs. Dubisson was a carbon copy of my roommate in terms of liveliness and energy, though a little taller and with a mane of perfectly white hair that she kept wrapped in a knot at the back of her head. Rather than donning the sweat suits that Miss Gloria favored, she dressed to the nines in trim trousers or capris paired with ironed blouses or sweater sets, and always her string of pearls.

"You look so pretty today," I told her as we got into the car, me in the front with Miss Gloria and Mrs. Dubisson in back.

"I don't have a daughter," she explained, "and no sign of any grandchildren either. So I might as well get as much use out of the darn pearls as I can while I'm still kicking."

Miss Gloria snickered. "Maybe I should start wearing mine. Do pearls go with bling?" She gestured at her Thanksgiving sweatshirt, the cartoon turkeys outlined in brown and orange sequins.

"We're at the age where anything goes," said Mrs. Dubisson. "Say, I was reading Facebook this morning while I put myself together and ate breakfast. Apparently that lady who fell ill on the food tour yesterday didn't make it."

"Good gravy, that poor woman died? This is already all over Facebook?

"You have to be careful about the Internet," I said, glancing over my shoulder at my backseat passenger. I pulled out onto Palm Avenue. "A lot of that stuff ends up falling into the real fake news department. And there are lots of evil trolls who want to suck you in and steal your stuff."

She waved her hand, shrugging me off. "I never take it too seriously, especially the Key West locals group. They love to gossip. Though I did get a heads-up when Kenny Chesney gave an unscheduled concert a couple years ago at the Hog's Breath Saloon.

I arrived ahead of the young people and nabbed a front-row barstool." She beamed, looking extremely pleased with herself. But then she straightened and frowned. "In this case, there was one of those six-degrees-of-separation things; the woman who died was related to somebody's mother-in-law's sister. They're already starting a GoFundMe campaign to pay for her funeral expenses."

"Those campaigns are overdone these days, in my humble opinion," said Miss Gloria. "People asking for other people to whiten their teeth and send their kids to language and tap-dancing lessons and lord knows what else. Whatever happened to people taking responsibility for their own lives?"

"What do they think was the cause of death?" I asked. This would make a huge difference for Analise and all the restaurants on her tour.

"I didn't get that," Mrs. Dubisson said. "But I'll check in later and let you know what I find out."

At 7:30 on a Saturday morning in Key West, pretty much the only vehicles you see on the roads are the great rumbling street cleaners that roll through Old Town to clean up the party from the night previous. So we reached our destination in under ten minutes. The library, a one-story pink stucco building, sat quietly three blocks off the main Key West drag, Duval Street. The front gates to the palm garden, located to the left of the library, were still locked. I backed the car into a spot in the lot behind the building so Miss Gloria would be able to pull straight out and have the smallest possible chance of nicking someone else's finish when she drove home later on.

"Maybe we'll be able to get the lowdown from one of the prisoners working the sale," said Miss Gloria. "Without cell phones and iPads, you wouldn't think they would know anything about the outside world, but they always do. I think my pal Odom will be here."

I eased the keys out of the ignition and got out of the car. Sometimes it felt like I was dealing with a couple of naïve teenagers rather than ladies in their eighties. "Be careful with those guys," I said. "Don't get too friendly. You know they ended up in those orange uniforms for a reason."

"It could happen to anyone," said Miss Gloria breezily as she trotted toward the back entrance with Mrs. Dubisson in her wake.

Library volunteers and trusties in orange jump-suits from the county jail were already busy unloading boxes of books from the storage room and moving them to the tables set up in the garden. Miss Gloria showed me where to sign in at the table by the back gate. By the time I'd turned around, she was hoisting cardboard boxes of hardcovers onto the table marked MYSTERY.

One of Miss Gloria's cronies directed me to the children's table, and I began to lift boxes of picture books onto this tabletop and arrange them so they could be easily viewed. I drooled over a complete set of hardcover Hardy Boys mysteries that I found at the bottom of the pile, though I resisted setting them aside because I couldn't think of anyone to give them to. And there was absolutely no spare room on our boat for poorly considered purchases. When I finished that chore, I was sent to the cookbooks and travel section, where I worked steadily until eight fifteen. Shoppers had already begun to line up on the sidewalk outside the black metal gates.

"We don't open until nine thirty!" called out a cheerful woman whom Miss Gloria had introduced as Marsha Williams, the president of the Friends' board. "If you're finished," she said to me, "you can start applying the stars to the spines of all the titles that don't have a circle on them. If they've been recycled through all the sales for the season and no one's been tempted to buy, we cull them out," she explained.

By this time, all the books had been unloaded from the storage shed and the jumpsuited trusties bundled off to their next job. Miss Gloria took the spot next to me, and we applied the star stickers in tandem.

"My buddy Odom didn't know anything about the death, but he's going to find out and let me know," she said.

I stopped working, stickers in one hand and my fist on my hip. "Find out from whom? And let you know how?"

She winked. "I'll keep you posted. Aren't you supposed to be going to *Key Zest* about now?"

I'd been dismissed.

I collected my backpack from the cupboard in the shed where we stored our valuables and walked down

Fleming Street and across Simonton toward the office on Southard. The whole time I was wondering how Miss Gloria's friend Odom would possibly know anything about a tragedy on a food tour when he was locked away without access to Facebook or any other Internet apps that might supply Key West news.

Activity in the town was beginning to pick up—our local grocery store, Fausto's, was already bustling with customers. And three people waited in line in front of the ATM near the entrance to *Key Zest*. I bolted up the stairs and burst through the front door. My friend Danielle, the receptionist, was already at work on her computer at the front desk.

"You're in early on a Saturday," I said.

"I needed to finish the holiday calendar," she said. "Wally wants it to go out with the next issue."

"Doughnuts?" I asked hopefully, looking around the small space, sniffing for the irresistible scent of glazed sugar.

"A fruit plate." Danielle scrunched her nose and pointed to squares of pineapple piled next to a bunch of red grapes on the TV tray near the door. "Palamina's request. She thinks we eat too many treats during this season."

Palamina was our co-boss, slim as a reed and not an inhaler of sugar and carbs like us.

I leaned over to whisper, "I'll bring some cookies on Monday."

Danielle grinned. "What kind? Oh never mind, you've never brought anything that wasn't delicious, so surprise me. What are you working on?"

"I took the seafood walking tour yesterday," I explained. "Every stop was wonderful until we got to the brewery, where one of the customers collapsed. Now I don't know if they'll even want to run the piece. I suppose it depends on what the authorities find out about this woman's illness." I glanced at Palamina and Wally's office door, where I could hear the soft hum of their voices.

"She's on a tear today," Danielle whispered. "My suggestion is whatever you're really doing, just look busy."

Chapter Five

For Jean-Remy, a scallop served in its shell with a teaspoon of velvety cognac and some exquisite whipped cream was more romantic than all the roses in the world.
—Nina George, *The Little French Bistro*

Nathan and I had settled on meeting with Steve over lunch in the back room at Camille's restaurant for our premarital counseling session. We'd gone around a few times about where to schedule this discussion. Houseboat Row was out of the question. All of my neighbors would have ears wide open—not in a mean way, just a matter of friendly curiosity. The truth was that Nathan scared them a little bit with his stiff-cop persona. Miss Gloria told me they all wondered how I'd managed to tame him. Ha! That would be a lifetime assignment. The interested listeners aside, it would be unfair to wedge Miss Gloria out of her own space.

The police department, with all those curious men and women in blue? When Key West froze over. Nathan didn't want anything to do with the teasing that would result if we were seen trooping into Steve Torrence's office to share our deepest joys and concerns. At least in the restaurant, our secrets would be muted by the busy hum of conversation from the other diners.

Nathan texted me at twenty to twelve to say he was waiting in the parking lot behind my office building. I felt a familiar shiver of excitement when I saw him leaning against a silver SUV. I ran the few final steps and enveloped him in a big hug.

"Too late to warn you that I've been up all night and don't smell that fresh," he said once we'd let go.

"You just smell like you, and that's all good," I said with a grin. "What's with the new wheels? Where's your police car?"

"In the shop," he said with a grimace. "The brakes felt spongy, so I didn't want to take chances. Ready to go?"

"Yes, and I'm ravenous. Apparently Palamina has put us all on a diet for the holiday season. What a dreadful idea. Doesn't she know that diets start *after* New Year's? And doesn't she know that most diets are doomed to fail anyway?" I slid into the passenger seat and he got in the other side.

"I suspect I'm going to pack on a few pounds, married to you," he said.

"Then you just work out a little harder," I said, running my hand down his arm. "I do so love these manly man muscles."

We exchanged a kiss that felt like it promised a lot more. His portable police scanner began to crackle, and he turned the volume down. "Whatever emergency that is, someone else is going to have to handle it. I have something more important to do— marrying you." He grinned and started up the engine, then drove us across town and parked on the street that ran along the side of the restaurant.

Decked out in rosy stucco, pink awnings, and aqua shutters, Camille's was a stalwart, old-school restaurant with a funky edge that was popular with the locals. The food was plentiful, solid, and inexpensive, a combination that customers couldn't get at fancier places in town. The waitress led us immediately to the most private booth in the back room. "Steve called to say he's running a few minutes late. Can I get you something while you wait?"

"Black coffee for me," said Nathan.

"I'll stick with water. Lemon if you have it, please," I said. "I've had enough bad office coffee this morning to rot anyone's gut." I turned to Nathan. "Where should we sit? Maybe side by side so he can look at both of us?"

He nodded and slid to the inside seat of the bench looking out at the other tables. Cops were vigilant all the time, I'd learned; they didn't like being surprised.

After the waitress delivered our drinks, his in solid white china and mine in a tall clear plastic cup, I asked him what he'd heard about the incident in the brewery. "It's not just morbid curiosity," I assured him, though he looked dubious. "You know I was right there when the woman took ill."

"Yes, and I find that astonishing." His eyebrows peaked in mock dismay. "Not."

I'd developed something of a reputation for showing up at murder scenes. And while there, I seemed to notice things more than other people did, and make connections that they might have missed. Friends knew I'd sorted out a few mysteries. And I was pegged as more approachable and less intimidating than the cops. Nathan wasn't thrilled about any of this. I rolled my eyes, peeled half the paper off my straw, and blew the rest of it in his direction.

"Really, can you tell me what happened?"

"We're investigating the situation," he said, ignoring my silliness and revealing his usual minimal facts. "I'm on another case, so I didn't hear the summary report this morning. But first, how did it go with the contractor?" he asked. "I'm afraid to ask that question."

"He had another emergency. We rescheduled for this afternoon. I'd ask you to meet with us, but I know you haven't slept. A crabby fiancé would probably not help the situation."

"Definitely not," he said, the skin around his green eyes crinkling with his smile. "I've saved every bit of available pleasantness for this meeting. Besides, I trust your mother completely."

He glanced at his watch. "About the food incident. Your friend came into the station yesterday. She was too upset to be very helpful."

"Understandably," I said. "She's not used to people getting sick and almost dying on her watch."

"And I hope she never gets used to it," he said. "If you don't mind taking our personal time to run over this, I'd like to hear more about what you observed during your food tour yesterday."

"Of course," I said, on instant alert. He didn't very often ask me for professional help. Like ever. Except last spring, when I'd acted as a decoy for a tense ten minutes to help catch a bad guy. And really, there had been no other choice. Maybe this pointed to growing trust between us?

My best friend Connie, who lived up the dock from me and was still a newlywed, had explained that in her experience, trust changed over time. "You think you trust someone completely, because why else would you marry them?" she'd mused. "But then you find that that feeling ebbs and flows. Overall, the ebbs get smaller and the flows get bigger and you end up with a net gain."

And my mother had said the same thing—that trusting someone entirely takes time, and that trust develops in a marriage as the relationship is tested by outside events. Inside events, too. I was finding that they were both right.

"Anything you want to know in particular?" I asked Nathan.

"Maybe first give me your impressions, and then I'll ask specific questions or have the officer in charge of the case call you to follow up. Honestly, I don't think it's going to amount to anything much more than an unfortunate stroke. But better to be thorough and consider all the possibilities now than be accused of negligence later."

"OK." I closed my eyes and began to think about how the day had started. "We met at Isle Cook Key West. Over on Whitehead Street near the Mel Fisher museum. It's a really cute space with a big chef's kitchen and an enormous island where the customers sit and watch the cooks at work. Chef Martha teaches a lot of classes there, and they bring in guest chefs as well. And they have wine-tasting events too. We should try one." I opened my eyes and grinned.

He made a face. "Maybe. I won't say no flat-out the week we're getting married." He took my fingers and squeezed. "OK, so you're in this room with a big kitchen," he prompted.

"They had us all take seats at the counter. And they gave us little jars of key lime pie sprinkled with Cuban crackers instead of regular crust. Martha makes her filling with lime juice fermented with salt. She calls this mixture Ol' Sour." I laughed, and then looked up at him, feeling a sudden rush of horror. "Please don't tell me this woman was poisoned with Martha's key lime pie."

My first interaction with Nathan several years ago had come after a death by key lime pie. That time, I had been a suspect. And he had scared me to death when he'd shown up at my houseboat. And then scared me even worse at official interviews that took place at the police department later.

He would have been quick to point out that I'd been a hysterical suspect.

And I would have responded that I had excellent reason to be—hysterical, that is. Being a person of interest in a murder case had been one of the worst experiences of my life. Even if I hadn't exactly mourned the victim (an understatement), I wouldn't have wanted to have been responsible for her demise. Honestly, I didn't ever wish her dead. Maybe swept away in a big wind like the wicked witch she was.

Nathan sighed. His chin sank to his hand, and with his change in position under the overhead fluorescents, the blue circles under his eyes became more prominent.

"You know I'll tell you what I can when I can. Nobody's saying anything about poison."

"I know you will. It's just that Chef Martha is such a sweetheart and they're doing such a good job with that new venture. I would hate to see anything knock the legs out from it."

"Of course you would. We all would, Hayley. We want every local business in town to succeed. Keep going, please."

"OK, so that's where we met the group." I described for him the one couple and the two other strangers, none of whom I'd seen before. "I wasn't paying that much attention at first because I was taking notes for my article."

"So you all had jars of key lime pie. Individual jars, or was it scooped from a bowl that everyone shared?"

"Individual. Little mason jars with lids that had the Isle Cook Key West logo on them. They were really cute. I think I saved mine, if you want to see it. I tasted it like everybody else, but I don't like dessert before my savory food—I always eat too much and then I'm not hungry for the main event. So I put it aside to finish later in the day."

"So noted. This jar you saved, is that same pie mixture still in it?" he asked.

I could feel my face sag with disappointment, and a flicker of matching disappointment in his eyes. "Darn it. That would have been too easy. Though I'm pretty sure there wasn't anything wrong with mine, because I ate the whole thing later and didn't feel a twinge of illness. Once I got home, I ran the jar through the dishwasher, thinking it would be the perfect size for making vinaigrette. Should I save it for you or bring it to the station?"

He shook his head no. Obviously a sparkling clean glass jar wouldn't offer clues to anything. "And then?"

"And then we walked over to Bagatelle's on Duval Street. Analise took us upstairs for their restaurant's special lobster macaroni and cheese. It was so rich, it could've put you into a coma. But delicious. Everybody loved it except for the woman who said she didn't eat carbs. Can you imagine? Life without carbs?"

He nodded. "I'm glad to know that isn't in our future."

I grinned. "Now that I'm talking about it, this no-carb person was the woman who died. Anyway, she tasted the dish, and then asked if anyone else wanted the rest of hers. We all said no. At first. Then her husband decided he couldn't let it go, so he ate a couple bites of hers too."

"You're sure it was the man, the husband, who ate the extra, rather than the woman who took ill?"

"I'm sure," I said. "Though that could have been the perfect way to sabotage a dish. Taste it yourself and then offer it to others. Except . . ." I ran my fingers through my curls. "Except how could she have been certain who would take her up on the offer? Anyway, she's the one who got sick, not her husband. And how in the world could you poison something while sitting at the table with a group of people? Someone would be bound to notice."

Nathan was beginning to look glazed.

Steve Torrence rushed up to the table, looking flustered himself. "So sorry to be late. I thought this was the slow season, but apparently our pre-Thanksgiving island visitors didn't get that memo." He kissed me on the cheek and reached over the table to shake Nathan's hand. Then he looked at the two of us, seated side by side.

"Maybe you two lovebirds might like to sit across from each other so you can look at each other directly as we talk?"

"Sure," I said, sliding out of Nathan's bench and onto the other. And feeling a bit like we'd failed the first premarital test. Torrence sat next to me and we ordered lunch, a rare hamburger with grilled onions and Swiss cheese for Nathan, bacon, lettuce and tomato on white toast easy on the mayo for Torrence, and the special Caesar with a scoop of chicken salad on the side for me. I didn't need to try something new because I wasn't taking notes on the food today, only concentrating on the future good of my relationship.

Torrence began. "Congratulations again on your upcoming marriage. It's really an honor for me to be part of this special day." The warmth of his smile made me feel as though he truly meant this. "I'll tell you my theory about what makes a marriage work—people who know how to talk to each other through thick and thin and assume only the best motives from their partner have the best chance of surviving. As you know, we can't predict what kind of life changes and challenges you'll face together. We can only work on how graciously you'll handle them."

Suddenly this all felt so serious and I was bursting with love and along with that, fear. I knew it was wrong, but I was overcome with a terrible urge to lighten things up. And a case of the giggles. I snickered, fighting to keep the laughter inside by taking a sip of lemon water and nearly choking.

Steve patted me on the back. "OK?" I nodded, wiped the tears from my eyes.

"What's so funny?" Nathan asked.

I winked at Torrence. "I've had plenty to face already with this guy's ideas about the wedding. First he wanted me to strip off my gown and throw it into the ocean after you pronounced us man and wife. I never did get the meaning of that."

"So you'd be left standing around in your underwear on the beach?" Torrence asked, an exaggerated look of horror on his face.

I thought he was on the verge of a major laughing fit—they both were. Which I did not appreciate, even if I deserved it for bringing the subject up.

Nathan leaned forward and tapped the table with his fingers. "First of all, I'd be stripping down too, and we'd have our bathing suits on underneath. The idea, sweetheart, is that we'd be throwing off the shackles of the actual wedding stuff and getting on with the fun in our life."

I rolled my eyes at Torrence. "Ridiculous. He'd never do it even if I had agreed. I'd be left standing there mostly naked and he'd be snickering in his tux."

"Maybe he was thinking of a James Bond and his golden girl effect?" Torrence asked.

"No tux," Nathan said quickly. "That was part of the original deal, remember?" He turned to face his friend. "She asked me for ideas, and the only things I could come up with were what I'd heard from guys around the department. As you know, cops can be kind of childish when they aren't being dead serious."

"*Kind of* childish?" I looked at Torrence again. "And then you know what his next idea was? Driving off into the sunset on a Jet Ski! In a wedding gown. A gown that I spent months searching for and plenty of money to score." I rubbed my fingers together to make the point, though honestly, I hadn't gone *that* crazy on the expense.

"Believe it or not, I've seen that done. It wasn't pretty. Somehow the bridal gown got caught underneath the Jet Ski and pulled the new wife underwater. She was dragged behind the ski for almost twenty yards. When she finally surfaced with her ruined hair and torn-up dress, she was beyond furious," Torrence said.

Nathan chuckled. "I get it, it's a bad idea."

"But really, let's be serious," said Steve. "I always like to start with a question about what each person is most afraid of in their future married life. What might happen that could jeopardize your relationship? You two will be in a special club, even more problematic than ordinary couples"—he directed this at me—"because you're marrying a police officer."

"Tell me about it," I said, taking a big gulp of air, and then reaching for Nathan's hand and giving it a squeeze. "Mine is easy: I know this guy doesn't like to talk about what's going on in his work life."

"And how does that make you feel?"

"Like I'm on the other side of a big border wall with no chance of scaling it. No handholds, no footholds, nothing. He thinks I can't understand, or something."

"Exactly," said Torrence, glancing at Nathan. "Maybe now would be a good time to try to explain to her some of your feelings about this."

Nathan shifted in his seat, pulled his hand out of my grip, and looked his friend square in the face. "I'm not sure what there is to say about it. It's hard for someone who doesn't work as a police officer to understand what we face. And I want to protect her from the ugliness."

Torrence said, "Try telling her a little more about what you think and feel about the ugliness and the danger. Talk to her, not me," he added gently.

Nathan sighed, shifting to face me again. "I could be in harm's way on a daily basis. We never know what we'll run up against during a given shift. If I told you every time I thought something bad might happen, you'd be on an emotional roller coaster. I know how worried you get about things and how you talk to your people, and then how your mother and Miss Gloria worry along with you. A police officer has to be aware of all the risks and problems but can't get caught up with every little blip of danger. We can't always be worrying, because that takes away from our ability to notice things and have sharp reactions." He looked over at Torrence and shrugged his shoulders, his hands gripping the edge of the table. "I can see I'm not explaining this very well."

"Oh, I understand what you're saying," I said, my voice a little snippy. "You're saying I can't handle it." I could feel my dander rising along with the color in my face. Nathan was getting mad, too.

"I'm not sure that's the exact translation," Torrence said. "Say it again," he suggested to Nathan. "Try another way."

Nathan nodded, looking down at his clenched fists. "Every day as an officer is a crapshoot. Even in my position. People get drunk, people get angry, and some people are just plain criminals. And if all this isn't handled perfectly—and even if it is sometimes— we get the blame for it. I don't think it's fair to come home and dump all of that on you." He ran his hands over his face. "And you're marrying into this. There's always a chance that something could happen to you too. You know that happened in my previous marriage."

"Yes, but that was unusual. And maybe her reactions were different than mine would be. Maybe I could have outsmarted the bad guy. And maybe you've changed, learned something from those mistakes." My lips quirked into a grin, but I knew my eyes were hopeful.

He smiled back. "I'm always learning things with you. But that wasn't the only reason we fell apart. I was so angry afterwards, thinking about how she could have been hurt by that psycho. And I felt so guilty. It wasn't fair that he would take out something he held against me on her." He sighed. "Don't you see, you mean everything to me now. I couldn't bear it if anything happened to you." This time he reached across the table to take my hands.

"I feel the same about you," I said softly, looking into his eyes and wondering if I'd ever felt happier.

"On the other side of this marrying-a-cop problem, I also worry that you fling yourself into situations where you're over your head."

The waitress arrived with our food and slid the plates onto the table. "Burger rare, special Caesar, and BLT. Enjoy your lunch!"

"We will," Torrence told her, and then added to me and Nathan, "I have a good feeling about the two of you. Remember, Nathan, Hayley is a people person. She can't help feeling sympathetic and getting involved when her friends are in trouble."

"Listening to her friends and not butting into investigations are two separate things," Nathan said. "I appreciate your thoughts and your insights, Hayley, I do. But I hate when you go further and put yourself in danger."

"I think I get that," I said, trying not to react too strongly to his use of the words *butting into*. This was hard work. "And I hope I'm getting better at it. Remember at the Little White House last winter? I didn't go meet up with the killer and mention it later. I called you ahead of time. That's progress, right?"

"Keep talking and you're going to be fine," said Torrence. "You've made a good start here, but my friend is right"—he pointed his fork at Nathan— "marrying a police officer brings an unusual set of stressors."

I took one of Nathan's fries and dipped it into a pool of ketchup. "What tips do you offer to couples you don't think are going to make it? Or can't you tell?"

"Lots of times it's fairly obvious," he said with a laugh. "Say the groom sleeps with the maid of honor the night before the wedding. Or maybe it's crystal clear that the bride has spent lots of energy on the wedding. And the groom couldn't care less. Like that. Bad start to a life together. And sometimes I can even see it in their vows."

"Yikes," I said. "We don't have those ready yet. Could we just borrow the winning script?"

Torrence said, "I'd make a fortune if I had one of those!" He glanced at his watch. "I need to get back." He looked at me. "You and I are meeting at Fort Zachary Taylor tomorrow afternoon to go over the ceremony blocking, right?"

"Right. And thanks for traveling the extra mile."

"There's one other thing we need to talk about for the ceremony—and I need both of you to weigh in on this. Do you want God or no God? Or I can do God light if that's what you prefer."

I looked across the table at Nathan, who shrugged and said, "Whatever you want is fine with me."

What did that mean? He didn't care? He didn't want to say? We'd have to talk about it later. I'd been raised as a casual Presbyterian, so I wasn't even quite sure what I believed. Though surely there was something out there bigger than us . . .

I winked at Torrence. "You heard us try to talk about hard issues. I think adding God wouldn't hurt us a bit."

Chapter Six

Sandy thought Anna still sounded angry. He had a picture in his head of a pan of soup standing on the Rayburn and ready to boil over.

—Ann Cleeves, *Red Bones*

As soon as I'd gotten back to the houseboat and settled onto the deck with my laptop, Analise phoned. "I'm so sorry about your customer," I said, sitting up straight and closing the computer. "I heard she didn't make it."

"This is my worst nightmare," she said. "I'm responsible for these people while they're on my watch, and I absolutely failed."

I opened my mouth to try to reassure her, but she barreled on.

"It's the truth and there isn't much you can say to soften the blow. But that's not why I called. Chef Martha wants to talk with you. I think she believes that someone wanted to sabotage her new success with Isle Cook Key West, and poisoning her food seems like a great way to go about it."

Thinking of the conversation I'd just had with Nathan and Steve, I stated the obvious, trying for firm but kind. "She should talk to the police. There's really nothing I can do."

"Of course I told her exactly that," Analise said. "She absolutely won't. I don't know why, but she won't. And it's not as if she's a flighty woman who makes wacky decisions. Maybe you could just stop over there and chat with her and try to encourage her yourself? You're the one with all the insider contacts at the police department. You could tell her how nice they are and welcoming of citizen input. And cute."

She laughed and then added, "Honestly, Hayley, I wouldn't ask you this if I didn't think she had a good reason to be worried. And an equally good reason *not* to speak with the authorities. And don't ask me what that would be, because she wouldn't tell me. You're the closest I can come to helping her."

I felt my urge to help someone in obvious distress overcome my urge to stay out of what was really not my business. Maybe I could persuade her to speak with Nathan. Or better still, Steve. She would like him the instant she met him. He had a very grounded way about him, a good sense of humor, and lots of common sense. And empathy. It would be very hard for anyone to see him as threatening. Though to be fair, I'd never been in a situation with him where he'd had to use force. Maybe his police hackles rose up like an angry dog's when called for.

"OK, I'll talk with her."

"Great. Do you have time today? She's working this afternoon prepping for a class. It's something about side dishes for Thanksgiving and wine pairings. She said you could stop in any time before five."

* * *

I parked my scooter near the Custom House, a handsome brick building with a metal roof designed for handling a snow dump that would certainly never fall on Key West. I walked two blocks to the cooking store, located on the second floor of a plain-looking building that included other shops. Though it was in the middle of everything—near Mallory Square, the Mel Fisher museum, and Duval Street—it was not easily findable.

Chef Martha was working at the chopping block set up on the wide island separating the shop from the professional kitchen. I recognized her from her former stint as chef at the Café at Louie's. Upstairs from Louie's Backyard, the Café features a more casual version of food than the downstairs restaurant, though both overlook the ocean. There as here, her cooking skills had been on full display for customers. I wondered what that said about her personality.

Most chefs work at the back of the house in cramped, hot, greasy spaces that diners never see. And they have little interaction with their customers, apart from an occasional appearance or command performance tableside. This kind of arrangement felt much more personal—and probably required more self-control too, as in no cussing, no yelling at the staff, no making fun of customers who demand out-rageous changes to the chef's menu. She was a wiry woman, a little taller than me but thin and muscu-lar, vibrating with energy, and covered in tattoos. She was chopping vegetables at a rate I'd seen only on TV cooking shows. I was afraid to interrupt her for fear she might startle and lose a finger.

When she paused to wipe her hands, I approached the counter.

She gave a wave and a smile so brittle I thought it might crack her face. "Hayley, right? I'm so grate-ful that you agreed to come. Can I get you anything? Coffee? A tipple of wine? A key lime pie?" She ges-tured at the large glass-fronted refrigerator, where one of the shelves was filled with the mini pies in small canning jars that we had been offered on the food tour.

Was she joking? To be honest, I was surprised to see those on display. If the mini pies had been a suspected cause of that woman's death, wouldn't the police have confiscated all of this? Or wouldn't Martha or the owners have thrown them out? Or removed them from the menu altogether? In any case, no way was I going to sample one. "Maybe just some water?"

"Sure thing. Have a seat right there at the counter and I'll come around and join you." She filled a large glass with water, ice, and lemon, slid it across the counter to me, and came to sit down, her fingers worrying the coffee cup she brought with her.

"Why don't you tell me what's up?" I asked. "I know you were upset about what happened with the food tour. Gosh, it was awful."

She nodded but didn't say anything.

"Are you concerned that the customer got sick with something you fed her?"

"Not exactly," she said, her eyes cast down to study the coffee.

I mentally pinched myself. I knew a better interview technique was to shut up and let the person talk rather than yammering on and feeding them half-baked possibilities that could obscure the truth. But I flashed on the conversation I'd just had with Nathan and Steve, and how I'd promised at the end that I'd try not to get involved where I shouldn't be.

"Listen, I feel like I have to say this. Analise mentioned that you don't want to talk to the police. But if you think you're in danger or if you know something about what might be a crime, they are the ones to help you. I can introduce you to a truly kind officer who I really trust."

She pinched her lips together and shook her head. "I can't talk to the cops." Her eyes were pleading now.

"Can you talk about why not?" I asked, working to stay patient and understand her point of view.

"Imagine that you did something in your life that was so awful you don't want anyone ever to know."

Now I was seriously curious. She motioned for me to close my eyes and think. So I did. I had some super-embarrassing incidents come to mind (like the time my belongings were dumped out on the curb in front of my ex's fancy condominium), and some other moments where maybe my best judgment hadn't been on display. But I thought of nothing so bad that I'd die if it became public. I opened my eyes.

"And this awful something, that you may or may not have done, are you thinking it might be related to this woman's death?" I stopped and waited. And waited.

"It's complicated," she said finally. "And it's going to sound ridiculous. I think it's possible that woman died because of me. I think someone I used to know is trying to hurt me, and this is the way that he went about it. The trouble being, of course, that he hurt everyone else involved and killed that poor woman—who was here on vacation, for god's sake."

"You mean something happened with your food and this hypothetical person was involved?" I was having a lot of trouble wrapping my mind around this. How could someone she knew from her past get into the kitchen and sabotage her key lime pies? And her pie was the only thing we'd eaten here. "You're saying someone you used to know came into your kitchen with the intent of getting you implicated in a murder?"

She covered her face with her hands. "I knew it would sound ridiculous. I can only say it's someone that I'd hoped I had left behind. Someone who didn't get free of some ugliness and didn't want to see me escape out of it either. I don't know how they contaminated my food." She looked as though she was struggling hard not to cry. And she did not seem to be the sort of woman who cried often.

"Did you recognize anyone from the tour?"

"I was only with you guys for a minute, remember? This is a super-busy week, so I only got a glimpse of your group." She gestured at the ingredients scattered over her counters.

"So it could be someone who lives in Key West?"

She shrugged. "I don't know where they are now. But you know you can live in this town a long time and never run into someone you know who also lives here."

I felt like I was playing twenty questions and not getting much out of it. "I don't see how I'm the person who can help with this—"

She cut me off. "Could you just talk with the people at the other venues and see if anyone noticed something off about the woman or any of the other customers? I know that you're good at observing and putting pieces together; lots of people have mentioned you. And besides, you have a perfectly good reason for interviewing people. You are planning on writing an article about the seafood tour, right?"

She had me there, but I still balked. "I can go about my work and maybe ask a few questions along the way. But if I don't find anything out and you really feel that you know something about how this woman died, will you promise me you'll talk to the police?"

She broke out in a sweat, glanced at the front door where a couple was coming in, and wiped her face with a clean towel lying on the counter. Without answering my question, she wheeled around and disappeared from the room through a back door next to an enormous wine rack.

I gathered up my empty notebook and unused pen and tucked them into my backpack. I recognized the people who had come in as the owners of this kitchen store, Eden and Bill Brown. I'd read an article about them recently in the *Key West Citizen*. They were both psychologists who'd retired to Key West to launch a new life and a new business, hiring Martha as head chef.

They began to unload bags of merchandise at the checkout counter near the front door. Both of them looked slightly worried, as well they should. If Martha was in trouble, their business would be too. She was conducting most of the cooking classes they offered, and probably setting up the guest chef slots as well. She was the ridge beam that supported their roof.

I thought they might respond more openly if I mentioned a connection with my pal Eric, also a clinical psychologist. So we'd have two degrees of separation rather than six. I walked over and introduced myself. "I'm a friend of Eric Altman—he's also a psychologist here in town."

"Eric's a darling man," Eden said. "Good for him that he's still out in the trenches. We loved our work with patients back in Ohio, but we love this change, too." She looked a little puzzled—obviously I wouldn't have come here to discuss Eric.

"I was here for the food tour yesterday," I said, wondering how much else to say. Would Martha have mentioned her suspicion about a personal vendetta to her bosses? I had no idea how much she trusted them and took them into her confidence. Considering that she'd bolted soon after they'd arrived, maybe not so much. So I didn't feel right repeating what she'd told me. But I didn't figure I'd get anything out of them without offering something first.

"Martha of course is concerned about the woman who died. If the cause of death ends up being food related, I know this would be terrible for you as well."

"She's quite naturally anxious," Eden said, in a no-nonsense voice. "We all feel dreadful about the poor woman who took sick, but Martha is taking it personally. We love that about her—she's absolutely serious about her cooking, while at the same time she makes everything fun for her students. And even with all that going on, our kitchens are spotless."

"Kitchens?" I asked.

Bill said, "There's a second kitchen in the back of the store. Lots of times if one of the visiting chefs doesn't want to prepare everything in public, he or she might start the dishes in back and then finish them in front of the guests. There's also lots of storage, walk-in refrigerators, all that kind of not-so-sexy stuff."

"You're writing an article for *Key Zest*, Martha said?" asked Eden. "If you plan to talk about the store, maybe you'd like to see the rest of our place?"

"I'd love to!"

She waved me on to follow her past the wine coolers, containing a wall of bottles of all colors, and to the door at the back of the kitchen through which Martha had disappeared. The hidden area was utterly neat and organized, lined with shelves that included cooking merchandise that I assumed would be sold in the store, cases of wine, and dried and bottled food. Against the far wall was a supplemental kitchen including a six-burner gas Wolf stove with a griddle and double ovens underneath that made me drool with envy, a chest freezer—ditto—and a walk-in cooler.

Bill opened the door to the cooler and gestured at the shelves, overflowing with turkeys, sacks of Brussels sprouts, slabs of bacon, onions in net bags, and more.

"She's teaching a class on Thanksgiving side dishes," he said. "My favorite is the brown-butter rosemary yeast rolls."

My stomach let out a loud rumble and they both laughed.

"You're welcome to join this class, on the house. She's including a tutorial on gravy from scratch," said Eden. "And her side dishes are like nothing you've ever seen on dinner tables. She likes to put a Thai spin on old classics, like sweet potatoes with charred poblanos or Brussels sprouts with Thai chilies and caramelized shallots. I can't wait for the habanero candy!"

I'd begun to salivate at the sound of those recipes, almost drooling like one of Pavlov's dogs. "Sounds divine, but I have plans with my family, and my mother would personally kill me if I bailed out. Another time, I hope." I exited from the cooler and circled the storage area, pausing by the bottles of key lime juice lined up on a top shelf.

We emerged from the back kitchen and I thanked them for talking with me, collected my backpack from the counter, and headed out the front door. I needed to stop in at the other places we'd visited on the tour, but maybe I'd save that for tomorrow. Today I was over-the-top exhausted, and had promised to pop in at my mother's place on the way home. I'd meant it when I'd told them that *not* showing up there would be considered just cause for homicide.

Chapter Seven

*Even the angriest person is soothed by the scent
of soup simmering on the stove.*
—Ruth Reichl, *My Kitchen Year:
136 Recipes That Saved My Life*

I trotted up the block to the parking area in front of the Custom House, where a tangle of rusted bike parts, rental bikes, and a few scooters rested. My trusty silver scooter was not in the place I'd left it. Had someone taken it? A lot of people passed this area coming in and out of Mallory Square. The scooter wasn't that valuable, but it was priceless to me—my only real form of transportation. I rummaged in my pocket and found the key. So at least I hadn't spaced out and accidentally left this in the ignition—a thief would have had to hot-wire the engine. Thoroughly irritated and a little rattled, I debated whether to call Nathan, decided yes, and punched in his number.

He answered, sounding sleepy.

"Oh my gosh," I said. "I totally didn't think— I'm so sorry to wake you."

"Is something wrong?" he asked, the sleepiness gone instantly from his voice. "Where are you? Are you OK?"

"I'm fine. I'm downtown. It's just, someone stole my scooter. I should have called the regular department phone number instead of bothering you."

"I'm glad you bothered me," he said, and began to bark out questions. "Where did you park it? Did you take the key? Did you notice anyone watching you as you left?"

As I was getting ready to answer, I spotted the scooter parked in the next rack over. "Shoot," I said. "It's here and now I've woken you for nothing. I was in a big hurry and I'm overtired and all is well. Will you able to go back to sleep?"

"I'll be fine, talk tomorrow," he said.

Ten minutes later, I parked outside my mother and Sam's rental on Noah Lane. For the last several years, they'd occupied this two-story home in the Truman Annex with a cupola overlooking the Navy's harbor and a covered deck with a dipping pool surrounded by tropical foliage in back of the house. It was much roomier than Miss Gloria's houseboat, and quieter too, with a glorious kitchen and a big dining room that could be opened up to the back porch if the weather was nice—the perfect place to host a dinner.

My mother and Sam were in the dining room, pouring over a handwritten page.

"Oh Hayley, I'm so glad you're here. The seating chart is impossible."

"We've hosted stressful dinners here before," said Sam with a wicked grin. "Remember how your Detective Bransford showed up when cousin Cassie and her husband were visiting? He was not exactly a gracious addition, and yet we survived that."

Nathan had appeared at a Christmas dinner party and interrogated my mother's guests at a moment when his murder investigation had stalled. The evening was going badly even before his arrival: Sam had just made a public marriage proposal to my mother and she'd said—nothing.

"I will never forget that night," my mom said. "I almost let the best thing in my life slip away. And having an irritable detective there didn't help." She smiled up at Sam, and he rubbed my mother's back in comforting circles.

"I promise he'll be better this time. For one, he won't have any reason to question your guests. I'm mostly worried about him and Dad—whether they'll hit it off." I hesitated, glancing at Sam and squinting my eyes. "And what about you and Dad? Will you be snorting and pawing at the dirt around my mother?"

Once Sam stopped laughing, he said, "We're not exactly rivals. He opted out of being married to your mother and I opted in. From what I can tell, that makes me both smart and lucky. And perfectly capable of being generous." He ended with an enormous grin.

I went around the table to hug him. "And she was so smart to snag you. Finally." I hugged my mother too. Then I peered down at the paper, which contained a line drawing of the dining room table with names penciled around it. "Assuming you and Sam are taking the ends of the table, I'd put Connie and Ray across from each other, and Allison next to Sam. Maybe Rory next to Mom on the other end because he'll be feeling a little shy. And then seat Miss Gloria in between Nathan and Dad. I'll sit next to Rory, across from that trio. She can get anyone laughing, even the worst curmudgeon, in case we have one. And knowing those two, we probably will. One or both. It scares me that I chose to marry someone so much like my father."

"Your father had some good qualities. Or I wouldn't have chosen him," Mom said in a brisk voice. "Time for a cup of tea? I could use a break."

We headed to the kitchen, where the counters were covered with Thanksgiving works in progress, even though we were days away from the holiday. She put the kettle on to boil. Sam retrieved herbal tea, mugs, and honey, and loaded a plate with delicious-looking cookies. I took a seat and read over Mom's recipe list.

"Cornbread sausage stuffing? That sounds amazing!" I said. "I don't remember you ever making that."

"It's Sam's specialty," said my mother. "He brought a whole recipe box from his southern grandmother as part of his dowry. None of this Pepperidge Farm-in-a-bag for him." We both giggled. As if either of us would ever serve food from a bag or a box or any kind of mix. We simply didn't have it in us.

Our genes dictated that everything be made from scratch, and my grandmother's training had reinforced that.

"I remember that your father was crazy for bacon, so I'm making the roasted Brussels sprouts with crispy bacon and onion and a little balsamic glaze."

I was curious about why she'd try so hard for my father. And wondered if Sam felt OK about that amount of effort as well. But why stir the pot when it didn't appear to be bubbling over? "Nathan will go mad for that, too—he loves anything bacon. But didn't Rory turn vegetarian this year?" Rory was my stepbrother who'd gone missing the last time he visited Key West. He'd started out looking for fun but ended with trouble way more serious than he could have imagined. Hopefully he'd grown out of the urge to bolt away from his family in a strange town.

"That's why we're making the roasted butternut squash and sage dish. Allison said he'll gladly eat cheese and eggs and butter, just not the animals themselves."

"As we all should eat if we walked our talk," I said with a sigh. I selected a perfectly light-brown pumpkin snickerdoodle from the plate in front of me.

My mother asked how things had gone during the meeting with Martha, and I explained how she seemed worried that the death was related to her. And how she didn't seem to have shared this fear with her employers.

"Honestly, it all sounds a little preposterous—or at least paranoid. So I plan to do a little looking online to see if I can find anything unusual about her history. Even though she fears that someone did this to damage her reputation, she won't talk to the police or give me any details."

"That sounds like a long shot, doesn't it?" Sam said. "Have you learned anything about the other people on the tour or the lady who died?"

"Those questions are on my list, too. And at some point I want to stop in at the other restaurants to see if they noticed anything about our group."

"Are you sure you want to take that on when you have so many wedding details to wrap up?" my mother asked. She was biting her lip, and I knew she must have worded that question carefully so as not to appear meddlesome.

"The thing is, I have to write the article on the seafood tour anyway. It's all I've got for this issue of *Key Zest*, other than a little piece on where to eat Thanksgiving if you're not up for cooking. And Danielle tells me that Palamina's on a tear."

"Again?" my mother asked. "What's wrong this time? For someone so high-powered, she sure seems high-strung."

I could only shrug.

"Have they definitely determined that the death was related to Martha's food?" Sam asked. "If so, I would think your Nathan could handle all this, or turn it over to someone who would."

"No, that comes from her so far. For all we know, the woman could have had a stroke or heart attack, unrelated to anything she ate. And I promised Martha I wouldn't say anything until she was ready." I crossed my arms over my stomach. Sam wasn't usually pushy this way—the stress of the season must be getting to him too. Luckily, my phone dinged with a text message to interrupt the conversation. Unluckily, it was the contractor, canceling. *Again*. A lump swelled in my throat. I held the phone up so they could see.

"I hate to say this, honey, but I don't think he's going to do the work," my mother said. She had that "I'm your mom and it breaks my heart when you're sad" look on her face.

"Maybe there's someone else in town who would take it on?" Sam asked, reaching out to put a comforting hand on my shoulder.

"Maybe." But in my heart of hearts, I suspected it would be years before that houseboat was renovated. Which wasn't the end of the world in the grand scheme of tragic things happening in the universe. But even so, I felt down in the dumps and ready to retreat to my bedroom with only my cat in attendance, a good book, and whatever treats might be tucked away in my freezer.

Chapter Eight

And fantasy is exactly what it's designed to be: the ooze of a buttery grilled cheese, the drip of a just-punctured yolk down the side of a double-stacked burger snowdrifted with truffles, a magically pink drink swirled with neon blue, a four-scoop ice cream cone melting in the sultry summer heat—these images are intended to elicit visceral, lizard-brain responses of hunger and desire, but somewhere between the screen and the mouth, things often go left.

—Amanda Mull, "Instagram Food is a Sad, Sparkly Lie," Eater.com

I woke up early, not surprising as I'd gone to bed before ten. I had a text message from Nathan, who'd sacked out at six AM but promised to call in the evening. And another text from Analise, who asked me to call her when I got a moment. While I brewed a pot of coffee, I mulled over what to make for breakfast.

On the counter sat a perfectly ripe avocado that would turn brown and mushy if I waited another day. I peeled it and mashed it up with a squirt of lemon and a few drops of Tabasco hot sauce. After popping two pieces of whole-grain bread into the toaster, I sliced radishes and dug out the arugula and cilantro sprouts I'd found at the Bayview farmers' market earlier this week. When the toast was done, I slathered it with avocado and sprinkled the radishes and sprouts over top.

Then I went out onto the deck with a big mug of milky coffee and the avocado toast to think through the day. Both cats nosed around my plate, seeming disappointed to find vegetables rather than bacon. The humidity that had hugged the island like a fleece blanket for the past few days had been pushed out by a cold front overnight, so I was glad to have my furry companions settle in on my lap.

I didn't have anything on the calendar until my meeting with Steve Torrence this afternoon at Fort Zachary Taylor beach, where we would discuss the rehearsal, which was scheduled for Thursday morning before Thanksgiving dinner. I realized that I was even more nervous about the wedding than I'd allowed myself to acknowledge. I didn't think it was the prospect of marrying Nathan. I loved Nathan and he loved me. We didn't have a simple relationship, but it was fiery at the right times and comforting at others. Committing myself to Nathan felt right and true. It was more the weight of history that was getting to me—my parents' divorce scared me. And Nathan's as well. Did two people who weren't that great at talking things over stand a chance of staying together?

On top of that was the group of disparate people gathering this week, despite my reassuring comments to my mom. To be honest, it was hard to picture Nathan and my father hitting it off. Dad liked to think of himself as an intellectual. He hadn't wanted me, his only biological offspring, to go into the food business, and I very much doubted that police officer would be on his list of son-in-law dream occupations. I suspected that both of our jobs felt blue collar to him. Though hands-on was more like it—he wasn't a snob. But his parents, my grandparents, had drilled the importance of moving beyond physical labor to intellectual work into his value system.

And despite Sam's insistence to the contrary, how easy could it be to be hosting my mother's first husband in his home? And how tense would this make my mother? Just thinking about it made me quiver with anxiety. What would help calm me down? Baking, of course.

Once I'd finished my breakfast and dislodged the kitties from my lap, I headed back into the kitchen, purposely avoiding looking at the pile of trash next door that was supposed to be my future home. I brought up my recipe for pecan pie bars on the iPad and began to pull out the ingredients: flour, sugar, salt, eggs, vanilla, butter, pecans, and the fat-inducing ingredient that I dared use in no other recipe—corn syrup. I'd made these once before for a potluck dinner and they'd vanished off the plate like a light frost in the sunlight. I whipped up the shortbread crust in my food processor, patted it into a parchment-papered pan, and slid it into the oven before starting on the filling. Once I'd finished the gooey pecan mixture, poured it over top of the piping-hot crust, and slid the whole thing back into the oven, I returned Analise's call.

"Did you get a chance to talk to Chef Martha?" she asked.

I filled her in on the little I'd learned. "Tomorrow I'll visit the other restaurants and see if anyone noticed anything. If I turn nothing up, Martha promised she'd talk to the police." I wasn't sure she'd follow through on that, but I had to hope. Or better still, maybe there'd be an announcement about the death occurring from natural causes and I could get out of this pseudo-investigation business altogether.

"Sounds fair enough." She hesitated, then added, "I have one more small favor. Would you have time to have a quick coffee with the dead woman's husband? He wants to talk with someone who was on the tour, and I can't reach any of the others. I know it's a lot to ask . . ." Her voice trailed away.

I heaved a mental sigh. "Could he meet me in an hour or so? At the Cuban Coffee Queen near the harbor?"

"Of course, and thank you. His name is Marcel. I admit I'm feeling a little desperate, too. Did you see the article in the *Citizen* this morning?"

"I haven't had a chance to read it."

"You'll see," she said. "Let me know if you find out anything new. And what I can do for you this week. I'm an expert on wedding stress after my brother's party."

While the pecan pie squares baked, I walked up the finger to the parking lot to grab our copy of the local paper. The headline that Analise had referred to was on the front page: WOMAN DIES FOLLOWING LOCAL FOOD TOUR. The Key West police spokeswoman, Alyson Crean, was quoted as saying the police would consider the possibility of food tampering as the cause of death, as well as natural causes. The short piece was accompanied by a large photograph of Analise holding a tray of small individual-sized key lime pies. This exact photo had appeared on the cover of *Menu Magazine* last year. The pies came from Blue Heaven restaurant, where the pastry chef specialized in mile-high meringue. This stop had been on Analise's original tour, before she'd cooked up the seafood tour. She had to be absolutely devastated. I was glad I'd agreed to another favor.

* * *

Marcel, the bereaved husband, was waiting in front of the colorfully painted mural that decorated one side of the original Cuban Coffee Queen. I realized instantly that I should have chosen another shop, as this one was very close to the spot where his wife had collapsed. I hurried up to him and hugged him before he had a chance to speak.

"I'm so very sorry about Audrey," I said. "I can't think of a worse way to end a vacation."

"Frankly, I can't either." He looked so upset and so bedraggled it was hard to witness. He had on the same clothing that I'd noticed during the tour—the jeans ripped in multiple places, the chains, the black T-shirt. Either he hadn't bothered to change, he had multiple sets of the same outfit, or some kind soul had washed the clothing and returned it to him. From the greasy look of his hair and the stubble on his face, I suspected he hadn't bothered with washing anything.

"What can I order for you?" I asked. "I always get the café con leche with one sugar. It's perfect almost every time. But the smoothies are good if you're hungry, or you may not have an appetite at all . . ."

I was rambling, because sitting in the presence of that much sadness was difficult and painful, and reminded me of what it would feel like to lose Nathan. Completely brutal.

"The coffee is fine," he said. "I'm not sure I'll ever want to eat again."

This original site of the Cuban Coffee Queen had a square opening in the wall where patrons ordered and got a quick look at the espresso machines and tiny kitchen inside. Employees popped out of the opening like puppets to announce pickups. As a regular, I knew most of them. Today, both of my casual pals Eric and Paulina were on duty. I chatted with Paulina about her new baby and Eric about his plans for Thanksgiving, then ordered the two cafés con leche and a cheese toast to go. Maybe the sight of me eating would stimulate Marcel's appetite. And toasted cheese was comfort food, through and through. And he looked like he needed all the comfort he could get. Several minutes later, I took the bag from Paulina and led Marcel toward a bench overlooking the harbor. I split the sandwich in two and left half on a piece of waxed paper next to his coffee.

"Analise told me you're helping investigate Audrey's death," he said, staring at me with damp eyes.

I nearly choked on a mouthful of cheese toast. "No, no, I said I'd talk to a few people while I finish the article I'm writing. No one has decided it was foul play, have they? And besides, even if they did, the police here do an excellent job with these kinds of cases, and I'm marrying a detective and I've promised him to stay out of police business."

His shoulders slumped even lower, as if I'd sucked away the only hope he was holding. A puff of wind blew across the harbor, clanking the masts and sails of the boats near us and causing us both to shiver. He picked up the paper cup of coffee and held it in both hands as though he was warming them by a fire. I began to feel frantic to fill the silence.

"What have you heard so far? Have they given you a cause of death? You seem to think it wasn't natural causes. Or maybe that's not at all why you asked to talk with me?"

"Honestly, now that I'm here, I'm not even sure why I wanted to meet. Maybe I just needed to talk with someone who'd been there with us."

"A witness," I said, laying my hand on one of his. "So they haven't told you why she died?"

"A stroke," he said. "They said she had a stroke. I thought they knew how to handle medical crises like that. How could a forty-five-year-old woman be alive one minute and half an hour later be gone?" A tear edged out of one eye, trickled down his cheek, and pooled in the stubbled dimple on his chin.

"You'd been to Key West before?" I was struggling to figure out how to keep the conversation going in a way that might be helpful to him.

"Years ago we stopped for a day during a cruise. It was our belated honeymoon. And we both loved it here and swore we'd come back." He set the coffee down at his feet, picked up the half sandwich I'd insisted he take, and then put it down again. "That might have been the happiest we ever were. Which is kind of sad, considering we were married over twenty years."

"I'm sorry for that," I said. "I can see why you fell in love with the place. The same thing happened to me. I followed a guy down here knowing nothing about Key West, and after that relationship quickly blew up, I got hooked on the place. And I've been here ever since. In fact, I'm marrying a local guy later this week." I twisted the engagement ring on my finger—we'd had it made using my grandmother's diamond—wishing I hadn't said this. "So you and Audrey were married over twenty years; that's impressive! What was your secret?"

"Secret? I have no idea. Put one foot in front of the other."

Yikes. If he'd been depressed when he got here, there were two of us in the dumps now.

"Shouldn't say things like that to a girl who is just getting married." He tried to push out a smile. "Audrey had a terrible case of depression. Most of her adult life. So it wasn't an ordinary marriage with ordinary problems." He gazed out over the harbor, his fingers tapping a rhythm I couldn't hear up and down the length of his thigh.

"I'm so sorry," I murmured, feeling like I was in way over my head here. This poor man needed to be talking to my psychologist friend Eric Altman. Or Steve Torrence with his years of experience counseling premarital couples. But Marcel didn't seem to notice my inadequacies.

"She had been so depressed over the past eleven months that it exhausted both of us. And no one could seem to help her. I think we'd both given up finding hope. Apparently depression runs deep like a river in her family.

"I'd lost patience this past year, I had. I even told her I was at the end of my rope. You can't imagine what it's like to always be wondering whether this is the day she takes her own life. And yet, I was done with quack hospitals and doctors and treatments that did nothing for her."

"I'm so sorry," I said again. "This sounds terrible." In fact, his hopelessness felt like it was leaking from his body and leaching into mine.

He shrugged and looked up, his face stained with tears. "She stopped telling me how she felt because I'd pretty much told her I couldn't handle it. Out of nowhere, about a month ago she started to feel a little better. She knew I'd planned to come down here to get away from our dreary November weather and do a little fishing. She insisted on coming along to celebrate feeling better and to renew our relationship. I tried to talk her out of it. Honestly? I thought she'd be a drag on my time." His fists clenched in his lap. "I didn't deserve things improving, did I?"

Again, I tried to puzzle out what he wanted from me. Reassurance, most likely. "My gosh, I don't think you can blame yourself for what happened here. She seemed joyful the other day," I said. "She was loving all the food—and loving you as well. I remember noticing how devoted to each other you two seemed."

He focused his blue eyes on me, pleading. "It sounds crazy to hope that your wife has been murdered. But that's all I can think: if someone else did it, then it won't be my fault. If someone put something in that food that killed her, at least I can live with myself."

I wasn't at all sure how learning that she'd been murdered was better than the stroke diagnosis, but I wasn't going to argue with him. "I'll keep my ears open," I said. "I wish there was more I could say."

He nodded briefly, then got up and walked away.

I was practically undone by the time I returned to the houseboat, feeling upset and hopelessly inadequate. I didn't believe I'd helped him at all.

The sheet of pecan pie bars was cool by now, so I slid the confection out of the pan onto a cutting board and cut it into squares. I ate one—so sweet and flaky and the tiniest bit salty—and then began to realize I could end up eating half the tray if I stayed here at home. Though my wedding dress was not tight, it would be if I power-grazed my way through the entire recipe. I packed the bars into a glass container, slid them into the freezer, and picked up the hammer and crowbar lying by the door, and my work gloves. I had several hours before I was due to meet Torrence at the beach. If no one else would work on the darn boat next door, I would.

Chapter Nine

Like plumage that expanded to rainbow an otherwise unremarkable bird, Kamala's ability to transform raw ingredients into sumptuous meals brought her the kind of love her personality on its own might have repelled.
—Mira Jacob, *The Sleepwalker's Guide to Dancing*

I let myself into Nathan's houseboat, wishing immediately that I had worn a mask or at least had brought a bandanna to cover my nose. The smell of mold and mildew was almost overpowering—like a beach house that had been left closed up too long, only worse. I could feel my throat constrict and my breathing thicken. This project had made me uber sympathetic to the people whose homes had suffered hurricane damage and had nowhere else to live. And there had been many of those, especially further up the Keys.

So far, Nathan and I had thrown out or recycled mounds of trash left behind by the previous owners, including cans and boxes of food in the cupboards—well past their use-by date—toiletries down to the last inch of goopy product in the bathroom, and sheets and towels so ratty we didn't even consider donating them to the homeless shelter. Either the previous residents had left in a big hurry or they no longer cared about this place—or about what the new owners would think of them. It had been empty since I'd moved in, and Miss Gloria had reported that the previous neighbors were frankly antisocial.

We'd also managed to strip up the shag carpeting that covered the main living area like a hideous orange pelt, faded in some areas where the sun streamed in and dirty in others.

Why oh why would someone choose to have their kitchen carpeted? I wondered for the umpteenth time. Especially with a shaggy pile carpet that would hoard crumbs and attract pests? In this warm climate where we never felt the snap of a good frost, pests were not easy to get rid of. Underneath the carpet, as Miss Gloria had predicted, we found a beautiful Dade pine floor. Or it would be beautiful once somebody—anybody other than me—sanded it down and painted it with clear varnish that would show its humble beauty. I mulled over what I could tackle that would work off some of my angst without hurting myself.

The original contractor, whom Nathan and I had hired last spring and both been delighted to snag, had fallen off a roof in April and injured his back. Before his accident, he'd told us that the wood paneling was cheesy and thin and would strip off easily. So that seemed like a good place to start. I wedged my crowbar into a hole and pried off the first section. Underneath the paneling was a thin layer of insulation, drooping between the studs like a dirty curtain. *Asbestos?* I wondered, wishing again for the protective mask. Nathan would kill me if he knew I was doing this on my own.

As I worked, I thought about the coffee date I'd had with Marcel. From my observations on the food tour, I never would have guessed that she had a history of depression. Nor that they'd had a long and rocky marriage. Did she have other medical problems aside from depression that might have led to a stroke? Did she take care of herself in the physical way that a person would who was attached to her life and wanted it to continue? Quite possibly not, if Marcel was correct about her suicidal tendencies. I realized that I should have asked Marcel if he'd felt queasy or ill during the tour or after.

I worked for an hour until my muscles were quivering and my hair was soaked with sweat. Then I carried the pieces of paneling out to the deck, added them to the pile of trash accumulating near the dock, and returned to Miss Gloria's boat. The house phone was ringing as I entered our home. I dropped the tools next to the door and rushed over to answer. It was a collect call.

Will you accept the charges from . . . ? Someone. The connection was too crackly to make out the name.

"No, sorry, wrong number," I said. The line cut off. Spammers had really upped their games on the Keys lately, and I refused to get sucked in. I went into the bathroom to shower and get ready to meet Torrence at the beach.

When I came out into the living room, much more presentable, Miss Gloria had arrived home. She looked up from the *Key West Citizen*, which was spread out on the counter.

"Where are you off to?" she asked.

I explained about my meeting.

"Are you around for dinner?" she asked, looking slightly wistful. The plate of pecan squares that I'd left for her on the counter was empty.

"I suspect I will be. Nathan's working nights through Tuesday, so I certainly won't be seeing him. What are you craving?"

An impish look crossed her face. "Thinking ahead to all the turkey and fixings that are coming this week makes me yearn for something rich and simple like macaroni and cheese with broccoli. Maybe with lobster instead of broccoli. Something that screams decadence to an old lady who could be living her final days on this earth."

She was shameless. "That dish was on the food tour at Bagatelle," I said. "It was delicious. And you know I'll make whatever you want, even without the drama." I grinned back at her.

"You mentioned it yesterday, and I've been jonesing for it ever since. Did it make an appearance before or after that poor woman took sick?" Miss Gloria asked.

"Before. Actually, we'd sampled everything on the tour by the time she collapsed. But she hardly ate any of that dish, so I'm pretty certain they're off the hook." I'd been thinking about the recipe too—the rich creaminess of the cheese paired with the even richer lobster. Heavenly. I'd even gone so far as to Google Ina Garten's recipe and noodle over what tweaks I would make before adding it to my "Coming Soon" Pinterest board where I stashed recipes that I wanted to try.

"Consider it done. We have the cheese and the good pasta I ordered from Eataly, that store in New York. I'll stop at Eaton Street Seafood Market and pick up the lobster on my way back from the beach. It would probably be a good idea if you called ahead? Say a pound and a half out of the shell?"

"Consider it done," she said, with a giant smile spreading over her face.

"I nearly forgot," I said. "The phone spammers are getting more and more clever. This time it was a collect phone call, which was obviously a wrong number or someone trolling for an idiot." As these words left my mouth, her smile was replaced with an annoyed grimace, and I suddenly realized that I was the idiot. It had probably been her friend calling—the man in the orange jumpsuit whom she'd talked to yesterday at the book sale.

"That was Odom calling me with news about your food tour."

"I'm so sorry," I said. "Let's call him back."

"He doesn't have a phone, Hayley, he's in prison. He can only call out. Collect."

I apologized again. "How in the world did he track down our home number?"

She looked at me like I was a simpleton. "I gave him our phone number."

Good gravy, was she really turning into one of those old people who could be taken advantage of, have her life savings ripped right out from one of her? I had to be gentle with her. "That doesn't sound sensible or safe."

She practically rolled her eyes. "He's not an ax murder, Hayley. He's not going to escape from jail and then come creeping onto the boat to murder us in our berths. He was an accountant at a law firm in Tallahassee and he made some bad choices, and fortunately or unfortunately, he got caught. The jury is out on our justice system, don't you think? I don't know if it teaches people a lesson to serve jail time, or produces hardened criminals."

I hesitated. She was already a little mad at me, but I felt like I had to warn her again. "I'm just not sure how safe it is to give out personal information to someone who's in jail."

"Hayley, he's a trustie; that's short for trusted prisoner. He's earned his way into that position with good behavior and volunteer work. And I've gotten to know him over this past year. He understands perfectly that what he did was wrong. And he regrets it and he plans to make amends. Starting with helping out an old lady." She parked her hands on her hips. "You should know that not everyone who's in prison is a bad person." She cleared her throat. "My son, for example." Then she marched into her room and shut the door—almost slamming it but not quite.

Now I felt like a complete heel. But why in the world hadn't she said something about her son before now? We'd lived together for, what, almost three years? And been friends before that. I wanted to be the kind of friend she could turn to when she had a problem, the way I felt about her. My mother had taught me how important friends were. And she lived her words, too.

The next thought stuck in my throat like a chicken bone. Had Miss Gloria told my mother and sworn her to secrecy because she thought I couldn't be trusted or wasn't mature enough to understand? That would really feel lousy.

Chapter Ten

Al dente pasta, swirled in a salty, creamy cheese sauce, macaroni and cheese is like a hug wrapped in a warm sweater, unparalleled in its ability to comfort and satisfy.
—Alison Roman, "Prepare to be Lusciously Comforted," *The New York Times*, April 11, 2018

The trouble with having seen so many weddings on the island was that I had found it impossible to figure out what I wanted and make some reasonable choices. Well, not impossible, but certainly difficult. I didn't choose Smathers Beach, because in the high season that strip of sand was like a wedding factory. Another option was the Southernmost Point, where I'd gone last year for the sunrise Easter service conducted by Steve Torrence. But they wanted to do the food at their café, and I had other plans for a very personal menu. Some couples hired a boat or a sailing vessel to go out on the water with a smaller group of friends and family. But I tended to get seasick easily—for the bride to upchuck during the ceremony would not be an attractive wedding feature.

I'd ended up deciding that the point of Fort Zachary Taylor beach, where my mother had planned to have her wedding (later diverted by a hurricane), was perfect. And then after the ceremony, we'd repair to the Hemingway house for the celebration.

Of course, the caterer had seemed like a slam dunk. Who made better food than my own mother? But I didn't want her and Sam to be slaving in the kitchen instead of enjoying the wedding. Luckily, Irena and Maria and their extended family, Cuban-Americans who had worked for my mother on the Little White House event last winter, had stepped up instantly to offer their services. I had had a hand in solving their relative's murder, and they were eager to help us in return. Our wedding food would reflect all the things I loved most about this island—the seafood, the tropical flavors, and a little dash of Cuba.

Nathan had insisted that all this was fine, he truly didn't have a preference. He only wanted me to be completely happy. As long as we served enough food to satisfy all the guests and enough wine to make them giddy without endangering their drives home or attracting negative attention from local cops, he'd be content. He hadn't wanted to discuss his first wedding in much detail, other than to say it was a dog-and-pony show that had cost a good chunk of his ex-wife's family fortune, not to mention good-will between him and his in-laws. Not a great way to start a marriage. Miss Gloria had encouraged me to run a Google search looking for the announcement of his previous wedding so we could get the dope on the story. But then we'd both come to the conclusion that that would be a breach of trust, not to mention bordering on stalker-creepy.

As usual, just being near the water calmed me down a little, allowing me to believe that this was indeed the right choice for our wedding ceremony. *Our wedding ceremony.* Yikes. Those three words brought back all the anxiety that the sounds of sloshing water had drained away. I parked my scooter and walked out to the point, where the beach met a large rock jetty and where cruise ships and other larger boats found the channel deep enough to allow them safe passage through the reefs surrounding Key West.

Before I arrived in town, one set of city commissioners had lobbied to dredge the channel deeper so that even bigger cruise ships could dock at our island. But the local residents rose up and rejected that proposal. Living wasn't always easy here, where one set of interests was often knocking into the interests of others, such as the rich people versus the homeless. The year-round working people versus the snowbirds who fluttered down for the winter season. The people with deep ties to business versus the people whose hearts were tethered to the environment. I supposed this might be true of anywhere I chose to live, but the small size of the island and the fragility of its vegetation and wildlife, and even the island culture, made the outcome of these struggles feel more poignant.

Steve Torrence appeared behind me and startled me out of my thoughts.

"It's a beautiful day," he said.

"Let's hope it can hold until next weekend," I said. "Probably won't."

"Oh," he said, circling his arm around my shoulders. "You're getting married, my friend—this is supposed to be a joyous time. I hope this isn't evidence of a downward spiral inside your head."

"Hope not," I said, and then pecked him on the cheek, just happy to be enveloped by his friendly aura. "But it's been a weird weekend. Have you ever had a day where it seems that everyone you meet either lies to you or is hiding something?"

"Are you kidding? You're talking about the life of a police officer. Out on the streets, people lie just for the sport of it." He cocked one eyebrow. "Don't tell me this is about Nathan."

"He doesn't reveal enough for it to constitute a lie." I laughed but without a lot of mirth behind it.

"Remember what I said about that yesterday . . ."

"I know, talk to him directly if I'm upset about something. And I will. But he's so wrapped up in whatever case he's got going on. What *does* he have going on?" I did not think he'd answer this, but he wouldn't hold it against me for asking.

"I'd tell you if I could. And he'll tell you when he can."

"Is he safe?"

"He's doing everything in his power to keep himself safe, as well as the people around him. That's always our first concern. And really, we go through so much training, physical and mental, that it's hard to get the best of us." He tapped one fist to chest and the other on his head.

I heaved a great sigh. "I think this food tour death has gotten to me. I'm worried about everything and everybody."

"That must've been a terrible thing to witness."

"It was. And then I met with the widowed husband for coffee." I held my hand out. "Don't get upset. I didn't go looking for this, but he was desperate for someone to talk with who'd been there. He seemed so horribly sad. Even so, I felt that he was lying to me the whole time we were chatting. But why lie to me? It doesn't make sense."

"Often it has to do with the person who's lying rather than the person they are hiding something from. Could he be holding back some kind of truth about himself that he thinks would look ugly in the light of another person's eyes?"

I nodded. This sounded both right and familiar. And it would help explain why he was hoping his wife had been murdered.

"The problem is that secrets grow poisonous after a while and begin to leak," he said. "Toxic spills."

"Speaking of toxic, I think the chef at Isle Cook Key West believes the woman's death was her fault," I said.

"Food poisoning?"

"Maybe, but maybe not accidental. Have you heard anything new about cause of death?"

"Natural causes, that's all I've heard so far," he said, pushing his glasses to the top of his head. "Tell me more."

"She won't talk to you—she'll barely talk to me. So I'm telling you this in a strictly confidential way." I fluffed up my hair, which had been flattened from my helmet. "And I chatted with her bosses on the way out. They are understandably concerned about their business; they don't want to get a rap for food poisoning or something worse. I'm sure all the restaurants on the tour are worried."

Steve frowned, slid off his glasses, and replaced them with sunglasses. "The cops are looking into all of this. Think about it, Hayley, if she didn't want to tell you something and she refuses to talk to the police department at all, what are the chances she did something illegal?"

He waited until I nodded.

"Pretty good I, suppose," I said. "But like what? She wouldn't have poisoned her own customer. Who would do something like that?"

"Supposing they had a connection from the past? Supposing she's been planning this since, well, since forever. Or supposing she'd planned a prank and it went badly south?"

"But how would Martha even have known that Audrey was in town? According to her husband, Audrey was a last-minute addition to the trip."

"And you've already said you felt like he was lying or hiding something as he talked to you. You can't absorb everything that someone says and assume that it's true. As cops, we assume there are always other sides to what a witness or suspect is telling us, many shades of truth. As you gather data, one version begins to stand out as more true than the others."

This seemed right to me. I'd done the same thing myself, the data-gathering bit, and seen my psychologist friend Eric build his understanding of his patients brick by brick this way, too. I nodded again to signal that I agreed with his thoughts.

He squeezed my shoulder. "Please don't get more involved. You did the right thing, trying to convince the chef to talk with me. You'll call me the instant you hear anything new?" he asked.

"Of course. And please do the same?"

He nodded. "If I can. No promises."

Which I didn't like, but I understood. "Enough about that," I said. "We were going to go over the ceremony and get ready for the rehearsal." I glanced over at him, and we started to walk toward the point where the Atlantic Ocean and the Gulf of Mexico came together, where our ceremony would take place. A suitable metaphor for joining me and Nathan together—the results could be a little bumpy, but exciting. "I know this isn't quite normal, rehearsing the rehearsal. I suspect it's downright neurotic."

He smiled, "You're right. I wouldn't do this for everyone. But you're a special friend and so is Nathan.

And you seem so anxious that I'm happy to help. What do we need to work on?"

"Most of the planning is easy—I stayed with tradition," I said. "Nathan goes up the aisle first, along with you. And the two of you stand there flexing your cop muscles and looking handsome while the music plays."

He laughed and pumped his bicep and patted his six-pack abs.

"Then my mother and Sam walk up and take seats. Then Ray helps his daughter strew the basket of petals. That will be so cute. Unless she melts down. With a toddler, that's always a possibility." I fanned my face with my hand, thinking I shouldn't have taken any chances with this wedding. I should have gone simpler. Like eloping.

"What's the backup plan if she falls apart?" Torrence asked patiently, pulling my mind back to the facts.

"Her mom, Connie, will be right behind her. So if the baby starts to shriek, she scoops her up and they come down together. And Connie always carries emergency snacks like Cheerios and fruit pouches. And I'm sure she'll have the baby take a nap before the wedding."

"Perfect," he said. "Then you and your father, right? Sounds like you've thought everything through. But . . . you still look worried."

I gnawed on my bottom lip. "Will it hurt Sam's feelings if he's not more involved in the actual ceremony? He is the one married to my mother."

"On the other hand, they haven't been married very long," Torrence said. "And he wasn't around during the time she was raising you, right? And he seems like a lovely man who doesn't easily take offense."

"All true," I said, my mind catching on something he'd said. "My mother had the most to do with raising me, so why isn't she walking me down the aisle? Why does she end up sitting on the sidelines watching my father walk me to the altar?"

He shrugged and I grabbed him for a quick hug, feeling a thousand pounds lighter. "I think that's the missing piece. Thanks." I hugged him again and left him looking befuddled as I trotted back to my scooter and headed toward my lobster mission.

* * *

Eaton Street is one of the busiest streets in Key West. Lots of tourists arrive in town on this route, as well as workers and delivery trucks and gigantic buses that sail around the curve from the Palm Avenue bridge. The road is narrow and runs two ways, making it utterly unsuitable for those tourists on wobbly bicycles who choose to navigate the street along with cars, trucks, and scooters. All in all, not the setting you might choose for an outdoor café. But if the food is good enough, I've realized, people will eat anywhere, particularly for lunch.

The Eaton Street Seafood Market is located inside what used to be a gas station, decorated with white art deco–style stucco with pink piping. This store serves fresh fish from local fishermen, and had recently added an outdoor café. It was here that we had enjoyed our Key West pink shrimp during the tour. One of the owners was replacing a sun umbrella as I parked my scooter.

"Miss Gloria called about the lobster," he said before I could greet him. "They're holding it for you inside—with her special discount, of course. I tried to talk her into the Key West pinks because the lobster is so pricey right now. But then she explained what you're making. What time is dinner?" He winked and grinned. Then his face got somber. "You were on the tour the other day when that woman took ill. So tragic," he said. "Hopefully it wasn't a seafood allergy. But why you would take a seafood tour if you were allergic to the stuff, I can't imagine."

"I haven't heard a word about an allergy. Her husband was told it was a stroke," I said, glad he had brought it up so I didn't have to find a way to finesse the subject. "Do you remember noticing anything off about her when we were here? We stopped at the brewery right after we ate your shrimp, and that's where she collapsed." I realized too late that he might take that as an accusation.

"After we delivered your pinks, I went back to work on the umbrellas," he said, gesturing at the canvas shading the tables on the sidewalk. "Hurricane Irma shredded our other umbrellas, and out here, we need the shade or our diners wilt. And it was very busy with other lunch customers that day.

All that to say, I wasn't paying a lot of attention. But from what I remember, she seemed fine. And nobody else got sick, right? If the shrimp had been off, everyone who ate it would've gotten sick."

"They tasted great," I said quickly. "And I remember her looking fine too. Call me if you think of anything that stands out?" I asked, handing him one of my *Key Zest* cards with my cell phone on it.

Then I went inside to collect the lobster and pay for it, learning that Miss Gloria had already given her credit card over the phone. I buzzed home, parked the scooter, and approached the houseboat, prepared to apologize again. But the door to Miss Gloria's room was still shut tight. She wasn't the type to sulk, so I assumed she was taking one of her senior-citizen power naps.

I stashed the lobster in the fridge, put a pot of water on to boil, and began to shred cheddar, Parmesan, and Gruyère cheeses. After sautéing a small chopped shallot and a few mashed cloves of garlic in butter, I added flour to the flavored butter and began to stir in milk. Once the roux thickened, I added the cheeses. When the pasta was cooked to al dente and the cream sauce thick and cheesy, I mixed it all together with the lobster meat, topped it with buttered panko crumbs, and popped the pan into the oven.

Then I texted my gym trainer Leigh and told her I would need to lose five to seven pounds in the next day's workout. She messaged back quickly with a horrified emoji face, and suggested I bring her some of whatever high-calorie treat I was making.

The house phone rang and I snatched it up. Collect call again; this time I accepted quickly. "I'm sure you're looking for Miss Gloria," I said. "So sorry about the misunderstanding this morning." I set the phone on the counter and went down the hall to roust my roommate out of her room. She emerged blinking and headed directly to the phone.

"Odom, how are you? I'm sorry my roommate hung up on you earlier." She listened for a moment and then laughed and listened again, turning away from me. I could hear only her side of the conversation, which consisted of a lot of *mm-hmm*s, *really*s, and *thank you*s.

She turned back to me when she was finished. "He hasn't heard anything about someone tracking Chef Martha. But he's got feelers out and will call back if does. Other than that, there is apparently a lot going on around this island—smugglers, both human and drugs, he thinks, plus some bad dudes moving down here for the winter. Neither of which has anything to do with your question."

"Thank you," I said, and then after a pause, added, "I'm so sorry if I sounded judgmental about your son. I had no idea." Tears pricked my eyes and hers looked a little damp too. "I'd love to hear about him if you're willing to tell me."

She sank down onto the couch and patted the cushion beside her, reaching for my hand. "It's so hard, you know, because you love these small beings more than life itself. You gave them life, and then they grow up and become separate little humans, and you nudge them out into the world like a little floating candle on the river, with so many hopes and dreams attached. But sometimes strong currents or storms come up and they get pushed away from the path you set them on and you're terrified their light will get blown out."

She took a shuddering breath. "You'll see one day when you have a child."

"*If*," I said with a smile.

"You will." She grinned back. "First of all, your mother will get grandmother fever and the pressure will mount and mount. And you'll want to pass on Nathan's gorgeous eyes to a baby."

"And my grandmother's recipe box when the green-eyed tyke gets old enough," I said. "But go on. Please tell me about your son. This isn't Frank, right?"

Frank was the older of Miss Gloria's two boys—men by now—and I'd met him once and frequently chatted with him by phone when he was trying to reach his mother. And he'd been the one to agree that my moving in with her would take a great weight off them and allow her to stay in Key West, something she badly wanted.

"It's so hard to worry from a distance," he'd said. Miss Gloria generally traveled up to Michigan to see them for a couple of weeks every summer, but none of her family had come to Key West since I'd known her.

"She's amazing," I remembered telling him. "Some days she has more energy than I do. And her mind is razor sharp. I promise I will look after her and let you know if anything changes." I didn't tell him that as often as I looked after her, she watched over me too.

"James. My second," she said, drawing my attention back to our conversation. "He was always so sweet and soft—a real-life cuddle bear." She held her arms to her chest, as if rocking an infant. "I fear I babied him more than I should have. He was very sensitive about criticism, so we probably said less to him than we did to Frank, who could roll with any feedback, absorb it, and come out stronger."

I nodded and waited, allowing her all the room she needed to tell me as much or as little as she wanted.

"Anyway, it was white-collar crime. Nothing vicious or physical, thank goodness. That would've been so hard to live with." She sighed and plucked at a glittery thread that had come loose on her sweatshirt. "Harder. He worked for an accounting firm, and he siphoned off money from his clients. Small amounts at first, and then when he didn't get caught, the numbers got bigger. He married a woman who wanted the best of everything—more than they could reasonably afford." She looked at me intently. "I tried very hard to get along with her, but we could tell right from the start—how much her family spent on the wedding—that she had big eyes and was full of envy. She was deeply disappointed in what we offered for the rehearsal dinner." She sighed, remembering the pain. "Over time, he fell behind on his mortgage and his credit cards, and the 'borrowed' money floated him out of trouble. Until he got caught."

"I can't imagine how disturbing it must have been to hear that news," I said, squeezing her hand.

She pressed her palms to her cheeks. "I was grateful Frank Senior was not alive to have to endure the shock. James himself said the same thing. He was so ashamed, and he's promised to pay back every penny. And I believe that he means it too. He's not a bad person, just a little weak. And talking with Odom has helped me to understand him a little better, because he got into similar trouble. And he's helped me figure out how to move on, keep loving him. Forgive him. And myself."

I opened my mouth to protest, but she waved me off.

"Your children are always a part of you. And you will always feel some responsibility for how they turn out, no matter if they are babies or you are eighty-something."

The oven timer dinged and I got up to remove our dinner, which had begun to perfume the houseboat with its cheesy, buttery scent and hints of the sea.

"Saved by the bell," she said. "Enough of that. Let's eat lobster and talk about your wedding."

I dished out two plates of the steaming macaroni, and Miss Gloria added a heap of salad to each. "A nod to keeping our figures trim," she said, laughing.

I took the first bite of creamy lobster and pasta, thinking a little midsection bulge would be a trade-off I could live with in order to eat this manna.

"Speaking of weddings and families, I had a lovely conversation with Nathan's mother today," Miss Gloria said.

My fork clattered to the plate and my mouth dropped open. "Nathan's mother? You're kidding! This has to be a joke."

I had never spoken to her, and Nathan had warned me not to try to call. So with my mother's editorial support, I'd written the warmest, most welcoming, most unthreatening note I could come up with and sent it off as soon as we set our wedding date. I'd queried him about his family dynamics, of course, because family and friends meant everything to me. And I'd hung around Eric enough to realize that who you become has a lot to do—like it or not—with your family of origin. I found it terribly curious—and a little worrisome—that Nathan seemed to have distant connections with his family, even though he'd let slip months ago that he had a mother, a father, and a grandmother.

"So you didn't spring out of Zeus's head like Athena," I'd teased him. When he said nothing back in response, I'd dug a little deeper.

"I can't imagine her son getting married and she hasn't even sent one line of congratulations," I'd said. "I guess I can't quite wrap my brain around that."

"Here's the thing," he said, looking sheepish and apologetic. "My mother adored wife number one.

They hit it off the second they met. And she blamed me completely for the breakup. And I wouldn't be surprised if they are still in close touch. My mother has never been the kind of woman who opens her heart easily. Once she does, she's all in. You might notice that I inherited some of that trait."

He waited for me to acknowledge that truth, and then continued. "After her heart was broken by the divorce, I think it was too hard for her to consider getting to know you. Too risky. Too much potential for disappointment."

I hadn't known what to do with this new information. I had so many questions. Why would anyone choose to take sides with an in-law over her own flesh and blood? An ousted in-law at that. What was so fabulous about Nathan's first wife that this chilly woman had fallen for her? How hard had Nathan tried to get her to come to the wedding, to open her heart to his new relationship? How had he described me? After he'd explained the situation, I'd felt a tiny bit angry and disappointed and sad. But he seemed to have closed the door on the subject so definitely that I didn't have the heart to bring it up again.

And now she'd called? Less than a week before the wedding?

"Yikes," I said. "What in the world did she say?"

Miss Gloria had just forked in a big bite of lobster and cheese, so she finished chewing and said, "She welcomes you to the family. She apologized for not contacting us sooner. And she wishes you and Nathan a very happy life."

I slumped against the back of the banquette. "I hardly know what to say. Is she coming to the wedding?"

"She sends her regrets, but looks forward to meeting you soon. You know what? I got the feeling that she's a tad agoraphobic. I think we may need to go visit her. And then she asked if you had registered for china or silver."

I shook my head and rolled my eyes. "She's obviously never set foot on a houseboat."

Miss Gloria giggled. "I explained all that to her, and I said she was getting the most amazing person as a daughter-in-law and that you were performing a miracle, loosening her son up so she might not even recognize him."

"Good gravy, what did she say to that?"

"She laughed, that's all. Like she understood exactly what I was saying. And then I told her that on top of all that good news, you were the most amazing cook. And I told her that the one thing you craved for a wedding gift was the Breville food processor. I said you hadn't even told anyone about it because you felt embarrassed about the price tag."

"You didn't."

"I did. And she said, 'Done!' She's going to buy it through the Restaurant Store and also give you a gift certificate to Martha's place. So two of your favorite local shops get a little piece of the action. I told her you were very big on shopping local. And then I told her we couldn't wait to meet her because we were all dying to see the woman who had produced the magnificent Nathan."

I covered my eyes and began to laugh helplessly. "Thank goodness we're only moving ten feet away from you. Would you mind coming over and answering our phone? You're the best personal assistant anyone's ever had."

Chapter Eleven

Another week, another chef down.
—Pete Wells, "Harassment Issues Need
an Answer," *The New York Times*,
January 3, 2018

I was up the next morning before dawn, determined to work off the calories I had consumed over the last few days. My best bet would be to jog to my appointment at the gym and then walk home. I planned to sprint from our houseboat over the Palm Avenue bridge to take advantage of the one hill in town, then jog along Frances Street, past the cemetery, down Truman to Bayview Park, and from there to WeBeFit. The return trip would be shorter, just enough time to cool down and limp home.

Beginning to pant as I crossed the bridge, I realized I had more ambition than stamina. I slowed down earlier than I'd planned, determined to avoid the humiliation of having to call someone for a ride. The morning felt hot and humid, even before seven, and I was sweating through my T-shirt by the time I passed the cemetery. I switched over to a trudge to catch my breath and cool off a little. My mind was circling around Miss Gloria's news about her son James. She was such a lovely, generous, warm person, and those traits shined through in everything she did and said. I pictured her as an amazing mother. So it seemed incongruous that one of her sons would have gotten into the kind of trouble that landed him in prison.

I cut across the final block of Frances Street to Truman and did a double take. I swore Nathan's rental car was sandwiched between two scooters and a battered Kia. Not his official Key West Police Department SUV—he'd told me that was in the shop for a week for a major rebuild of his spongy brakes. I retraced my steps to be sure—and yes, in the back seat of the little silver SUV, I spotted the pink plaid seat cover that his dog Ziggy favored. And a giant fleece bone that I'd given him as a gag gift. Ziggy had taken to it instantly.

What in the world was he doing here?

For the most part, the buildings on this street were small single-family homes, probably some rentals, but mostly year-round residents who appreciated somewhat reasonable rents in exchange for the not-so-desirable proximity to busy Truman Avenue and the gentleman's bar called the Buoys' Club. And yes, although I'd never set foot inside myself, that establishment was exactly what it sounded like: inebriated men watching mostly naked girls on impossibly high heels pole dancing. Some of the men were probably hoping for more than the view. Surely

Nathan wasn't there for the so-called entertainment. My breathing quickened at the thought. I knew him too well as a decent, devoted man, soon to be my husband—he would not patronize such a place. So why was his car here? It had to be police business of some kind.

I wound through the residential streets around the Horace O'Bryant School, past the low-income housing, to WeBeFit on First Street. This gym where Leigh worked was high-tech and hosted the best personal trainers on the island, though the quarters were tight. The space would not work for the claustrophobic client or those who were certain they'd be too fat or out of shape to make a public appearance. Leigh was waiting inside the door with her iPad. I was six minutes late to a half-hour appointment.

"I'm totally serious. I need to lose five to seven pounds before Friday," I said, grabbing a stainless-steel water bottle out of the cooler. "It's not my fault, really. Miss Gloria insisted on the lobster mac and cheese last night, and then I had to sample the pecan pie squares because I wanted to be sure the recipe turned out well. We're hosting a madhouse of guests for Thanksgiving."

A couple of the other patrons who regularly worked out at the same time I did began to hoot with laughter. "Maybe you could drape something gauzy over your wedding dress," suggested Cathy as she completed a set of impressively hard pull-ups.

"Or switch over to a burlap sack," said Roger, another regular customer who entered triathlons and had probably never experienced an extra ounce of fat in his life. I stuck out my tongue and followed Leigh to the back of the gym.

"You know it's too late for any of this work to show up for the wedding, but it might cut some of your anxiety, which appears to be in overdrive. And your sore muscles might remind you not to sample so many treats." She leaned forward with a grin and whispered: "Did you bring me something?"

I grinned back and passed her the pecan bars that I'd wrapped in foil and tucked into my pull-string backpack. "Watch your molars," I said.

We started the day's workout, focusing on my abs, my biceps, and my shoulders.

"You're quiet today," Leigh said. "Is something bothering you?"

"What do you know about the Buoys' Club, the bar on Truman?"

She cocked her head to one side and squinted a little. "I used to know some of the women who worked there, when I was doing writing workshops out at the jail. You know it's a strip club, right?"

I stopped midcrunch. "Yes. But surely they weren't in jail for stripping?"

"Mostly alcohol and drugs, which is what it probably takes to tolerate working in a place like that." She looked disgusted. "Do you know that those women don't go by their names, they go by channel-marker numbers? Makes my blood boil to think about it."

I couldn't help asking, "Have you been inside?"

"Only by accident. And I'll never go back again. Why do you ask?"

"I noticed it as I was jogging by. Usually I'm on my scooter and it doesn't register." I didn't have the heart to tell her about Nathan's car. What if he really was there for his last hurrah before we got married? I didn't believe that, but the thought was too humiliating to even bring up with a friend.

At the end of the half hour, we threaded back through the small gym to the front desk to make my next appointment. As Leigh brought their computer up to my account's page, a text buzzed through on my phone. It was from Martha Hubbard.

CAN YOU STOP BY THIS MORNING BY ANY CHANCE? WOULDN'T ASK BUT THERE'S BEEN ANOTHER INCIDENT.

WILL DO. ABOUT AN HOUR, I texted back.

Leigh knew most everyone on our island, and those she didn't know, she knew something about. So I asked her opinion about Martha's mental stability.

"She's a good friend," Leigh said, her expression thoughtful. "And as long as I've known her, she's always been a rock. She went through some wild times a number of years back, but nothing recent that I'm aware of."

"Do you know of any kind of rotten boyfriend or boss who might be out to get her? Who might have held a grudge against her, waiting for the right time to strike back?"

Leigh handed me a card with my appointments scratched out on it. "Since coming to Key West, she's worked as a chef at both Nine One Five and Louie's Backyard—the upstairs part."

I nodded, having seen her there and tasted her food several times. She'd even sent a few extra dishes over to my table that we hadn't ordered—the mark of a chef who recognizes a valued customer.

"As far as I know, people loved her at both those restaurants. She was super-reliable and her food was good. And that is a very good combination for a chef. And I've never heard a word about anyone being out to get her." She finished tapping my next appointments into the computerized schedule and gave me a hug. "I hope you have a wonderful week. Don't get too knotted up—in anything. OK? We'll see you at the beach."

Ulp. That meant at my wedding. I trotted home to Houseboat Row to shower and change, every muscle in my body screaming for mercy. My heart insisted that I really wanted a glazed doughnut for breakfast, but my head steered me to a bowl of home-made granola with sliced bananas and almond milk. Feeling fortified and more than a little tired, I hopped on the scooter and headed south to the cooking store.

* * *

The door to Isle Cook Key West was locked, but I could see Martha working at the counter of the open kitchen. I rapped on the glass and she startled, glancing about like a trapped rabbit. But then she recognized me, smiled, and came over to let me in. She gave me a hug, but not before locking the door again behind us. She looked more frazzled than she had at my last visit, pale and tense, as if poised to run at any moment. And maybe she was.

"Thanks a million for coming," she said. "I know you have a lot to do and I appreciate it. And I wouldn't have called you if I wasn't—" Her voice broke, and I could see her struggling not to lose her composure. "Anyway, let me show you what happened." She led me into the back storeroom that I'd seen briefly on my other visit. "You know I make my key lime pie with Ol' Sour."

This was the foundation for her special recipe—lime juice and salt. "Yes. Analise told us all about it on the tour."

"If you're making a lot of it, you have to keep the 'mother' going," she said. "It's kind of like making sourdough bread—you need a starter, and you carry that over to the next batch and the next. So this is where I store the mixture." She pointed to the middle of a tall rack of shelves in the center of the room. Among the other supplies—including folded dish towels, a box of wine glasses, large cans of sweetened condensed milk, and boxes of Cuban crackers—were four bottles of cloudy, brownish liquid. The mixture had been made up in recycled wine bottles, decorated with white line drawings of flowers.

Martha saw me studying the labels.

"It's French wine from the Languedoc region. A very popular varietal, and the empty bottles are so pretty. So we wash them well and reuse for the sour mixture."

"Got it," I said.

"It takes about two weeks to get the solution ready, so I always have some brewing. These bottles sit back here, and every time I go by, I pick up each of them and shake them enough to stir things up."

"OK, got it," I said. "But sounds like something went wrong this time?"

"Yesterday, I came in to make a batch of the mini pies in mason jars for an event we're having later tonight. The bottles seemed a little out of place, but I didn't think anything of it. Eden's a neatnik and sometimes comes in and straightens things up behind me. So I shrugged it off." She wiped her forehead with the red-checked towel she had draped over one shoulder.

"I made the pies and left them sitting on the counter to cool. Bill was starving, and he loves my recipe and I saw him eyeing them. So I said he should go ahead and try one—I'd made a few extra. He took one bite and spit it out." She choked a little on the next words. "He didn't even have a napkin; he spit the stuff right into his hand."

Not much worse, I guessed, than having a diner so dislike a dish that he actually spat it out. In front of the chef.

"Naturally, I asked him what was the matter. I told him not to worry about hurting my feelings. We can't afford serving something crappy to our guests." She swiped at an imaginary smudge on one of the bottles, using her checkered dish towel again.

"He said it tasted really, really salty—like something you might gargle with if you had a sore throat."

"I was actually surprised when I heard how much salt goes into Ol' Sour," I said, "because the pie didn't taste the least bit salty to me."

She nodded. "That's exactly the point. The salt is supposed to intensify the lime flavor, not grandstand itself. So anyway, I got a spoon to check it, and he was right. Salty as hell. Someone had tampered with my food."

"Did you save it?" I asked. Wouldn't she have set it aside to have someone else check it out if she was that worried?

"I was so horrified, I threw the entire batch out. And then I checked every single other ingredient I am using in the lesson tonight to make sure everything was OK."

"And?"

"Nothing else tasted off." She led me back out of the storage area. "I can't imagine how you're going to figure this out, but I really need to know who has it in for me."

I stopped, my hands on my hips. I'd agreed to ask a few questions as I visited merchants, not to take on the case like a real detective. "Maybe it's time to bring in the police," I said gently.

"No," she said, taking off her apron and slapping it onto the counter. "After you've talked with everyone, and if you can't find any real facts, I promise I'll do that." She glanced at the clock on the wall, the minute and hour hands made out of a fork and spoon. "I have to run out to Fausto's. I've used up my last stick of butter. Who could do Thanksgiving dinner without butter? But text me the minute you know anything." She ducked into the back room, leaving me standing behind the counter, bewildered as when I came in, if not more.

I gathered up my stuff and started out the front door just as Eden and Bill were coming in. I explained that I'd stopped by to chat with Martha.

"We're really worried about her," Bill said without my prompting. He repeated the same story Martha had told me about the terrible-tasting pie.

"How long have you known her? I'm imagining a while, given how important she is to your business."

"We thought we'd checked everything out," Eden said. She looked at her husband. "Let me restate that. We *had* checked carefully. Since we are new to town and since we were trying something very different and sinking our retirement funds into the venture, we wanted to hire someone completely reliable."

She paused again, fingering the lace on her collar. "I feel funny talking about her like this. Years of working as a shrink, you know? All that training in confidentiality doesn't just leave you if you move on to something else."

"I know," I said. "Eric is the same way. He's very careful about talking out of school." I tugged on the gold hoop in my earlobe. "The difference here is that she asked me to look into this situation."

They exchanged another glance and then both nodded.

"I'm not suggesting in any way that Martha put something into her own food," I said. "What could she possibly gain from that? I feel like I need every bit of background that might help me understand what happened. You checked references when you hired her, right?"

"Absolutely. Both places where she worked previously couldn't say enough good things about her. I gathered she'd had an issue with drinking at one point, but everyone said she hasn't touched a drop in years. Honestly, her work here has been magical. People love the food and they adore her teaching. When we schedule the class where she takes people out fishing and then brings them back to cook the fresh catch? Those sell out almost before we get them listed. Honestly, this has all grown way beyond our expectations."

I nodded thoughtfully. "That's the same thing I hear from everyone. Looking at this from another angle, it seems to me that what you noticed about her state of mind could be important to what happened the other day."

"Yesterday afternoon, I should have known something wasn't right because the key lime starter looked a little funny—cloudy, almost shiny. And yet, Martha's made the recipe, what, a thousand times?" Bill asked his wife.

"Something like that. She joked that we could pass it off as salted key lime pie, but obviously it was a no go. Even our salted caramel–loving customers would have spit that out." Eden ran her fingers through her curls. "But anyone who's a little distracted could make that mistake, no?"

"Maybe," Bill said.

"Possibly," I repeated. When I'd made cooking errors because I'd been in a hurry or distracted by something personal, they had tended to run in the opposite direction—leaving things out, like sugar or baking powder, rather than tripling the amount. Although even for a professional chef, wouldn't it be easy enough to read three teaspoons and use tablespoons by mistake, or something along those lines?

"Was it only the amount of salt that tasted different? Or could it have been a different kind of sea salt—something that might have tasted metallic? I know Chef Paul Orchard likes to use local salt in some of his dishes. He collects it himself on the beach."

"I don't think that was it," Bill said. "It tasted like someone had dumped in triple or even quadruple the amount of salt that her recipe calls for. It wasn't a minor glitch."

"Just supposing that someone did tamper with her mini pies, how could they go about doing it? Does she make everything on the premises?" I asked.

"Oh, definitely," said Eden. "The health department would never allow food to be cooked elsewhere.

They have to examine our kitchens and make sure they're up to snuff."

"So then it would have to be someone coming into the store from outside," I suggested.

They looked at each other again, their faces mirroring dismay.

"How would a person gain access to her food? I can't imagine that you wouldn't notice someone entering the front door and going into the back room."

"Certainly not on an ordinary day," Bill said. "We don't depend on foot traffic for our business so much as the folks who come for specific events."

"Those times can get a little crazy," Eden agreed, "so it's possible that during a wine-tasting event, for example, someone could slip into the storage area and the back kitchen."

"Can anyone access this back area from the outside without a key?"

"I certainly hope not," Bill said. "We keep that back door bolted so no one surprises us while we're in the storefront. Though I suppose if the perpetrator was also a locksmith, all bets would be off."

"This is really scaring me," Eden said. "Are you working for the police? Did you agree to investigate? Is this official?"

I gulped. Nathan would absolutely kill me if he heard this conversation. "I wouldn't call it investigating, but I did agree to Martha's request that I continue to look around and ask questions as I visit the other venues. I'm not at all affiliated with the police department."

Looking at the concern on their faces, I now realized how truly devastating the possible poisoning would be for their business, as well as to Chef Martha's reputation. "I'll let Martha know if I discover anything. And if I don't, she's agreed to talk with the cops."

Chapter Twelve

But the goal of the arts, culinary or otherwise,
is not to increase our comfort. That is the goal
of an easy chair.
> —Jeffrey Steingarten, *The Man Who*
> *Ate Everything*

Since both of the other places I'd planned to visit this morning were within easy walking distance, I decided to leave my scooter where it was parked. On the way to Bagatelle, my mind spun and swirled around the conversations I'd had in the cooking store. Clearly Martha feared someone from her past and believed they had tampered with her lime juice mixture. On the other hand, Bill and Eden seem to have settled on another explanation for the salty juice: a mistake caused by a distracted chef.

If Martha was right, how did this person get into the back room unnoticed, and why? Yes, someone attending an event could have slipped in, but it seemed like a risky proposition. Had one of them accidentally left the back door open while taking out the trash or bringing in supplies? Despite how it might have been accomplished, spiking the lime juice seemed like a shotgun approach to wreaking havoc on a chef.

Once I got home, I planned to hit Google hard, looking for any relevant threads in Martha's history, along with facts about the woman who had died and her husband. Better to be overprepared with too much information than to miss an important clue.

Bagatelle restaurant was located on the busier end of Duval Street near Sloppy Joe's Bar, and still had the appearance of an old two-story conch house, with its double porches and carved gingerbread trim. Fans were positioned every few yards on the ceiling, rotating in lazy circles to circulate air over the diners. On the food tour, we had been guided up the stairs to the second floor and seated at a table near the back of the room. So I took the same route.

The wooden floors felt authentic, the uneven slats lending the impression that I was visiting an old sea captain's home. Floor-to-ceiling French doors stretched along the front and sides of the building. On nice days, they could be opened so diners would feel steeped in the atmosphere of Key West, while remaining far enough removed from the Duval Street hubbub to enjoy their meal in relative peace.

I approached the bar and asked whether the waiter who had delivered our food during the tour was working and available for a quick chat. Caroline, a tall woman with a long blonde braid, came over to the table where I waited, looking concerned. "I'm the manager, but I help with special events like your group tour as well. Was there a problem with the service? Or the food?"

"Oh, not at all," I said, patting her hand. "We had a wonderful stop here. But you may have heard that one of the guests fell ill at the end of our tour and has since passed away."

She gasped and pressed her hand to her mouth. "Oh my gosh, no, I hadn't heard. I'm so very sorry."

"Thank you," I said. "That's why I came to talk with you. I'm hoping to find out what you remember about our visit. I'm trying to pinpoint what exactly happened before she took ill. I'm not looking for something in particular, just anything you might have noticed about that stop." This sounded like a wild-goose chase as the words left my mouth, and I suspected nothing would come of it. "And I understand absolutely that a lot of people come through the restaurant, so you might not have these details impressed in your mind. Especially you being the manager too." I smiled with reassurance; at least I hoped it came across that way. "Maybe we could start with what you served and what the reaction has been from customers in the past?"

Caroline reached back to smooth her braid and then straightened her service apron. "The chef and I chose our lobster mac and cheese to serve to the tours because it's our signature dish, and quite a showstopper. Were you able to try it?"

"Yes, indeed," I said. "And it was fantastic. In fact, my roommate got so enamored with my description that she talked me into making it for us last night. I don't think my rendition came very close to how fabulous your dish was, unfortunately."

"I'd be happy to get you a bowl for lunch," she said. "Something to tide you over while we chat?"

I was tempted. But if I ate this for lunch, every calorie I'd worked so hard to burn off in the gym would be replaced—and more. "Thanks so much for the generous offer," I said, "but having eaten two helpings for dinner last night, and with Thanksgiving coming later this week, I think I'll be sticking with salad and fruit. Anything stand out in your mind from our visit?"

She perched on the stool next to mine and fell quiet for a moment. "People who come on these tours tend to be omnivorous eaters. And Analise makes clear that allergies and preferences can't be individually accommodated because this is a group tour. So folks know that going in."

"That makes sense," I said. "They aren't choosing which dishes to order, as they would if they were going out to dinner."

"And often there's not much left on the plate after we serve our mac and cheese. Most frequently we get nothing but empty dishes on the return trip. But one member of your group took a little taste and then pushed her bowl away. That sticks out in my mind, because I remember joking with our chef when I brought the plates back to the kitchen. I teased him that the only reason that plate was even half empty was because the woman foisted her leftovers off on her husband. Chef takes pride in those empty dishes. He wondered if maybe she had a seafood allergy? Or lactose intolerance? Or was she one of those people who thinks pasta is the invention of the devil? We both laughed at that. And then he tasted her food himself to be sure there wasn't something wrong with it."

"And was there?"

She shook her head no.

That sounded like Audrey, but I had to be sure. "What did she look like?" I asked.

Caroline described a middle-aged woman who dressed like a tourist in light-colored, loose clothing.

"That was Audrey. Did she look well when you saw her?"

"Honestly, I couldn't say. All of you seemed to be having a blast, and we love Analise to pieces, so we're always happy to welcome her group. More often than not, people come back for a whole meal after they've sampled the lobster mac."

I rustled in my backpack for my phone. "That reminds me. While I'm here, I'm also writing an article for *Key Zest* and would love to hear what goes into that dish. As long as your chef wouldn't go ballistic for sharing his state secrets . . . Do you use local lobster or import it from New England? And how many kinds of cheese?"

"Florida lobster tails and three cheeses—sharp cheddar, Gruyère, and Havarti or sometimes Parmesan. And don't skimp on the butter or use skim milk in the sauce."

"Believe me, my roommate was watching me like a hawk," I said. "I put in half the stick of butter and about a ton of cheese. Clogged arteries be damned!" I gathered my things together and started to leave.

"Wait," she called. "One other thing." I turned around and walked back. "There was another couple with you. They didn't say a lot, but the man—looking back I would say he was watching her."

"Watching Audrey? Worried about her? Or something else?"

"More like tracking her reactions, waiting for her to say something, maybe? Watching what she ate?" She shook her head briskly. "Now I feel like I'm making things up. I so hate hearing that she died when that looked like such a happy day."

I left Bagatelle and walked the few blocks on Duval to Caroline Street, realizing my interview technique was a little clunky. Once I'd introduced the news of a dead customer, quite naturally my interviewee would become defensive. At the next place, I decided, I would start with the food.

A block south of Duval, I reached the little Airstream that housed Garbo's Grill. A line had already formed at the open window in the trailer and I could smell the heavenly scent of grilling meat and fish. I was tempted to fall right into the queue and order myself one of their unbelievable hamburgers. Or perhaps the mango hot dog wrapped in bacon. Or Korean spiced beef tacos. But I knew I needed to get the information I had come for and get the heck out without succumbing to temptation. I needed to face my fruit salad head on.

I did not recognize either of the people working in the trailer, but I popped my head in the side door and called out a cheery hello. I explained that I was there to follow up for a *Key Zest* article about the food tour and asked a few questions about their fish tacos. The woman closest to the door stopped work to chat, offering the names of some of the spices they used and emphasizing that fresh and local fish and shrimp were absolutely key.

I wrote all this down, and finally mentioned that one of the food tour attendees had fallen ill and died after the event. "I'm following up on that, asking if anyone saw something a little off. The authorities are still trying to figure out what happened. It's so sad." And then I stopped, forcing myself to leave a silent space that she could fill.

"Good lord," the woman said, her face flushing pink. She glanced over at her coworker, who had paused to listen. "Honestly, we didn't notice a thing wrong with your group. You were sitting at one of the tables, right?" She pointed to the round metal tables that lined the path from the street to the trailer.

I nodded.

"We can't see much from back here. And everyone got the same dish, so if one of you got sick from our food, all of you would have, right? And we are super, uber careful with hygiene, because food poisoning can destroy a business in an instant." She hurried on before I had a chance to answer her question. "We make everything here except for the prep of the sauces and such—the health department insists that happens in a kitchen. So we share space with some other mobile eateries."

"You share a kitchen?" I asked. Thinking that if the kitchen was as busy as it sounded, anyone could slip something untoward into someone else's food and probably not be noticed.

"You should really be talking to the owners," she said, a dismayed look crossing her face. "They are excruciatingly careful about cleanliness and fresh food. We've heard no reports of anyone taking ill."

Back out on the sidewalk, I realized that I needed to check in with Analise about whether there was any further news about the cause of Audrey's death. I would also ask for the names of the remaining customers on the tour. I didn't remember one of the others watching Audrey eat, as Caroline at Bagatelle had mentioned, but I hadn't been focused on them either. Audrey had been chatty and loud throughout most of the morning, so it seemed possible that the quieter customers might have been feeling annoyed. But it was also possible that Caroline's memory was distorted. This was a subject for a call, not a text, as the more I learned, the faster I thought we needed answers. As soon as I got out on the street, I dialed my friend's number.

"Can you send me the names of the other two people who took your tour with Audrey and Marcel?" I asked.

"What are you going to do with them?" She paused. "I feel a little uncomfortable passing out my customers' names."

I sighed. This was getting more and more complex, bordering on ridiculous. "I'm still looking at things off the record as you and Martha requested. However—and I'm telling you this confidentially—there was another incident at the cooking store."

I explained about the salty, cloudy key lime pies, and how Martha believed someone was sabotaging her. Though her bosses were not so sure. "I talked with the owner at Eaton Street Seafood Market yesterday—he doesn't remember seeing or hearing anything strange during our visit. Today I visited Bagatelle and Garbo's, but I wanted to do some nosing around on your end, too. Maybe it will become obvious if one of the other customers knew Martha or could possibly have had a reason for sabotaging her work. Or for that matter, knew Audrey herself."

Analise remained silent.

"Has anyone else asked you for those names?"

"No, and I'm sorry to be weird, but it doesn't seem right to give them out. Isn't there an expectation of privacy when you sign up for an activity like this?"

I felt another zip of annoyance, thinking this was only a food tour after all, not a financial transaction. Or someone smuggling drugs or other contraband. I couldn't help sounding snippy.

"You asked me to explore; otherwise I wouldn't press you."

"You're right. Let me look things up and text them to you. If you feel you have to turn them over to the police, give me a heads-up?"

"Of course." I signed off and started to walk toward my scooter. Minutes later, her text came in.

JanMarie Weatherhead, who appears to be a local resident, maybe something of a foodie—or at least she likes to eat. And Zane Ryan. He's a chef at the Perry Hotel on Stock Island. I have a feeling he was doing some undercover research for when he opens his own little restaurant. And of course, Audrey and Marcel Cohen. Stay in touch.

Chapter Thirteen

*It's one of my top ten rules about living alone:
Never eat from the carton. You'll only feel
more pitiful.*
—Roberta Isleib, *Asking for Murder*

Finally back at the houseboat, I booted up my computer and began to research the two names Analise had texted me. JanMarie had lived in Key West for the last thirty years and was active in Steve Torrence's church, according to her Facebook profile. She was a regular at Cooking with Love, a program that operated out of the church basement and provided hot meals to seniors and shut-ins on Saturdays. She'd posted many photos of the meals they cooked and delivered. I looked at the church's website and found her name on the list of volunteers. She was spearheading the production and distribution of their Thanksgiving meal this coming Thursday morning. Unless she was on the hunt to steal Martha's recipes for the soup kitchen, she seemed an unlikely suspect.

Zane Ryan, however, was more complicated. He had opened a restaurant on Sugarloaf Key three years ago that had closed a year later. I did a search for reviews and learned it had been slammed by disgruntled customers on Yelp and OpenTable. Some diners thought that his food was crummy—undistinguished and not worth the prices on the menu; others that he was reaching for a brand—nouveau Keys—and had fallen short of what he'd promised.

Why would a chef with some significant experience take a food tour, a busman's holiday? Did he have a connection to Martha Hubbard? I didn't remember any interaction between them, though she'd only made a cameo appearance while we sat at her kitchen counter. Without some bad history, he would have no obvious reason to sabotage her. Or Analise either, for that matter. Even if he was wildly ambitious about opening another restaurant, neither Analise's tour business nor Martha's cooking classes could be considered serious competition.

And why would anyone who wanted to get at Martha arrange for Audrey's death on the last stop? It seemed like such a roundabout—and difficult to the point of near impossible—way to punish an enemy.

I turned away from these questions and worked for a while putting together the article about the food tour, but found it hard to remain focused. Would my bosses even want to run this after news of the death on the tour spread like melted butter across town? I sent in my short piece on where to eat Thanksgiving dinner, and then texted Wally and Palamina to ask about the tour. Meanwhile, the vision of Nathan's car parked near the Buoys' Club kept popping into my mind. After noodling over the right words to use, I shot him a text.

> Worried about how hard u r working this week. Can I help in any way? And can u share anything about what's going on? I'm going to be a police officer's wife soon enough and I might as well start learning the ropes right now.

He texted me back a few minutes later.

> I'm fine, I'm safe. There's a bad actor in town and it's crucial that I play my part. Absolutely plan to be at the dinner with your father on Wednesday, and Thanksgiving dinner with your family Thursday, and the wedding on Friday.

And then he'd added a smiley face blowing a kiss. All of that was great, and slightly reassuring, but also vaguely unsatisfying. A bad actor? That didn't do much to lower my anxiety. A second message flashed in.

> But there is one way you could help. Ziggy's dog sitter bailed for tomorrow morning. Can you pick him up early and

take him for a run or something? I've got
meetings at the police department until
noon and then plan to come home and
crash for a couple hours.

Absolutely! Stay safe and sleep well.

My best girlfriend Connie came up the dock and
hollered out hello just as I was setting my phone down.
"How is our bride-to-be holding up?" She hopped onto
our deck and perched on Miss Gloria's chaise.

I grinned. "I think I'm OK. If it wasn't for everything else going on, I'd be doing great. Though I'd
feel better if my groom wasn't on the night shift."

She clucked in sympathy. "I read about the food
tour this morning in the paper. Tell me this isn't the
one you were attending for the magazine?"

This confirmed my fear that nobody would be
interested in a review article about stops on this tour.
Not for a while, anyway. Unless they had some grisly
interest in seeing the place where Audrey had died.
"Unfortunately, yes. And it was an awful thing to
witness. And then this morning, I had coffee with the
husband of the woman who died. That was even
worse."

"What do they think happened?"

"Allergies? Stroke? Sabotage? Jealousy? Love,
lust, and lucre, as P. D. James used to say?" I sighed.
"Nobody's really saying. Not to me, anyway."

"The paper said she collapsed at the brewery,
right?" Connie asked.

"Exactly."

Then she glanced at the notes I had sitting on the table beside my chair. "You're not involved in this case, are you?"

"I'm just asking a few questions as a favor."

"Does Nathan know?"

Connie understood perfectly my tendency to get mixed up in dangerous situations and his concern that I not.

"He doesn't know anything about it because I haven't seen him for days. And it sounds like I won't see him until my father and his family show up tomorrow for dinner. He's the one we should be worried about." I told her about the so-called bad actor.

"You poor thing. I guess you have to get used to stressing out since you're marrying a cop. Or even better, get used to *not* stressing out. But I'm sure he's fine. They are not going to send him into danger three days before his wedding."

"It's his second marriage," I said with a laugh. "If it was the first time around, they might have given him the week off."

"Speaking of time off, I came by to see if you could use my massage appointment with Renee this afternoon?" She held up her iPhone tuned in to a camera that showed her baby girl sleeping in their houseboat. "My babysitter canceled, so if you can't, I'm going to have to cancel."

She and her husband Ray had both raved about how Renee had ironed out their muscular kinks and reduced the stress of raising a lively toddler. "Why don't I watch Claire so you can go?"

"Absolutely not. If you're free, I'd like you to take it. I think you need it more than I do."

I rolled my shoulders, which felt more like a sack of rocks than muscles. The idea of taking an hour to calm down and chill out felt amazing. "Are you sure?"

She nodded vigorously. "But you need to leave right now." She gave me directions, and I gave her a big hug and went out to the parking lot to grab my scooter.

I found the salon easily enough—the Tranquility Spa, located in a little strip mall on North Roosevelt. When I arrived, a slender woman with curly hair and lots of tattoos came to the door to greet me. "Hayley?"

"Yes. You look so familiar," I said. "I'm Connie's friend. But I don't think we've met, have we?"

"I don't think so," she said as she led me down the hall. She showed me to a small room with a cork floor, a tin ceiling, a massage table, and not much else. She left me to undress and get on the table. As I positioned myself with my face in the cradle and settled the white sheet across my shoulders, I realized where I had seen her before. She was married to Chris, the owner of Fogarty Builders, the guy who had helped me solve the mystery of Gabriel Gonzalez's murder last winter. When I'd gone to talk with him at his office, I'd seen Renee's wedding photo on his desk.

She returned to the room, turned down the lights, turned up some soothing music, and started to work. And I felt my tension begin to dissolve.

"You had a few knots in your back," she said once we'd finished and I was dressed again, sipping on a cold glass of water.

I snorted with laughter, nearly choking on the water. "Only a few?"

"Connie said you're getting married this week? That would explain it."

Then I told her how I had met her husband last winter, and how discouraged Nathan and I were about getting our houseboat renovated anytime in the next decade. "And I don't know where the heck we're going to live. My fiancé has an apartment, but before the hurricane hit we'd agreed that he would let the lease lapse starting in December. They've already rented it to a new tenant. The other choices are to live with my mother"—Renee snickered—"or my octogenarian roommate."

When she'd finished laughing, she said, "What you need is a new contractor."

"I know that much; we've had two bail on us already. Everyone's so busy after that hurricane blew through in September. This last guy's attitude was essentially 'I'll get to it when I get to it,' and underneath that, 'I don't need you; you need me.'" I sipped more water, feeling the calming effects of the massage already beginning to fade. "I'm afraid he's right."

"I'll text Chris right now—I think he had a customer pull out this week."

Minutes later, she came out of her room with a big grin on her face. "He says he can be there in fifteen minutes."

* * *

Chris was a tall rugged man with a nice smile, intense blue eyes, and a beautiful yellow Lab dog who bounded out of his truck and dashed to the end of our dock, her leash trailing behind. The animals living on the pier scattered, crouching under chaise lounges or hiding behind potted plants.

Chris whistled for her and shouted, "Lulu!" The dog ran back and sat at his feet, staring up at him with adoration, her tongue lolling. "Sorry," he said. "We recently adopted her and she's not completely trained."

Evinrude the cat peered round the miniature fig tree we had growing on Miss Gloria's deck, the fur on his neck and back puffed up so that he looked twice his normal size. He growled at the dog, who instantly cowered. "That's my guy," I explained. "He's the top cat and dog in town, and he'll let anybody know it." Evinrude lifted his lips and hissed, never taking his eyes off the intruder.

Chris laughed. "She'll get a lesson in cat-iquette today. So show me the project," he said.

By now, two of his workers had pulled into the parking lot and were standing behind him. We started up the finger, and I pointed at Nathan's houseboat. One of the men's eyebrows shot up and the other one whistled under his breath.

"I know it looks bad. My fiancé and I have tried to pull some of the trash out, but life has a way of throwing distractions in our path. We're getting married on Friday, and this was supposed to be finished by next week so we could move in."

"That's ambitious," said Chris, gesturing for his two workers to quit sniggering. They followed me onto the deck of the boat, kicking at the piles of debris—the carpet, the paneling, the pink bathroom sink, and some random beer cans tossed by passersby that I swore were a new addition since this morning.

Once inside, Chris paced around the small space, examining what was left of the plumbing, the kitchen, and the lighting. "Surprisingly enough, the bones of the place look a lot better than I'd expected."

"That's exactly what my roommate said," I said, feeling a tiny bit of my despair recede.

Then we discussed what I had in mind for the renovation, what I had already ordered, and how much chaos we were willing to live in while they worked.

"Can you show me your architectural renderings?" Chris asked.

I begin to giggle, almost on the verge of hysteria. I led the men over to two pencil drawings that were tacked on the one wall that remained untouched. "The last guy said we didn't need an architect, so this is what we've got. I know we want to keep the Dade County pine floors that we found under the rug and on this wall. Unless you think we're asking for trouble with termites?"

"Most likely not," he said. "That pine is much sturdier than many types of wood because it has more resin. And so as it dries, it becomes denser than concrete. That's why it was used so often in Key West before they overforested. Though we often pretreat the wood before we build with it if we harvest it from demolition projects. Have you thought about using it for your kitchen cabinets?"

My shoulders slumped. Again, the last contractor who bailed out had said he had a contact for recycled Dade County pine, which was hard to come by—and a craftsman who could fashion the wood into built-in cabinets and shelves. Obviously, he wasn't going to share either of those names with me—I couldn't even get him to call me back, never mind divulge insider tidbits. I explained all that, and Chris made a few notes in his phone.

"Do you cook?"

"I love to cook. Cooking and eating are in my blood. I've been dreaming of a double oven, and I've already ordered a German refrigerator that I think is narrow enough for this space. It's sitting in my mother's garage, along with some vintage drawer pulls and doorknobs."

"I get the picture." He grinned and went back to his truck for a pad of paper, on which he quickly sketched and jotted down measurements as his workers read them out. He asked me a few questions about where I might want the cooktop, the dishwasher, the ovens, and how much of the view I was willing to sacrifice for cabinets. Then he scratched down some figures.

"This is the general estimate of what I think it might cost. That will depend, of course, on the cabinets and fixtures you use in the bathroom and kitchen. I have a stash of old Dade County pine that I got in a barter with a decorator. And I know a guy who could produce your cabinets."

"Could he do built-ins in the bedroom with drawers under the bed and lots of bookshelves?" I described Miss Gloria's beds and how useful it was to have the extra storage space.

"He can do anything." He wrote that down too.

This all sounded way too good to be true. "How long do you think it will take?" I cringed, preparing for the worst, like maybe a year from now we could finally move into our place.

Chris said, "I'm guessing three to four weeks for the cabinets. Two months, possibly three, to finish the job."

My eyes nearly popped out of my head. His estimate was one-third less time than the contractor who had just dumped us.

"If you're interested, I'll go back to the office and run the numbers," he said.

"Absolutely interested. Nathan will need to see everything too, but I bet he'll be thrilled."

"Where is your wedding?"

"We're getting married at Fort Zachary Taylor beach, and then going to the Hemingway Home for the reception."

"Are you planning to entertain here this week?"

"None of the big parties will be held here on the pier. But knowing my family, they'll be dropping in and out all weekend. My father and his wife and her son arrive in town tomorrow." I glanced at the pile of junk on the deck and felt my heart sink a little.

He turned to the two guys watching our discussion and poking around my disastrous piles. "Let's get all the trash loaded in the back of our pickups." He turned back to me. "If you're having a bunch of out-of-town guests, you don't want the place looking like this. If your fiancé approves of the price, we'll start next Monday."

He stuck his hand out to shake.

But because I couldn't help myself, I gave him a big, full-body squeeze instead, too overwhelmed with gratitude to answer.

Chapter Fourteen

It was not what Eli had said but the way he'd said it, as if he'd rolled a piece of bitter melon in sugar and was now passing it off as candy.
—Camron Wright, *The Orphan Keeper*

It felt weird to have a night to myself, with Miss Gloria gone to her mah-jongg group, my mother and Sam out to dinner with friends, and Nathan who knew where. I made a salad with one of Miss Gloria's homegrown tomatoes and other produce from the Bayview farmers' market and heated up a serving of leftover lobster macaroni and cheese. I felt a little let down not to have someone else to celebrate the new contractor with, but I'd have to make do with the congratulatory texts that had flowed in from Nathan and Miss Gloria and my mother after I'd announced the great news. I picked up a culinary mystery that I hadn't had time to read more than a few pages in and went out on the deck to eat my dinner and enjoy the evening.

After I finished supper, I closed the book and went back inside to watch an episode of *Say Yes to the*

Dress. The panicked bride on the show sent my anxiety skyrocketing and had me running to my closet to make sure I had chosen well. My dress wasn't a long slinky column of satin like the girl on TV had picked, nor the frothy fairy-tale wedding gown that I'd pictured growing up. Instead I'd be wearing a sleeveless white douppioni silk with a sweetheart neckline and a full skirt that fell gracefully from a cinched waist to midcalf. It would be dressed up during the ceremony with my grandmother's antique lace veil, but it would also be comfortable on the dance floor.

My mother had cried when I'd tried it on in the store. When we brought it home, Miss Gloria had clapped her hands and then pumped her fist. And Connie declared it perfectly stunning. It *was* perfect, for me anyway. The one question remaining was shoes: whether to wear the white platform sandals my mother had surprised me with or the red-sequined high-tops that felt more like me. I could decide that at the last minute—maybe sandals on the beach and sneakers while dancing?

I got out my computer and surfed through lukewarm Yelp reviews of Zane Ryan's defunct restaurant for a second time. "Lost its umph before it ever got any," "Staff was pretentious and rude," and "Food fair, staff sullen" were some of the worst comments. I wondered how accurate these were. The most recent was a rant about why a local chef would import fancy ingredients to make dishes only a New Yorker would enjoy when he was blessed with the freshest and most delicious seafood in the world.

Not a bad point, really, though founding a restaurant, hiring the right staff, and churning out good meals every day was a lot harder than it looked from the outside. I didn't blame a new chef one bit for wanting to exert his creativity over the menu. My phone rang, jarring me out of my imaginary argument with the online reviewers: Analise was calling.

"How are you holding up?" she asked.

"It's been a good day. I think we have a new contractor for the houseboat, and they already moved tons of trash off our deck, which will mean fewer comments from my father when he sees it."

"He would do that?"

"He hates the idea of me living on a boat in a hurricane zone, and a trashed-out boat would've been even harder to defend. Worst of all would be if he said something to Nathan, who's probably already having serious second thoughts about his decision to buy it."

"I suspect Nathan can hold his own in any conversation with your father," said Analise. "He doesn't strike me as a man who is easily cowed."

"True!" I laughed. "I think he's in the right business."

"So you're not feeling desperate or overwhelmed about anything—am I reading that right?"

"Yes," I said slowly, bracing for what was to come.

"I had another phone call, this time from Audrey Cohen's sister. She doesn't believe Marcel about how Audrey died and she's asked to speak with you."

"Oh good gravy," I said. "She should talk to the medical examiner—I don't know anything. And how would she have any idea that I'm involved?"

"Once I admitted that I'd already left the brewery by the time her sister collapsed, she flipped out." Analise described what sounded like a terrible mixture of wailing, fury, recriminations, and regret.

"But how did my name come up?"

"I'm so sorry; I let slip that you'd met with Marcel for coffee, and then she wouldn't let it go until I promised to ask whether you'd talk with her too. I'll simply call her back and tell her you're not available. That you're getting married this week and your plate is full."

I hated to let my friend down. And I couldn't imagine how terrible it would be to have to deal with a loved one's death and tie up details from a distance. Key West can feel like the end of the earth even under the best of circumstances. A friendly voice could really make a difference. "I'll do it. One phone call won't hurt, right? But I wish I had some training in grief counseling. I guess I can beg off and hang up if it gets too painful."

A moment of silence. "Well, it wouldn't be a phone call. She's in town now. She flew down as soon as she heard about her sister."

"Don't tell me, she's waiting somewhere with a glass of wine?"

"The bar at Seven Fish."

That at least told me the sister had good taste. I'd loved that restaurant from the first time I'd eaten there and used it for my trial-run restaurant review for *Key Zest* a few years back. And now that it had moved to its new spiffy location, you could actually get a seat at the bar without calling a month ahead or knowing the owner. On top of that, I was way too wired to go to bed this early. And besides, it was an easy drive from Houseboat Row, and only blocks away from the Buoys' Club. On the way home, I could circle around the block and see if Nathan's car was still parked there. Though I felt guilty even thinking that.

"One glass of wine. I'll meet her in half an hour after I finish up what I'm doing. But truthfully, I don't know what I can possibly tell her that you wouldn't have already said."

"You're a good friend. I'll make this up to you, I swear."

Before I went out, I decided to have another chat with Audrey's husband. I'd ask him if he knew either JanMarie Weatherhead or Zane Ryan. And maybe he'd have something new to report about his wife's death that the official sources hadn't yet released. And I was super-curious about what he'd say about his sister-in-law.

He picked up on the first ring, answering with a curt "Yes?"

"This is Hayley Snow; we spoke the other day? I'm following up to see how you're doing. I imagine some of the shock must be wearing off, and I've been thinking of you."

"Thank you," he said.

We sat in silence for a moment, and I wondered whether the conversation was over before it began. I decided to mention Audrey's sister to stir the pot a little. "I'm going to have a drink with your sister-in-law tonight—"

"That bitch!" he shouted. "Sorry, but I wouldn't listen to a word she says. She's an old sourpuss who never approved of our relationship and did her best to poison it from the beginning. And she had a completely skewed view of her sister."

"In what way?" I asked in a quiet voice.

"She had no idea how hard it was to be married to Audrey. She had no idea what I gave up. Or how bad things had gotten."

"Tell me," I said.

Now the words poured out of him. "Honestly, I was ready to call it quits. I could not take the mood swings, the accusations, the way she spent money, the men she slept with, the way our lives had gotten so far off the track of what any reasonable person would consider normal."

"Men she slept with?" I repeated.

He huffed into the phone. "That's a little bit of an exaggeration. She had one boyfriend. She insisted that was over and that it hadn't meant a thing."

"Sounds so very difficult," I said. "I'm sorry." I simply didn't have the guts to ask him who the boyfriend was. Maybe Audrey's sister would tell me . . .

"Audrey wanted to make things up to me by coming on this trip, and insisted that she was feeling better and that things would change for real this time. They changed all right." It sounded as if he was either crying or hyperventilating, and I felt like a heel.

"I'm so sorry," I repeated. "Have you had any other news about the cause of death?"

"Her sister demanded an autopsy, and that could drag on for weeks, I'm told."

"She doesn't believe that Audrey had a stroke?"

"Apparently not. She despises me, and the feeling is quite mutual. She's exactly the kind of woman who would suspect me of dropping a poison pill in Audrey's wine glass. I would have fought her on the autopsy, but that would make me look guilty as hell, wouldn't it?"

Yikes. He'd laid that right out on the table. I made some sympathetic noises.

"One last question and then I'll let you go. Did you know either of the other people on our tour? I'm supposed to be writing an article about the experience, but in the rush of your wife's illness, I forgot to get their names."

His breath seemed to hitch, and the next words tumbled out. "Never laid eyes on either of them before and wish I'd never met any of you or come to this godforsaken backwater town." After that, he hung up. He had obviously moved past the stage of denial about his wife's death and was well into anger.

I took a couple of deep breaths, trying to remind myself how sad he must be and how none of his rage was really directed at me. But by now, my neck and shoulder muscles had tensed back into hunks of concrete. I ran a comb through my curls and trotted out to the parking lot.

Within minutes, I'd arrived at Seven Fish. I paused in the entrance to get my bearings—swearing to myself that this was absolutely the last person I was going to question.

The new restaurant had a soaring ceiling, so it wasn't as cozy as their old space, but it had more seats and less noise. The bar and counter were stunning, constructed of wavy metal to simulate the sea. I spotted Audrey's sister in the far corner seat of the bar, nearest the kitchen. She had on a red shirt, as Analise had described. I approached her and introduced myself. Behind her tortoiseshell glasses, her eyes looked red from crying.

"Thank you so much for agreeing to come. I'm sure it's not convenient right before the holiday. I wanted so much to talk with someone who had been with Audrey on her last day." She glared. "Someone other than Marcel, I mean, who couldn't be bothered to spend the evening with a member of his own wife's family."

"It's no trouble," I said. "I'm so very sorry for your loss."

She wiped away a tear with her sleeve and signaled for the bartender. I ordered a glass of Spanish white albariño and she ordered a double scotch, though the longer I sat here, the clearer it seemed that she was already on the verge of drunk.

"I gather that you and Marcel are not great friends," I said, once the bartender delivered my wine.

"I *blame* him. We know she was a handful, but he was a terrible match for her. She never felt that he loved her enough; she always felt that he considered her to be damaged goods." She took a big slug of her new drink. "And I suppose she was, if you have to look at that way. But a more stable person might have been able to balance Audrey. Honestly"—she looked at the mirror behind the bar, then back at my face—"nobody in the family ever liked him."

I tried to reconcile what she was telling me with what I remembered. "They seemed so cozy on the tour, holding hands and talking together. And she had a million plans for how they were going to celebrate this visit to the island," I said, wanting to give her some kind of good news to take away. "I understand that she suffered from depression."

"Ha," said Audrey's sister. "She was sheer cuckoo, bordering on nutso. We shouldn't have been surprised that Marcel gave up on her over the years. We tried everything: psychotherapy, Reiki, meditation, electroshock, inpatient therapy, outpatient therapy, group therapy. She was a tough customer, but that didn't mean that we didn't love her. But he married her and whisked her out of Seattle to Minnesota, so it was harder for us to keep track of her, and to help him with her. He promised to love her and care for her, and I don't believe he was doing either."

"Wonder why he didn't file for divorce, if things were that bad?" I asked.

She frowned, sipped her drink, and rubbed her fingers together. "All the money was hers," she said.

"If he divorced her, he got nothing. And that would mean no more funding of his wacky schemes from our family's trust, no more anything."

"What line of work was he in?" I asked. I wanted to ask if there was a clause in her will about the distribution of her money in case of suicide or murder, but I didn't have the nerve.

"The food industry, but he never held a job for long. He fancied himself to be a great chef—ha! When that didn't pan out, it was as if he thought everything else was beneath him. As if he'd been destined for great things and refused to do anything normal. Well, let me tell you, we all start out thinking we're destined for great things. Did he think that Audrey wanted to be sick her entire adult life? Did he think that I wanted to work as a clerk in the Department of Motor Vehicles? All day long, I have to listen to annoying people with their sob stories."

She sounded so bitter and angry that I was finding her increasingly difficult to sit with. I still didn't really understand what Marcel had done for a living over the years, but I didn't believe I would get many facts from her. Outside on Truman, sirens wailed and two police cars with lights flashing sped by in the northbound lane. "Did you ever get the sense that she felt she was in danger with Marcel? Did he hit her, for example?"

"If he did, my sister wouldn't have told me." She plucked an ice cube out of her glass, popped it into her mouth, and crunched it to nothing. "Even the times she called when she was way down in the dumps and we begged her to come home, she refused to tell us what was going on. It was like he had a hold on her, emotionally anyway." She rambled on, describing more instances of him behaving like a lout.

"Was there ever any hint that she was having an affair?" I asked.

That shut her down like a quick twist to an old garden hose. "I don't know," she said finally. "And if she was, more power to her."

"Is there anything else I can tell you about my time with your sister before I go?" I asked. "I have a date with my fiancé. We're getting married on Friday." We were getting married, though I sure didn't have a date with Nathan tonight. But neither did I want to stay here for the evening absorbing more of this woman's venom. It seemed as though the one thing Marcel and his sister-in-law could agree on was Audrey's mental distress. I couldn't help wondering whether the seemingly impossible had happened: Marcel had become desperate enough to poison his own wife in such a way that it looked like a stroke. Maybe he did it by using something that would get into her bloodstream from her skin and leave no trace?

How could a relationship get that bad? Where did the slip-sliding even begin? I found it painful to think about for too long, with my own wedding only days away.

After wishing Audrey's sister well and expressing my sympathy again, I retrieved my scooter, and took a left onto Truman. I drove the two blocks to Watson, turned left, and paused next to the Buoys' Club parking lot. The cop cars that I'd seen rush by while in Seven Fish were parked in a semicircle around the dumpster behind the gentlemen's club. The police were out of their cars, flashlights bobbing, and I could make out the shapes of at least four officers. I was relieved to see that none of them was Nathan. Nor was his rental car parked along the side street where I'd seen it the other day.

I hit the redial button for Marcel's number, thinking I'd really like to talk with him one final time so I could compare his description of Audrey's cycles of depression with that of his sister-in-law's. The phone rang a few times, then went to voicemail, so I left a short message, asking him to call me when he had a moment.

Once home, I changed into pj's and settled on the couch with the cats and a pecan pie bar to wash away the grimness of Audrey's sister, and Audrey's life. I tapped the website for the strip club into my phone's Google search bar. The description promised sexy, nude dancers, and the perfect place to host a bachelor or birthday party. The FAQ for dancers promised earnings of $200 to $700 per night, plus inexpensive housing on the premises.

What would convince a woman to take this job? I couldn't imagine working there under any circumstances. This would be a good question for my psychologist friend Eric. I was lucky not to have to consider a choice like that, and I knew it.

Chapter Fifteen

He was eating the soup, lifting his spoon with mechanical regularity, chewing and swallowing as if his life depended on tipping the steaming liquid into his mouth.
—Ann Cleeves, *Red Bones*

Early the next morning, I rode over to Nathan's apartment to walk Ziggy. To be honest, except for the exuberance of the dog, my guy's place was not a warm and welcoming space. But Ziggy more than made up for the guy-style furniture, the bare walls, and the refrigerator empty of everything other than grocery store–brand condiments, good beer, and cereal. Each time I saw the dog, he made it clear he couldn't believe his luck that I'd turned up again. And that right there was the difference between a cat and a dog.

Though I loved Evinrude with all my heart, he would never come running up to fling himself on me and lick my face to show his complete adoration. A cat's affection was more subtle, expressed by lap lying and purring, all at his convenience. Having both kinds of animals would be a joy, at least for me. I was not so sure that Nathan would interpret the early-morning feline face patting as a sign of Evinrude's affection. Nor would he appreciate it.

I tiptoed to Nathan's bedroom, tapped on the door, and stuck my head in, in case he was sleeping. But the bedcovers were neatly made and there was no sign that he had been there the night before. I was tempted, sorely tempted, to rustle through his night-stand and the top of his dresser to look for hints as to what he was up to. He would kill me for that inva-sion of privacy, and rightly so. So I grabbed Ziggy's leash and raced him down the stairs and out into the dawn instead.

"Which would you rather do, my little pal?" I asked the dog, who was bounding from one side of my feet to the other, doing his best to wind the leash around my ankles. "Shall we take a fast walk along the Atlantic? Or go to the dog park?"

Those last two words, *dog park*, sent him into paroxysms of doggy joy.

"Dog park it is, buddy," I said, "and luckily for you, this happens to be the time of day that Eric goes there with Chester. And Chester and you are a match made in heaven."

I texted Eric that we were on the way, strapped Ziggy into the crate on the back of my scooter that I use to carry groceries home, and drove to the Higgs Beach dog park located across the road from the water. The city had planned to move the road so the parks and playground could be located directly on the water, but during an infrared survey, graves were discovered and identified as the remnants of an old cemetery, and the renovation was scrapped.

Eric and his dogs were waiting inside the double-latched gates, and Ziggy began to leap and bark when he saw them. "Let me unhook you before you hang yourself," I told him once we'd made it through the second gate. I unhitched him and he roared off with Chester, with the smaller, shorter-legged Barkley in hot pursuit.

"Phew," Eric said. "That's a lot of energy. Chester has certain pals he plays with. I bet Ziggy will love them too." He pointed out Bella the Boston terrier, in a purple dress, Roman the Yorkie, and two mini Aussies. Eric introduced me to a few of the other dog owners on the way toward a concrete picnic bench, where we could watch the dogs and chat privately. The dogs tore around the fenced-in space, looking as happy as any creatures I'd ever seen. Across the road, the turquoise ocean lapped at the beach, with seagulls calling overhead.

"How are things going?" he asked once we were settled. "You look a little tense."

"I'm worried about Nathan. He's been working nights and he won't share what it's about. I know I'm signing on for more of this in the future, but it's hard to strike a balance. There's nothing I can do about it anyway. But every day I read about police officers in the news—and it's rarely good."

"That is hard," he said. "There has to be a lot of trust."

"But that's not what I needed to talk to you about, though thanks for asking."

I described what had happened on the food tour and how Martha Hubbard was so worried about someone stalking her. Or sabotaging her, or something. Then I told him about meeting with Audrey's widower. "He said the strangest thing—he wished his wife had been murdered rather than any of the other possibilities that might explain her death. Does that seem odd?"

"That's one thing I've never heard, and I've learned to expect anything and everything from a person who's grieving," said Eric. "Tell me more about him."

So I described what he'd told me about their difficult marriage and her history of depression and possibly infidelity and how the darkness had suddenly seemed to lift from her psyche and she'd insisted she come along with him to Key West. And how it was like the early days of their marriage and then suddenly she was gone and he was left completely blindsided. And how completely different Audrey's sister's vision of Marcel and their marriage had sounded.

"She hated Marcel and blamed him for how badly Audrey's life turned out."

"If Audrey hadn't died right there at the table," Eric said, after mulling this description over, "I might have said that she could have been experiencing the euphoria a depressed person sometimes feels once they've decided to take their life."

"I don't see how that could've happened—how she could have killed herself right in front of everyone else and no one saw her do it?"

"She probably didn't," he said. "Unless she had something lethal and quick acting on her person. If everyone was talking and laughing and drinking beer and so on, would they have necessarily noticed someone swallowing a pill?" He paused and hollered for Barkley, who had begun to hump his brother on a nearby picnic table while the other dogs looked on. "But that's kind of a wacky theory. And probably the medical professionals would have picked something like that up. What about prescription drugs? Do you know of anything she might have been taking?"

"I don't. Both Marcel and Audrey's sister made it sound as if she'd tried every treatment out there."

And then a light dawned on his face and he asked me to describe what we'd eaten.

So I scrolled through my memory, listing the pie, the smoked fish dip, the seafood, the cheese, the beer.

"All the things," he said slowly, "that interact very badly with an MAO inhibitor."

"And in plain language, that means?"

"It's an antidepressant. Not a new one. And it's not that commonly prescribed because of the strict dietary limitations that must be carefully followed while taking it. People don't like being told what they can and can't eat. Also, if a patient is bipolar, the MAO inhibitor should only be given in combination with a mood stabilizer like lithium, in order to reduce the risk of inducing mania. But lithium sometimes makes people feel logy and they gain weight and feel tired, so it's not unusual for patients to quit taking it. Did she seem like she was getting a little manic?"

"Hard to say, not knowing her baseline. Though she seemed quite happy overall. And the day was perfect. And she wanted to visit every tourist attraction on the island in the next day and a half. And she was very wound up about where they should eat dinner. Which I know is important, but still . . ."

We both laughed and watched Chester and Ziggy run laps around the perimeter fence of the park in hot pursuit of the mini Aussies. "What happens if you eat the forbidden foods?"

"The drug works by blocking the breakdown of tyramine, and that can help relieve depression. But if you eat foods high in that compound, like strong cheeses or smoked fish or beer—especially tap or home brew—the tyramine can build up. And that can cause severe headache, spikes in blood pressure, and in the worst cases hemorrhagic stroke."

"And that's exactly what her husband said was the preliminary diagnosis."

"Sounds like it's worth reporting this to Nathan so the police can follow up. I have to get to work," said Eric, glancing at his watch. "Would Ziggy like a drink of water before we go?"

"Whatever your guys are doing, he'll want to do," I said, watching Nathan's wiry little black dog trot behind Eric's Chester and Barkley. The dog wearing a purple dress waded into the large pan under the faucet, and the other three slopped big gulps of water around her legs.

"On another subject, there was a big brouhaha at the strip club last night. And that got me thinking— what do you think would possess a woman to take a job in a place like that? And what else goes on in there, anyway?"

"Our favorite bartender from a restaurant near the airport quit to take a job at the Buoys' Club. I'm sure the money was good—imagine someone without a whole lot of education suddenly making three to five hundred a night. But still, it made me sad."

"Sad?"

"Sad that she felt she had to work there. It's soul crushing. Do you know that they label the dancers with numbers instead of their names? The numbers correspond to nautical location points. I don't know how a woman can go in there every night and come out emotionally OK." We hugged and he held me at arm's length. "Try to think happy thoughts the rest of this week, OK? I've heard there's a very special wedding coming up."

I clipped Ziggy's leash on and headed back to Nathan's apartment. Once inside, I rustled around in the papers stacked by his phone to find a pad so I could leave a note. Sticking out from underneath his Key West Police Department mug filled with pens and pencils and a screwdriver was a brochure from Analise's food tour. I slid it out. Isle Cook Key West and Garbo's Grill were circled in blue ink. The other stops had black check marks beside their names. What the heck?

Underneath that was a copy of *Menu* magazine, a free insert published quarterly and distributed in the *Citizen*. It might have been considered a competitor to my beat at *Key Zest*, though it did not provide reviews or articles, only menus and ads. Was he using this to order takeout? I doubted it, as he was a creature of habit and rarely branched away from his favorites, unless dragged by me. I flipped through the pages and noticed several had been dog-eared: Martin's, the Perry Hotel, Santiago's Bodega, Michael's. That last name made me smile, as we'd had our first attempt at a date there. He'd been sidelined by a case and never showed up. Some things hadn't changed much since then.

I pulled his notepad out and scribbled down the information about the side effects of an MAO inhibitor, followed by *Miss you* and a series of *x*'s and *o*'s.

Chapter Sixteen

Something has gone grotesquely wrong when chefs brag that the chickens they buy lived happy, stress-free lives, but can't promise us that the women they employ aren't being assaulted in the storage room.
—Pete Wells, "Scandals Keep Breaking, but Restaurateurs Have Yet to Own Up,"
The New York Times, January 2, 2018

After leaving Nathan's apartment, I drove downtown and parked behind Preferred Properties to go to the office. Since I hadn't received any feedback about whether my piece on the food tour would run, I thought maybe it would be better to hash this out in person. And besides, I needed some direction on what articles Wally and Palamina wanted me to work on for the season leading up to Christmas. I'd been so busy with plans for the wedding, there hadn't been much space in my brain for thinking ahead. Not that I'd honestly get a word written this weekend, but I could make some notes and pretend it might happen.

Danielle was sitting at her desk in the hallway with a plate of fruit in front of her. Surely these weren't the exact same grapes and chunks of pineapple, but the fruit looked droopy and forlorn and so did my friend.

"Oh my gosh, I told you I'd bring cookies this week. It's been so crazy I completely forgot." I bent over to hug her.

She shrugged and said, "Don't worry about it. My mother and her sister are going all out for Thanksgiving, so one tiny week of dieting won't hurt me a bit."

"Who else will be at your family dinner?" I asked.

Her fair skin flushed pink. "I've invited my guy to come and meet the family."

I clapped my hands with excitement. "That's a big step. They don't mind you dating a cop?"

"We'll see," she said, grinning.

"Bring him to the wedding," I said. "We'd love to meet him, too. Unless you think that would scare him off." Then another thought popped into my head. "Unless Nathan is his boss and that would be too weird."

"But I didn't RSVP that I was bringing a date," she said. "That messes up your count for the caterers and all."

I laughed. "You know my family; they'll make sure there's double the food we need. And alcohol, too. Then my mom will end up begging the guests to take leftovers home. She's neither Italian nor Jewish, but she's generous like them when it comes to food."

"I'll ask him," she said, blushing again. "He can always say no. Speaking of no, you missed Wally by fifteen minutes. He's heading up to the mainland to share the holiday with his brother. Is he not coming to the wedding?"

"He sent his regrets." I couldn't be sure whether he was really busy or just plain didn't want to come. Either way was fine. I would hate for someone to feel uncomfortable at my celebration. I tipped my head in the direction of Palamina's office.

"Is she in? I wanted to do a little brainstorming before I turn off my mind for the weekend."

"She's there, but I've barely heard a word out of her. She's very glum," Danielle whispered. "Even more than normal."

Palamina could wax hot and cold, and she definitely tried to keep clear boundaries between her and us staff. "Do you know why she's upset?"

"You can be sure she wouldn't confide in me," Danielle said.

"Is she headed to New York today? I would never travel on the Wednesday before Thanksgiving—it's the worst," I said. I had done it once to fly back up to my mother's place in New Jersey. A freak snowstorm had brought travel in the entire southern half of the East Coast to a screeching halt. And that had meant I'd spent ten extra hours in the Atlanta airport with a lot of other cranky travelers. I'd arrived in the early-morning hours of Thanksgiving and gone directly to bed.

I tapped on my bosses' door and went inside when invited. Palamina was sitting at the desk she shared with Wally, squinting at her computer screen. Her face looked even more pale and gaunt than usual. "Have a seat," she said, waving me to the folding chair beside her. "I didn't expect to see you today. Or any day this week, to tell the truth. Aren't you getting married?"

I tried not to get ticked instantly, without much success. The stress of the week had torn my politeness filters right off. "So what, you were expecting bridezilla, bridal basket case, Queen Bride or something? All me, me, me—"

"Cut!" she said, finally smiling. "That wasn't fair on my part. My only exposure to brides was my sister—and she tortured us for a full year. The last week before the wedding was the worst—she insisted that every moment revolve around her. We were all screaming banshees by the end, and then she ended up divorced a year later. So I'm not used to seeing a normal bride—the kind who would even come to work two days before the big event." She grinned and I felt glad that I'd decided to stop in. "I'll start again. Good morning, Hayley. How's it going? What's up?"

"I'm plenty nutty this week," I admitted, astonished at how quickly her apology had punctured a hole in my ballooning outrage. "Maybe more than I expected. But I'm finding that channeling my anxiety into work and thinking about other people's problems helps me tamp it down. In other words, I'm not off the clock. Not until this afternoon." I grinned back at her.

"Tell me what you're thinking," Palamina said, smiling again. This much warmth was a side of her I hadn't seen lately.

I explained how I'd planned to write up the food tour article and my concerns about whether we ought to be running it before the questions about Audrey's death had been settled. "I'm also thinking ahead to the pre-Christmas season."

"What are your thoughts about the food tour bit?" she asked.

I wished I didn't always feel as though her inquiries were a series of traps set to finally uncover the weak spots in my mind. I tapped a finger on my chin, focusing on the tiny water feature she had installed last week in a corner of the office. It made a hissing noise that she found relaxing. For me, not so much. It suggested that a trip to the ladies' room was overdue.

"I have a bias because Analise is my friend. And I hate to run anything that will damage our local merchants. Unless, of course, the food at a place is consistently awful or makes people sick—that's a different story and they're fair game."

She interrupted. "So that leaves us where?"

"My instinct is we should wait until the police clear up the facts about the death before we run the piece. Otherwise, it looks like we didn't know about it and we look foolish. And if we did know about it but don't mention it, we lose our credibility in the community. People are bound to find out, and then it appears like we've joined the Bubba pipeline." *Bubbas* was the name for the old boys' club in Key West, suspected of protecting each other's interests, often at some considerable cost to the town or its people.

"I agree. What do we know about the death so far?"

How much to tell her? I hated her to think I was nosing around when it wasn't my job, but on the other hand, she was smart and might have some good ideas. And we were kind of on a roll. So I described how Analise had asked me to speak with both Audrey's husband and her sister. And how Eric had mentioned the possible medication interaction, and that other stops on the tour hadn't offered any seriously useful observations. "In other words, we're nowhere."

"Let's hold off on publishing the article," she said. Then she fell silent, fiddling with the pen lying next to her computer. "I suppose now is as good a time as ever."

I could feel the sweat pop out all over me. What was coming next—reduction in salary? It would be hard to go lower than what I was making. Cut my hours? Spend more time in the office? I couldn't imagine anything I wanted to hear.

"I think you do food very well," she said, "and you know I'm not a particular fan of food. I eat," she laughed, "pretty much because I have to, but it's not in my DNA to care about it like you do. Or maybe," she mused, "it's not a DNA problem; it's that my family didn't care, so I never learned to appreciate the pleasures of food. What mattered in my household was being smart and thin—you could never be enough of either. Neither of my parents liked to cook or eat—I envy your relationship with your mom."

She'd never been so open about anything in her personal life. I felt sorry for her description of her family—180 degrees from my own. I nodded gravely.

"Anyway, I've been thinking that although you do food well, you could do more. You could write bigger stories, and I suspect our readership would be very interested."

"Like politics?" I asked, thinking of Frank Bruni, who'd started out as a food writer, landed a job as the *New York Times* restaurant critic, and now wrote essays about political and social problems.

"Not that big," she said. "I was thinking of staying within the realm of food and restaurants but going bigger than reviews. You did a little of that with the Cuban food and influence piece last winter, and it worked well."

I flushed with gratitude. She didn't dole out a lot of compliments. "So maybe food trends," I suggested. "Who's trying what and how are they doing it and how is it working out?"

"Maybe," she said. "Pitch me some ideas and let's see where we go. I'd like to see you try to get at the psychology behind the trends, rather than simply describing them. But in addition to that, we've heard so much about the MeToo movement this year. Even in the food world, haven't a few celebrity chefs been taken down?" I nodded. "How does that play out here on the rock? Have local cooks experienced harassment? Have locals in the food industry noticed things changing for female chefs?"

"I would love to take a crack at that," I said, thinking immediately of Martha Hubbard. She would surely be willing to talk to me about her experience as a female in this man's world. Or what had been a man's world up until now. She sort of owed me at this point.

"Shoot some ideas over to us. I'm curious—what's your technique when you approach a subject and ask them to talk about something like this? Best buddies? Good cop, bad cop? Motherly?"

"Honestly, I don't think a lot about it. I'm curious about what makes people tick, and I think they appreciate that." I started to tell her more, but she began to rustle around her desk as if she was anxious to return to work.

"I won't keep you. But I'm glad we had the chance to chat." I stood up and grabbed my backpack. "When are you leaving for Thanksgiving? Or do you have some people coming here?" I was almost certain she had mentioned plans in New York.

"He broke the relationship off," she said in a flat voice. Though if I listened carefully, I thought I could hear it tremble.

"Oh geez, that's awful timing. I'm sorry." I paused for a moment, picturing how lousy she must feel—dumped on the cusp of a major family holiday. And her with a family who didn't care about celebrating with food. "If you don't have other plans tomorrow, come to my mother's house. We're doing Thanksgiving together. It will already be chaotic, so one more can't possibly make it worse. She'll insist. And you'll like my stepmother. She's not a big foodie either, but smart as a whip."

"I'd feel like a fifth wheel," she said. "Thanks anyway. And there will be all that food . . ." She flashed a smile that was half grimace, or maybe more than half.

"The problem is, once I admit to my mother that I invited you, she'll be calling to pester you until you give in. Might as well save yourself that trouble. And you can bring a bottle of wine as your contribution."

"Oh, why not?" she said, a real smile creeping over her face. "Thank you."

I left Palamina's office and went to the end of the short hall to my tiny space, enough room for a small desk and chair. Period. But I'd covered the slanting ceiling over my desk with some of my favorite articles, and photos of friends and family around the island. When I came in next week, I would add a photo of Nathan and me getting married at the beach. And maybe for a laugh, I'd change the name on my door from Hayley Snow to Mrs. Bransford. But probably not—I liked my name and had pretty much decided to keep it. And as with most things having to do with the wedding, Nathan had insisted it was up to me. I got the strong sense that he'd fought for things in his previous marriage that really didn't matter in the end. He wasn't going to repeat that mistake with me.

I pulled my computer out of my backpack and jotted down the rough ideas that Palamina and I had brainstormed. *Go deeper!* I added at the end. *Think psychology!*

I also jotted some notes about the life and death of Audrey Cohen, from the points of view of her husband and her sister, and Eric Altman's idea about the drug to treat depression. My mind skimmed over the events of that morning, looking for bits of information that I might have forgotten to add.

I paused for a moment to puzzle over Martha's secret, wondering what she could have done that felt so awful. Was it something really terrible? Or was it something only moderately dreadful that took on more and more weight the longer it remained undiscovered? Didn't we all have things from our past that we wished we hadn't done? Why would she be so intent on keeping a secret if it would help solve the mystery around Audrey's death? Or at least keep her out of the pool of murder suspects, if it came to that? Had she actually done something illegal, as Steve Torrence had suggested? I had to think I was squandering brain bandwidth that wouldn't amount to much in the end. Because it made no sense that she would purposely cause the death of a customer and ruin her own reputation and that of her bosses, Eden and Bill.

Unless. Unless she had actually known Audrey Cohen, had some prior connection that would translate to a motive for murder. Which so far she'd denied.

I tapped Audrey's name into the search bar and came up with very little other than a mention of her death in the *Citizen* and *Konk Life*. She seemed to have lived her life quietly, except perhaps within the close circle of family where she hadn't been quiet at all.

Next I Googled Martha Hubbard. At the top of the search, I found several recent articles about her new venture as chef and food curator at Isle Cook Key West. As I suspected, her partnership with the owners was based partly on her knowledge of food and culinary expertise and partly on her knowledge of local chefs.

Below those articles, she was mentioned briefly in a piece about the history of Louie's Backyard and several glowing reviews of her classes on TripAdvisor. Before that she'd had an exhibit of her photography at a local gallery. But nothing about the rest of her work history or any past problems—just a long, historical white space.

I needed to make another visit.

Chapter Seventeen

Chefs are not going away; we are evolving.
—"Martha Hubbard: Resident Chef at Isle
Cook," by Jennifer White, *Florida Weekly*,
October 12, 2017

A few last-minute shoppers were browsing in the Isle Cook Key West shop, which I thought would be to my benefit. I could sail past the front checkout without attracting attention and go directly to Martha, who was working in the kitchen at the back of the store. I could smell the delicious scent of butter steeped in garlic.

"Don't tell me you have a class the night before Thanksgiving?" I asked when I arrived at her counter. "If a person doesn't know what she's serving by now, I'd say make reservations."

She looked up, startled. The anxiety did not fade from her face when she saw it was me. "Is there news?" she asked in a low voice.

"Not really," I said. "Only more questions." I slid onto one of the high stools at the counter. "Are you certain you'd never seen Audrey Cohen before she entered the store last week?"

"As I said, I barely paid attention to the customers that day. Just waved hello." She patted a stray wisp of hair back into her ponytail. "If the guests had been other people I recognized, like you, I would have noticed."

I nodded. "We were all in our own worlds, I guess. I was taking notes on what Analise was telling us and thinking about how to write up the article. From what I'm hearing, though, it's possible that Audrey died because of a bad reaction of food and beer with her antidepressant."

She glanced up, a whoosh of relief in her eyes. "I'm sorry to hear that, but in some ways it takes the pressure off. If it's true." She dumped a blue ceramic bowl of dough onto her floured counter. Then she began to knead it, stopping at every turn to sprinkle fresh rosemary leaves on top and knead those into the mixture.

"What are you making?" I asked.

"Rosemary garlic brown-butter rolls," she said. "I let them take the second rise in the fridge. Then I bake them before dinner and slather them with more garlic butter right before bringing them to the table. Guests go mad for them."

"Sounds fabulous," I said. "What else is on your menu?"

"Smoked turkey with a honey vinegar glaze and red-eye gravy, confetti succotash, mashed potatoes with cream cheese, sour cream, and scallions, the usual," she said, finally cracking a smile.

"I'm practically drooling," I said. "You take Thanksgiving to a new level."

She paused for a moment, looking puzzled. "Did you need something else?"

"I stopped by because I've just come from a pow-wow with my boss. She wants me to write a piece about the effects of the MeToo movement on the restaurant business, specifically on our island. I figure you're a good place to start because you've worked in different places in town and you know a ton of chefs."

She punched the dough with more force. "I don't know what I'd have to add."

I watched her sprinkle sea salt onto the dough—a lot of sea salt—and then plop it back into a greased bowl. She stretched a length of plastic wrap over top of the bowl. "Crap," she said. "I forgot to add the browned butter." She removed the wrap, swung around to the stove, grabbed the small pan of melted butter with garlic, and poured it over the top. Then she rolled the dough in the butter until it glistened.

She wasn't going to talk about this as easily as I'd hoped. "I'm wondering how common harassment is in restaurant work? I've read the pieces about celebrity chefs getting taken down since the MeToo movement surged into public awareness. Seems like there are lots of men in positions of power in this business, so maybe this problem appears in regular restaurants as well?"

Martha began to peel and chop onions, her knife slicing quickly through the white flesh, filling the air with its sharp, eye-watering tang. "I've worked in kitchens since high school, when I took a job at Denny's to make enough money for the senior class trip to Disney. Of course there's a lot of joking around and cursing, and some of it is in bad taste. But from what I've seen and experienced, it's lower-level stuff, not the big stuff like you read in those articles."

"What kind of smaller stuff?" I asked.

"Things like a guy saying, 'Your coat'"—she paused her chopping and pointed at her chef's coat with the tip of her knife—"'would look good on my floor tomorrow morning.'"

"Really? That blatant?"

"Oh sure. And I'd say something like, 'Geez, dude, take a shower once in a while and change your grease-spattered pants, and maybe you'll get lucky.'"

I laughed. "You gave it back as good as you took it."

She wiped her forehead with the sleeve of her coat, waving the knife in the air. "It was a rite of passage, you know? When you said something like that, you were showing that you were one of the guys and you could take a joke. And I can take a joke. You probably haven't seen that this past week, but I can play along with pranks and jokes. Some of them were even funny."

"But . . ." I raised my eyebrows, hoping she'd continue.

"No but," she said, scraping the onions into the oil that sizzled in a frying pan on the front burner. Hot grease splattered the back of her hand, but she didn't flinch. "End of story."

"You'll let me know if you think of anything else?"

She shrugged. "Sure."

She was looking a little irritated, and I realized I was overstaying my welcome. "One other thing before I leave you to it," I said. "My boss wants me to write 'bigger pieces,' like psychological trends in the food world in Key West. Any thoughts about what's going on here in town?"

She scratched her head with one finger and stirred the onions with the other hand. "I'm not sure what she means by psychological trends. Some of the chefs around here have begun to feel very possessive about their food. They don't want patrons making demands about ingredients and so on."

"So how does that play out in restaurants?"

"If a diner asks the server to leave off the lemon or the spicy rub or the artichoke sauce or something, the server is supposed to say our policy is not to make changes to our menu. Because if you take off the rub or the sauce, it's no longer our recipe, is it? People should understand this coming in—we do a limited menu and we do it super well."

Honestly, I thought this was a little mean-spirited. What if someone was severely allergic to salt or onions? Those ingredients were included in practically everything. Out of luck, I guessed. Maybe chefs felt about their food the way writers felt about their words—these were their darlings, carefully crafted pieces of art and no one should mess with them. But on the other hand, I had learned since joining *Key Zest* that a good editor often made a piece of writing stronger.

"One other topic to think about—I'm just putting this out there before my wedding gets any closer and my brain turns to mush. What about trendy ingredients on our island? Anything unusual turning up lately?"

She turned off the gas burner and moved the pan to the back of the cooktop. "There's always some competition about finding a flavor that no one else has or using it the way no one else does. That's why I like going out to dinner from time to time—it's important to check out what other people are doing. Of course, I read cookbooks too, and read some of the bigger chefs' blogs and follow their Instagram feeds." She pulled a large package covered in butcher paper from the fridge and began to unwrap it. Sausage. "Saffron seems like it's big around here lately. And making desserts that glitter in the candlelight. Customers love ending the meal with a showstopper."

"Yikes," I said. "We're wrapping up our Thanksgiving dinner with good old-fashioned pumpkin pie and whipped cream. Although I did slide a little chai spice into the filling. But don't mention that to my father if you see him; he'll have a heart attack."

"There you go," Martha said, laughing. "Sometimes diners want the same thing over and over. But no one likes to cook the same thing ad nauseam. No matter what the fussy customers insist they want done." She wiped her hands on a clean dish towel that read, SORRY, I'M IN A COMMITTED RELATIONSHIP WITH BUTTER. "If you hear anything different about the death, you'll text me?"

I nodded. "Of course. And have a fabulous holiday." On the way out, I glanced back at her once more. She was dumping the ball of rosemary dough into the trash.

As I drove home, I thought about what I'd learned—if I'd learned anything. Martha seemed tense to me, as if still worried about a lingering threat. Watching her liberally sprinkle ingredients into the bread dough, I'd thought of her salty lime juice. And I could imagine her getting upset, making a quick mistake, and then forgetting she'd done it.

Why did I always leave a conversation with her with the sense that she'd left out half the story?

Chapter Eighteen

Spending your days trying to one up your own palate is exhausting. Stepping away from the wood-grilled matsutake mushrooms with nasturtium agrodolce, and towards an uncomplicated hunk of meat is the gastronomic equivalent of collapsing into your bed at the end of a long day.

—Helen Rosner, "On Chicken Tenders," *Guernica*, June 12, 2015

I had planned to pick up my father and stepmother at the airport in Miss Gloria's car, but my father, true to form, wanted to have his own transportation. I honestly didn't mind, as it took some pressure off. What bride wanted to have to worry about how her extended family would get to the various events, and how to help them escape if the parties ran long or were dull? Instead, I met them in the bar at Casa Marina, the large Waldorf Astoria resort on the Atlantic Ocean, where they were staying. Allison looked wonderful, slender and elegant, with her blonde hair pulled back into a ponytail and a pair of thick gold hoops in her earlobes.

She pulled me into a warm hug. "You look wonderful," she said, "glowing just like a bride should."

Which left me feeling instantly guilty. At her wedding to my father years ago, I'd been a terrible brat—reluctant in every way, from shopping for a dress with Allison (which I refused to do) to standing with them at the altar in that hideous choice (which my mother insisted I do). But what preteen wants to see her father sign his life away to a woman who isn't her mother? And honestly, the dress was cutesy-squared with a lace collar and full skirt and sash—something a five-year-old might have loved. The only saving grace was that Rory, Allison's little boy, had acted even worse.

Today, Rory hung back behind her but accepted my embrace. "Let me look at you," I said, holding him away for inspection. "You're practically all grown up. And you cut your hair. And you have on real clothes."

That made him laugh. Last time he'd been in town, when he'd disappeared into the spring-break crowd and we'd thought he was gone forever, he'd sported a shaggy haircut resembling Farrah Fawcett's (and oh how he would have despised that comparison) and refused to change out of a grungy T-shirt decorated by the rock group Purple Moan. (Yeah, I'd never heard of them either.)

Finally I turned to my dad, who looked tired and maybe more gray-haired than last time, for a hug. "I'm really glad you're here." He squeezed me back.

"No way in the world we would miss this," Allison said. "Your father is all verklempt, though he won't tell you this himself," she added in a stage whisper. "But where is the famous Nathan?" She looked around the cavernous lobby as if he might be hiding behind one of the pillars.

"He's on a big case," I said, adding a cheerful smile. "He said he'd meet us at the bar at six." I herded them outside, and we settled at a table close to the water. Who could be grumpy when sitting with a view of the Atlantic Ocean, especially when the weather was balmy compared with northern New Jersey?

A waiter in a crisp white polo shirt came over to take our order.

"Two glasses of your top white wine for the ladies, Dos Equis for me, and a Coke for the young man," my father told him without consulting any of us.

Allison rolled her eyes and patted my hand. "He's feeling a little bit out of control," she said under her breath. "My advice is to give him some leeway. We're so excited for you and your new life course, but he's got some mixed feelings burbling underneath and he's not too good at identifying and understanding them. Or sharing them."

"Understatement," I said, snickering along with her. Then I spotted Nathan's familiar form across the patio. My stomach clenched with nerves. What if they didn't like him? What if he didn't like them?

"Don't worry," Allison said with a wink. "If you love him, we will love him."

I blew her a kiss of thanks and got up to meet Nathan and bring him over to the table. "This is my famous Detective Bransford, soon to be husband. Yikes," I added, "that still sounds so weird. Nathan, this is my stepbrother Rory and my stepmother Allison."

"I believe we met you a couple of years ago at the police department," he said to Rory, who I was glad to see did not shrink away. "Glad to have you here under happier circumstances."

Allison insisted on pulling Nathan into a hug and then patted him on the cheek. "We are delighted to welcome you to our family."

"Thanks."

"And this is my father." I stepped back a bit to allow them space to jostle for position. They shook hands a little too long and too hard before breaking apart. Nathan stood about four inches taller than my father, and probably outweighed him by twenty-five pounds, all of it muscle. My father looked pale and almost wispy in comparison.

"A pleasure to meet you, finally, under better circumstances," said Nathan, smiling so that his dimples twinkled. "I've heard so much about you from Hayley."

"And you," my father grunted, signaling for the waiter. "I'll order you a beer. Or would you prefer whiskey?"

"Sounds great, but I'm on duty tonight. I'm sorry I won't be able to have dinner with you either"—he looked apologetic as he glanced in my direction, as this was news to me, bad news—"we've had a fast break in one of our cases."

"Crime waits for no man's dinner nor his wedding," I said, muttering nonsense to cover my disappointment. If he was bailing out now, would this continue to happen all weekend? "Wasn't that something from Shakespeare?"

My father looked puzzled, but Allison laughed.

"Sit, sit," said my father, gesturing to the one empty seat at the table as if inviting Nathan to perch on his living room sofa.

I tried not to get annoyed. I had to keep reminding myself that what Allison said was true—this must be hard for my dad. He wasn't in charge and it wasn't his turf. And it would only get harder, watching my mother's ease with my friends and my island, and watching his daughter—his little girl—get married. Truth was, I hadn't been that girl for a very long time. But maybe he hadn't realized that in his gut until now.

"Is this a busy time for the police department?" Allison asked, taking a sip of her wine and nodding her approval at my father's selection.

"Ordinarily, not so much," Nathan said. "We often have a lull before and then right after Thanksgiving, leading up to Christmas. And New Year's, which is one of the busiest times of the year." He explained how visitors to the island came in waves, usually based on the weather and special events. And this meant visitor shenanigans and crime came in waves, too. And during these high times, extra law enforcement types came in from out of town, and all that took some managing too.

"We chose Friday after Thanksgiving for the wedding, thinking it would be a downtime," I said. "But Nathan's bad guys aren't cooperating. And the tourists aren't either. I nearly got mowed down by a gaggle of scooters that ran the red light on Eaton and Duval. And none of the walkers pay a lick of attention to those lights—I guess we should all bow down to their vacations."

"There's so much to see in this town," Allison said. "It's hard to pay attention to the necessary details of life. Which folks in your family will we get to meet this weekend?"

An uncomfortable silence fell over the table. Finally Nathan said, "No one. My parents got divorced about seven years ago, and my mother hasn't been the same since, I'm afraid."

Allison looked mortified. "So sorry to hear that."

"Miss Gloria had quite a conversation with your mother," I told Nathan, my eyebrows peaking. I wasn't going to spill all the dirt about Mrs. Bransford in front of my family, but I kind of wanted Nathan to squirm a little. "She can't wait to meet all of us. But she's not able to make the wedding." He flashed a strained smile.

After another ten minutes of chitchat about the weather in New Jersey, Rory's sports schedule, and a polite inquiry about my mother's catering business, Nathan announced that he had to leave. "I'm very sorry to miss dinner, but I feel certain there will be more opportunities in the future." He squeezed my wrist and gave me a kiss, and then stood up to kiss Allison on the cheek. He shook my father's hand, another mano a mano display, and chucked his fist into Rory's shoulder. "Until tomorrow," he said.

"I'll walk you out," I said, getting to my feet and moving toward him.

"Stay with your family," he said, hugging me. "You don't get to see them very often." Then he lowered his voice. "Can we possibly do the rehearsing thing Friday morning instead of tomorrow? I'm afraid I'll be out all night again tonight, so I'd love to get some sleep."

"Excuse me a minute," I said to my family, and to Nathan, sweetly but firmly, "I'll walk you out."

"What about Thanksgiving dinner?" I said, once we'd walked across the patio by the pool back to the hotel. "Are you going to be able to make it?"

"Of course I'll be there. Wouldn't miss it. I've already checked with Steve and your mother about moving the rehearsal, and it's fine with their schedules."

"You checked with them *first*?" I couldn't keep my hands from dropping to my hips.

"I didn't want to make you crazy for no reason, if either of them couldn't switch." He had a funny expression on his face, half impish, half imploring.

I wasn't thrilled about this change—in fact, I was both irritated and unsettled. But I remembered the conversation we'd had with Steve Torrence about learning to be a cop's wife. Flexibility and communication were key. It would not do to pitch a fit the first—or second—time something didn't go exactly to my plan.

"Did you get my note about the antidepressant Audrey Cohen might have been taking?" I asked.

"Yes," he said, squinting. "I passed that along."

I wanted to ask him what he was doing at the strip club, but I felt nervous about bringing it up. "What really goes on in the Buoys' Club?" I asked. "I jogged by the place this morning, and it registered for the first time. I don't think I'd ever really thought about it, except as kind of an island joke about visitors too dumb to watch their credit cards. Is it just tourists and naked dancing women?"

His entire body seemed to grow rigid. "Why do you want to know?" he asked. "What could this possibly have to do with you?"

"I met Eric at the dog park this morning, and he mentioned that they knew a woman who went to work there. He seemed so sad about it. And that got me wondering."

He took both of my hands in his and looked directly into my eyes, as if he knew I wasn't telling him everything. "You saw the TV show *The Sopranos*, right?"

"Yes, Tony ran his crime business out of the Bada Bing. But that wasn't a real place." I could see he was getting upset. But I couldn't tell the truth without telling him I'd been snooping around his car and had seen Ziggy's stuff. And he was in a hurry, and we didn't have time to have a blowout and then sort out both our feelings.

"It's not a nice place," he said. "Let's talk about this after the wedding, OK?" he asked. "Please. For now, just stay away from that place. I know you're softhearted and I love that about you. But it's not good people there, and you could get hurt."

I kissed him again. "OK. I'll be glad when this case or stakeout or whatever you're calling it is over so we have time to talk. About your family, too. No one is coming, right?"

"Obviously you've already talked to my mother." He glowered a little. "My grandma wasn't up for the trip." A look of pain flitted over his face. "I promised we'd visit her after the wedding. You'll like her, and I know she'll like you. I spent every afternoon after school at her house. She baked a mean cookie."

"If she helped raise you, how could I not love her?"

"My father is a no," Nathan said. He had a grim set to his lips, bending the usually soft curves into steel lines. "He's mule-stubborn. I've been told I take after him that way too. I promise we'll have the rest of our lives to figure this all out," Nathan added. "You can talk until you're hoarse. And I will listen like the big lovesick dope that I am." He hugged me close and hard and then wheeled away.

I returned to my family, where my father was watching Nathan disappear into the lobby of the Casa Marina. "What did you say he's working on?" he asked, turning back to me.

"I don't think she did say," said Allison, nudging him in the ribs.

I shrugged. "I didn't because I haven't a clue, which makes sense if he's working on something top secret. He can't be leaking the details to me and my family."

"I bet it's a sting," Rory said, his eyes lighting up. "Did you see the episode on *Live PD* where the night-shift cops were hiding from the bad guy in a boat? And it turned out he had accomplices and the good guys got ambushed. And one of them was shot and started to bleed out—"

"Rory!" Allison said. "Enough about that show. This is Key West, not La La Land."

"Yeah," Rory said, sinking from excitement back into a teenage slump. "Nothing happens here. Nothing bad, that is. Nothing fun."

The muscles around my father's mouth tightened, as if he was on the verge of reminding his stepson that he would have died last time he visited had we not rescued him. But Allison squeezed his arm and he remained silent.

"Right," I said, feeling glum too, but trying not to sound that way. "Nothing except murders and kidnapping and drug runners from South America—"

"Do you think he'd take me on a ride along?" Rory interrupted.

"Rory," my father said, "get that out of your mind. You aren't going on a ride along with anyone but us."

"He thinks he's too old to feel this way, but he's very excited that you're marrying a police officer," Allison explained.

"I'm sure we can arrange a visit to the station," I told Rory. "Nathan or my friend Steve Torrence could show you the command center and the gym and one of the patrol cars. We'll make sure to fit that in."

"Where are we eating tonight?" Allison asked.

She was a marginal cook, despite being an accomplished chemist. But contrary to what I'd told Palamina, she did share my love for eating, even if she wasn't obsessed as my mother and I were. In the end, her kindness and warmth toward my father and me and the rest of the family were all that mattered.

"I made a reservation at Santiago's Bodega tonight. They always have lots of choices and we don't have to share the dishes unless we want to. I was thinking I'd follow you over on my scooter so I can stop at Mom's on the way home."

"How is your mother doing?" my father asked.

"She's blossomed down here," I said. "At first when she told me she was planning to start a business in town, I wasn't so thrilled."

"This was your adventure, after all," said Allison with a smile.

I nodded. "But she's so busy and so happy, and Sam seems happy, too. You'll like him," I added, thinking my father *would* like him. If he allowed himself to relax and not let the weight of his own past mistakes color his view.

"Let us know if we can help with dinner tomorrow, too," Allison said.

"You're already on the hook for wine for both dinner and the reception," I said. "That's all we could possibly ask. Nathan feels uncomfortable about even that much."

"We wanted to help you celebrate," Allison said, and my father made noises of agreement. "He's still your father"—she pointed to my dad—"and you are his one and only daughter. And we all three love you to the moon."

I blew him a kiss, and then another to her. "We should get going. It's probably a busy night for eating out, and I'd hate to lose our table."

"Can we swing by the Sunset Celebration on the way to dinner?" Rory asked.

It wasn't exactly on the way, but if we parked a couple of blocks away and took a quick tour through the performers, we would still be on time. And if Rory was enthused about anything in Key West, I hated to discourage him.

Mallory Square, where street performers and visitors gather to salute the sunset, was crowded with tourists, but not so packed that I couldn't hear the voices of seagulls flying overhead. My mouth watered at the smells of popcorn and conch fritters and the scent of crushed mint wafting from the bars. With a plan to meet back at the street in ten minutes, we left Rory and my father admiring a man juggling fire on a high wire. Allison and I headed to Lorenzo's booth, recognizable by its brightly colored umbrella, a deep-blue tablecloth dotted with silver stars and moons, and a beautiful lamp that might have been at home in my grandmother's living room. Lorenzo was dressed in a white dress shirt and plaid tie, his dark hair curling in the humid air.

He recognized Allison instantly and got up to greet her warmly. Then he gave me a hug too. "We don't have time for a reading," I said. "We just stopped by to wish you happy Thanksgiving. We'll see you on the beach?"

"Would not miss that occasion for the world," he said with a grin.

"Where are you having Thanksgiving?" Allison asked.

"I'm not celebrating this year," he said, after a slight pause.

"You don't believe in Thanksgiving?" she asked.

"I don't have anything against it; it's just the stars didn't align this year. Sometimes that happens and it's OK, really." He adjusted the knot on his tie and flicked at an invisible spot on his white shirt.

I suspected that meant he hadn't been invited to join anyone's dinner table. Allison must've had the same thought at the same time. I gave her a little nod.

"Why don't you come to Hayley's mom's tomorrow? Honestly, this family always prepares more food than anyone can eat. And if they're willing to invite the ex-husband and the wicked stepmother to the Thanksgiving table, they couldn't resist including you."

We all laughed, and I chimed in: "Absolutely, please come. My mother would be furious to know you were eating by yourself and we hadn't done anything to fix that. You know what she's like. She loves you to pieces."

"I do know. And I thank you." He crossed his hands over his chest and bowed his head. "What time, and what shall I bring?"

"Nothing to bring, and five o'clock." I reminded him of my mother's address on Noah Lane, and we headed back to the car and my scooter.

Chapter Nineteen

If there's one thing you should cut from your diet, it's fear.
—Aaron E. Carroll, "You Don't Need to 'Eat Clean,'" *The New York Times*, November 5, 2017

After a fabulous dinner of spanakopita, skewered shrimp and chorizo, beef tenderloin with blue cheese butter, and the veggies and salad Allison had chosen at Santiago's, I got on my scooter and drove the back way to my mother and Sam's home. These streets took me past the corner of the Naval Air Station, housing an old artillery bunker that I'd heard contained remnants of missiles from the sixties' Cuban Missile Crisis, abandoned brick buildings near the new city park that formerly functioned as a Keys Energy coal-burning plant, and then into the southern end of the Truman Annex. The City of Key West had agreed to buy those brick buildings for practically nothing. As often happened with those decisions, the buildings still sat empty while officials argued over their proper use, and the money it would require to rehabilitate them, and then what to do with them after they'd spent gobs of taxpayer cash on the purchase.

This end of the island was eerily quiet during nighttime hours—a little spooky unless a concert was scheduled in the new city amphitheater. I was glad to pull in front of my mother's place in the peaceful Annex neighborhood. I knocked and then let myself in. The house smelled delectable, so I made a beeline for the kitchen. Two trays of biscuits were cooling on the center island, but there was no sign of my mother or Sam. I broke off a piece of one of the biscuits that had obviously been taste-tested and popped a little corner of it into my mouth. It was light and flaky and tasted like pumpkin or more likely sweet potato with the faintest hint of cinnamon, followed by a late kick of cayenne pepper— and loads of butter.

I traced the sound of classical music and found my mom and Sam enjoying a glass of wine on the back deck. They were reclined on side-by-side lounge chairs, holding hands.

"Sorry to barge in—I just wanted to check in and see how things are going," I said. "Your biscuits are killer good."

"Thanks. New recipe. Get a glass and have a nightcap with us," Sam said, swinging his legs off the chair and beginning to get to his feet.

"No, no, I just wanted to touch base."

"How was your dinner? And how did Nathan and your father get on?" my mother asked.

"Dinner was great. Something for everyone. As for Nathan and Dad—" I shrugged my shoulders. "The little time we spent together, they seemed to be fine. Then Nathan had to go back to work, so he couldn't have dinner with us after all. He's on some top-secret undercover mission."

I could hear my voice hovering between annoyance and worry, neither of which I wanted to pass on to my mother. She had enough on her plate without fretting over my husband-to-be. "We stopped at Sunset on the way to dinner, and I wanted to let you know we invited Lorenzo for Thanksgiving. It's a little late to be asking, but is that OK?"

"Of course," my mother said. "We adore Lorenzo. There's always a place for him at the table."

"Thanks." I grimaced. "I also invited Palamina because her beau dumped her. She won't eat much," I added quickly. "I should have checked with you first—"

"Absolutely no problem," said Sam. "It's Thanksgiving, a time to celebrate family and welcome people who don't have as much to celebrate as we do. And besides, Connie and Ray had to cancel because the baby is sick. Palamina hasn't tasted our food. Maybe we can tempt her into overeating on turkey day like the rest of us."

"Maybe. She's a tough sell."

"What else?" my mother asked, studying my face. "You look bothered."

"We've moved the wedding rehearsal to Friday morning instead of tomorrow," I said. "Nathan was afraid he'd be up all night and that would be the only time he could rest."

"Perfect," my mother said, not letting on that she'd already approved the change. "That actually works better for the turkey and a million other things. But you're the one getting married. Is it OK with you?"

I puffed out some air. "None of this is my favorite way to run a wedding. But since I'm going to be married to a cop, I figure I'd better get used to adjusting."

"That works for every marriage," Sam said, drawing my mother into a hug and then blowing me a kiss.

After bidding them good-night, I buzzed back up island to our pier. The sound of sixties rock music drifted across the water from the boat next to Miss Gloria's best friend Mrs. Dubisson's boat. A new couple had moved into that big blue boat at the end of the pier, and they loved a party. The fairy lights on our houseboat were twinkling a friendly welcome. As I got off the bike and lifted it onto its stand, our next-door neighbor, Mrs. Renhart, returned from her nighttime walk with her elderly Schnauzer.

She picked up Schnootie and squeezed her close to her chest. "It looks like you finally got someone to work on that old tub," she said. "Let's hope they last longer than the other fellows."

She smiled a little, and I imagined this was her attempt at friendly pre-holiday conversation. "I get a good feeling from these contractors," I said. "Thanks for noticing. And that reminds me to put some lights up on that boat before Friday. Are you sure you won't change your mind and come to the wedding?"

Not that I was dying to have her and her curmudgeon husband in attendance, but it had seemed too sad not to send them an invite.

"Thanks, but on Fridays, Mr. Renhart insists on meatloaf and mashed potatoes, and watching reruns of *Columbo* on the telly. He's gotten too old and set in his ways to deviate."

Did she sound wistful, or was it more like resignation? I wondered what she'd been like as a young woman, and whether she might at some point have been happier without her husband. Some people's marriages seemed to be such a bad fit that they'd be easy to end, while others might turn sour so slowly you would hardly notice you were no longer happy. Gloomy thoughts for two nights before my own wedding.

I gave her a little hug and kissed Schnootie on the head before trotting up the finger to our boat. Miss Gloria had already gone to bed, but she'd left the living room light on. I poured myself an inch of white wine and went out to the porch to sit with the cats. A Rolling Stones lick floated through the night air . . . *Pleased to meet you* . . . and Mrs. Renhart's wind chimes pealed a chorus.

I couldn't keep my mind from circling back to Nathan's mysterious case. I felt intensely curious. Why wouldn't he tell me more? The answer wasn't obvious like the time last winter when he'd been in charge of security for the Havana/Key West event and its many major celebrities. As far as I knew, there was nothing coming up in the next week in Key West, no special events aside from the Thanksgiving Hog's Breath 5K Hog Trot and our own wedding. The more secretive he acted, the more curious I got. And that was something we could probably both work on—he could tell me a little more and I could be a little less nosy.

Chapter Twenty

Contrary to popular opinion, pumpkin pie-lovers are adventurous, quizzical, good in bed and voluminously communicative.
—Kate Lebo, in "Gemma Wilson's Eat Your Words," *City Arts Magazine*, October 24, 2013

I rose early the next morning to finish work on the pumpkin pies. I had made the dough for the crust two days earlier, cutting butter and cream cheese into the flour, moistening it, and refrigerating the lumps to be rolled out later. I let the dough warm slowly on the counter while I drank coffee and flicked through my email. Thinking about the events of the week, I rolled out the crust, then folded the pie dough in half, dropped it into the glass pans, and fluted the edges.

While the pie shells prebaked, I whipped up the filling, which included my top-secret ingredients— maple syrup, extra vanilla, and chai spice. I had made this recipe dozens of times before, so I could let my mind wander. While the beaters hummed in the background, potential opening sentences for my article on culinary trends circled through my head. When the crusts were ready, I poured the filling into them and slid the pans into the oven.

An hour later, I pulled the two pies out of the oven and left them cooling on the stovetop. The filling had come out a rich orange, puffed up beautifully by the whipped eggs, with only the slightest cracks. Not like the year when I'd taken the pies out too early and the pumpkin filling had collapsed into wrinkles resembling an old man's neck. This time the crusts had turned out golden and perfect, too. Hearing Miss Gloria stir in her room, I slid two ginger scones into the oven to warm and made another pot of coffee.

Miss Gloria and I were enjoying the scones with lots of butter and coffee out on the deck when the house phone rang. I dashed in to pick it up and recognized the UNKNOWN as likely coming from the Stock Island jail. I accepted the collect call from my roommate's jail pal, Odom, and apologized again for hanging up on him the last time.

"Not a problem," he said. "Not everyone can be as kind and openhearted as your roommate." Which felt like a slap in my face that I probably deserved. I brought the phone outside and handed it over to Miss Gloria.

"Good morning, Odom," she said. "Happy Thanksgiving. Hayley is here with me; do you mind if I put you on speaker phone?"

His voice piped out of the phone. "Sure. I heard another bit of news," he said, "and wanted to pass it along." The volume of his voice dropped lower as though he might be worried about who else was listening. "It seems that some kind of smuggling ring has moved into town."

This didn't really surprise me, because with all the water around us, the Coast Guard was often intercepting shipments of illegal drugs and sometimes immigrants.

"Is it drugs?" Miss Gloria asked. "I'll never forget the day my Frank and I went out puttering on the reef in his little motorboat and came back with a bale of marijuana onboard."

We all laughed, imagining the two older folks figuring out what to do with their discovery.

"That's always possible in this town," Odom said. "It's easy enough for boats to land and things to get unloaded before anyone is the wiser."

"What about human trafficking?" Miss Gloria asked.

"It could be that also," Odom said, practically whispering now. "Apparently the Joint Interagency Task Force is involved, along with the local cops and the sheriff's office. So in other words, it's a big deal."

I knew I shouldn't get annoyed at the lack of specificity, but I could feel the anxiety gathering in my chest. After all, he was in prison and should not be expected to have much decent news from the outside.

"Maybe you heard something more about my friend's food tour and that awful death?" I asked.

"Not exactly." He paused for a minute. "But I might have heard something that's more to do with you and your detective."

My heart sank with a clunk I could almost hear.

"A man he put away ten years ago up in Miami has escaped from the Florida penitentiary."

"What was he put away for?" Miss Gloria asked.

"He committed a vicious streak of home invasions and robberies that ended in a big chase all the way to Islamorada. I wasn't in the courtroom, of course, but word has it he threatened the detective that he'd come after him first chance he got."

"How could they let a man like that go?" I asked. "Why would they allow a hardened criminal who hurt so many people back on the streets? Where is he now?" I was beginning to feel frantic, out of control, terrified for Nathan.

"I can't answer that," Odom said. "Remember what I said, they didn't let him go. He escaped. Besides, one thing I've learned in here is don't count on fairness. Sometimes the worst criminals figure a way to get out, and the little guys who didn't do much get trapped inside."

In the background I could hear voices complaining that his time was up.

"Thank you for letting me know," I said.

My anxiety shot even higher as Miss Gloria ended the call and went inside to replace the phone in its cradle. Surely Nathan knew about this? Surely they were protecting him? How could I check? I convinced myself it would be best to delay worrying, put it out of my mind for the moment and ask him later at Thanksgiving dinner. He would already know about this and I'd insist that he tell me. Though he'd be furious to learn that an inmate of the Stock Island jail was phoning Miss Gloria on a regular basis. Really, did I have to say that? Maybe it wasn't my news to tell.

I couldn't help myself, I picked up my open laptop and surfed to the Monroe County Sheriff's Office website, where I found the list of current inmates. The charges were terrifying: "manslaughter," "domestic battery by strangulation," "murder dangerous depraved with premeditation," "cause bodily harm," "use of two way communication device to facilitate felony," "possession of a controlled substance without prescription," "convicted felon failure to register." From there I found a link to the Florida Department of Corrections and navigated to inmate escape information, aka the "Absconder/Fugitive" information list. There were, horrifyingly enough, 420 of them. However, I couldn't go any further without a name. And studying the crimes and the names was a sure path to crazy.

For the second time in so many days, my phone buzzed with Analise's number popping up on the screen.

"What's up?" I asked, my heart pounding a little harder, anticipating more bad news. Because, honestly, she would text with the good stuff.

"Did you see the front page of the *Citizen* this morning?" she asked. And then barreled on without waiting for me to answer. "They found a body in the dumpster behind the Buoys' Club."

"A body? My god, who was it?"

"They're saying his name is Marcel Chaudoir. But they've posted a photo and I swear it's the guy from my tour—Marcel Cohen. And how many Marcels could be visiting Key West?"

Her voice trailed off. "At least they can't say it was food poisoning that killed him. Because how would he have put himself into the trash? And why?" Her voice choked up. "Sorry. That's gallows humor, I know, but this has been the worst week ever."

"Let me read the article and I'll call you back."

After hanging up with my friend, I went inside and grabbed the newspaper from the coffee table in the living room where Miss Gloria had been relaxing earlier. On the first page, sure enough, was a story about a man who had been found dead in the dumpster, presumed murdered. My stomach skidded as I realized the grisly discovery must have happened last night, around the time I'd been cruising by looking for Nathan. That explained the police presence I'd noticed.

As Analise had told me, the newspaper identified the deceased as Marcel Chaudoir. And his photo looked quite a bit like the man I'd met on her food tour, though less scruffy. Police department sources mentioned that all leads were being followed, and that if anyone had information about the death, they should call. The last line mentioned that the victim's wife had died several days earlier, possibly due to a hemorrhagic stroke.

Before I could think too hard about it, I called Audrey's sister. She might be able to explain the discrepancy in names, and she surely would have been informed about Marcel's death.

"Yes, I saw his mug in the paper," she said as soon as she answered. "And no, I did not kill him."

Which honestly, I hadn't considered, though it made a little bit of sense, as bitter as she had sounded. "Why are they calling him Marcel Chaudoir? Do you have any idea?"

"Marcel Chaudoir was a made-up name," she said. "He probably still had it on his driver's license, though he changed it back to Cohen after he failed to make a go of his restaurant. That was years ago. Audrey said he once knew a man with that name and he'd always loved it, fancied it would help him become the French chef he wished he was. So she changed hers too. Audrey and Marcel Cohen became Audrey and Marcel Chaudoir." She pronounced his name with a faux-French flourish.

"He owned a restaurant?" I asked. This made it seem like he'd been a bigger deal in the foodie world than what she'd implied last time.

"French fusion or some such nonsense. We ate there once when I went out to visit Audrey. The food was downright weird and there wasn't much of it. Not for those prices. I literally left hungry."

"Is his family coming into town, or do you have to handle all this?" I asked.

"I'll have as little to do with it as your cops will allow," she said.

I thanked her and hung up. Both members of one couple dying on vacation struck me as way too bizarre to be coincidence. What could have happened this time? On the one hand, if Marcel had been frequenting the Buoys' Club, he might easily have consumed too much liquor and ended up in a drunken brawl out in the parking lot.

This was not unheard of in our town. Perhaps the police would find that the brawl was related to a fight over one of the dancers. Or possibly something else, something bigger, like drug deals or something worse—maybe even related to the gossip we'd heard from Odom. I had no idea what really went on in a place like that, aside from the dancing girls and drinking. But considering that Nathan had been staking out the establishment this week—and that he'd warned me to stay far away—it must have been something big.

Whoever killed Marcel could not have thought things through. Tossing a body in the trash did not seem like a reliable way to dispose of it if you were trying to keep the death a secret.

I Googled the new name, Marcel Chaudoir, adding "Chef" at the last minute.

The first item to come up was a story written by a food critic before Marcel's restaurant failed.

Enter Marcel Chaudoir's new restaurant, Sur Ma Table, and you realize at once, perusing the menu, that you may be in the presence of culinary genius. Stay long enough, and you also might notice that enough people have told him he's a genius that it's gone to his head.

As this reviewer works, she tries to go to dinner without pre-established opinions. That means no reading reviews online, no listening to friends who say you must try the duck pate en croute or the beurre braised baby mushrooms and veal or even grandmother's yellow cake with caramel icing that you need a small hammer to break into.

But I tried them all, plus half a dozen other dishes split among my dining companions, and we all agreed here was a chef who worked on a plane higher than most restaurants could imagine. There were a few glitches—the tension of the wait staff was palpable. They crept around like dogs who'd been beaten. The hostess was wound tighter than a proverbial top. But most critical, we all suffered serious gastrointestinal distress later that night and into the next morning. One of our party ended up in the hospital.

I adored the premise of this restaurant, which promised a meal at the chef's table inside the kitchen for every diner. I adored every dish that we tried, sauf the pistachio-crusted sweetbreads. And I could have chosen to blame our problem on a theoretical bad clam. But my mission is to be transparent, and that means calling out the problems in the places I visit as well as the culinary masterpieces.

Then I scanned the history of this critic and was very interested to learn that she'd been active recently in writing about the #MeToo movement for chefs and restaurateurs. She'd be a great get for the article I would be writing after this weekend. Several minutes into her website, I realized that this woman now lived in a fifty-five-plus community in Naples. I couldn't believe the serendipity—that she was less than a day's travel away. But I also couldn't see myself taking the four-hour ferry to Fort Myers and then a taxi to Naples, considering that my family was in town and I was due to cohost a Thanksgiving dinner that might rival Chevy Chase's vacation movies, and that I was getting married on Friday.

So I did the next best thing—tracked down her phone number and dialed her up. I explained who I was and how Marcel Chaudoir aka Cohen appeared to have been murdered in Key West.

"My beat is food, like yours," I said, after she expressed her shock and horror. "I'd love to write something about who he was in the food world and what happened to all that early promise, a perspective that might otherwise go unmentioned. Do you have time to chat for a few minutes about what you remember about Marcel? I found your review of the dinner after which you and your guests got sick."

"I'm so sorry to hear this; what a loss," she said. "He was a remarkable talent and so entrepreneurial. He had big plans for his restaurant. I do regret that my review might have contributed to taking down his empire. Sometimes I wonder if I made a mistake."

She paused and I heard a clattering noise in the background, as if she'd dropped the lid to a pot on a stone counter. "These days, it probably would have come out anyway in Yelp reviews or on OpenTable. But those things were not common even fifteen years ago—people paid attention to what was in the newspapers. And I was a big fish for a while, right after the *LA Times* and the *New York Times*.

"I'm in the middle of preparations for a dinner for twenty. Is it possible that we could continue chatting next week? Meanwhile, I will look through my files and see if I can find any other notes from those days."

"Of course," I said. "But one more quick question before you go?" I didn't leave her the time to say no. "I realize this was a long time ago, but can you remember anything illegal that Marcel might have been involved with, anything that might have led to this awful result? His murder?"

"I'd like to take the time to think this over, but off the top of my head, he was a ruthless man, extremely ambitious. Now whether that would set him up to be murdered, I can't say. Lots of people are ambitious and they don't end up dead."

"Did you follow his career after your review?"

She sighed. "A review like that, mixed as it was, was bound to have an effect on business. As I was quick to say in my write-up, his cooking could be brilliant. But to tell the truth, if the food critic and all the people accompanying her get sick as dogs after they eat at a restaurant, would you make reservations? And mind you, the prices were steep for the time."

"I don't suppose I would, not right away, anyway. And as you said, these days you can read online reviews that might refute such a claim, or include a response from the owner explaining the situation. So I might watch and wait for a while."

Her comments reminded me of the responsibility I balanced in my job—letting diners in on my opinions while staying mindful of the effects my words could have on a restaurant. "I'll let you go, but please stay in touch, especially if you remember anything more about him?" I read off my email address and phone number, wondering if she was bothering to write them down.

Once off the phone, I returned to the kitchen and poured the dregs from the coffee pot into my cup, wishing I had time to zip up to the Cuban Coffee Queen for a real coffee. I tried to think about what I knew. How odd it was that two talented chefs, Martha and Marcel, had ended up in that small space in her industrial kitchen at the very same moment and did not know each other . . . Was the meeting really coincidental? Key West was a small town on a small island in the end, but that stretched even my powers of suspension of disbelief. I wondered if she could shed any light on the food poisoning incident. Had she ever heard of Marcel before the events of these past few days?

My mind suddenly flashed like a warning light on Martha. Not that I could picture her killing him and disposing of the body that way, but I believed she had to know more than she'd told me so far. I considered calling her, but decided to swing by the cooking store on the off chance that she'd be there. She'd be more likely to tell me the truth in person. And she had mentioned the other day that she was hosting her own dinner on Thanksgiving but that she'd gotten so spoiled by the store's kitchen that she preferred to do the prep work there. Eden and Bill had been very kind about letting her work in their space off hours.

I folded the front page of the newspaper and tucked it into my pocket. Then I walked to the little back porch, where my roommate, decked out in her best Thanksgiving sweat suit, was crouched in our mini garden of container pots, trimming herbs.

"I'm going out for an errand. Back in a jiffy, OK?"

"Remember that I'm having a drink and a snack with my mah-jongg group this afternoon in the Truman Annex? Not all of them are so lucky as to have personal chefs in their families. In fact, some of them don't have families at all." She grinned and waited until I confirmed. "Mrs. Dubisson is driving. I'm thinking I'll have her drop me off at your mother's place afterward and I can take a little catnap in a spare bedroom?"

"Sure, why not."

"Do you want me to bring the pies and pecan bars now? Then you can buzz down on your scooter later with just the whipped cream?"

"Perfect," I said.

"Listen." She scrambled up and came over to take both of my hands. "Try not to worry about Odom. Imagine you're in that enormous jail and news spreads through the inmates, who are itchy with boredom and full of gossip like a bunch of old ladies. And it's even worse than usual because it's a holiday and they really, really don't want to be stuck there."

She squeezed my fingers until I nodded.

"Remember playing telephone as a kid? By the time any kind of news reaches Odom, it's probably distorted as all get-out. And what are the chances that an escaped criminal is going to drive the length of the Keys to wreak havoc? You'd be really dumb to do that, because there's only one road out. A sheriff's department roadblock is a given. And besides, Nathan's a very good cop and a strong man. Honestly, he can take care of himself."

I felt tears prick my eyes. I so wanted that to be true.

Chapter Twenty-One

In the kitchen there is nothing new and nor can there be anything new. It's all theft. Anyone who claims to have "invented" a dish is dishonest, or delusional or foaming.
—Jonathan Meades, *The Plagiarist in the Kitchen: A Lifetime's Culinary Thefts*

The roads on the way down to the cooking store were still quiet, except for occasional joggers and walkers, many wearing green and pink and blue tutus and goofy hats and carrying beers after finishing up the traditional Hog's Breath 5k Hog Trot. I was able to park right behind the store and walk around the Mel Fisher museum to the store entrance. The front door was unlocked, and Martha was busy at the stove. She looked up. The expression on her face was not welcoming.

"Happy Thanksgiving," I said. "Do you have a minute?"

"The habanero candy is just getting to the soft ball stage. I can't leave it now. Can you hang out for a bit?"

"Sure," I said, trying to think of words that might relax her. "You know I love this place. And my mother-in-law-to-be gave us a gift certificate as part of her wedding present. I don't know if I'll succeed in convincing Nathan that one of your dinners would be fun, not torture. If he says no, I get to pick out all kinds of cool cooking stuff. Or else bring a friend. My mom would love it."

She gave a tight smile in return and resumed her station at the stove. I wandered around the store, mentally adding merchandise to my list of possible purchases. I didn't want to leave Miss Gloria's kitchen bereft, if and when I finally moved next door. And Nathan should have a chance to veto my selections, though I doubted very much he would care about what was in our kitchen drawers or about any potential china patterns or Italian ceramic serving dishes. As Miss Gloria had explained to Nathan's mother, fancy dishes didn't belong on a houseboat anyway.

On a shelf containing cookbooks and cooking magazines, I spotted one I hadn't seen before with a glossy cover showing two chefs at work at a magnificent professional stove with a copper exhaust hood. I leafed through the pages displaying stunning kitchens and perfectly groomed chefs standing behind their showstopper dishes. This was a serious restaurant chef catalog, not so much for novice home-style cooks. As I flipped through the back pages, I noticed listings for peculiar ingredients. Some chefs were looking for sources, other vendors were selling—Iranian saffron at ten thousand dollars a pound, Indonesian vanilla at thirty dollars a bean, Lambda olive oil at seventy-five dollars per 500ml. Who ordered these things? And what did they cook with them?

In my talks with Martha this week, I had been recognizing that cooking the same dishes over and over could get tedious. Yes, in the right restaurant as a head chef, you could make plenty of money. But how many plates of fried yellowtail snapper could one chef make before her soul cried out for something more adventurous? Martha's cooking was both idiosyncratic and ambitious. She wouldn't have taken a job like this one if she hadn't been willing to take risks.

Then I thought about my own cooking and the food I prepared and what a big part of my life it had become. But some of the great pleasure of the meals I made was serving them to people I loved, and let's be honest, eating them myself. If I had to make the same thing over and over and send it out to waiting strangers, would I too begin to chafe at the constraints? Would I be looking for newer ways to make things, techniques or ingredients that would bring more acclaim?

Martha finished pouring her molten candy out on the countertop and came over to where I stood. "What's up?"

"They found the body of the guy who was on the food tour with me in the dumpster behind the Buoys' Club."

"Which guy?" she asked, her eyes narrowing.

I pulled the article out of my backpack and smoothed it on the counter. "Marcel, the one whose wife died."

As she studied the photo—a younger version of Marcel without the scruffy beard—the look on Martha's face turned from slightly annoyed to truly terrified. Whatever she was afraid of felt very real.

"Maybe you'd better tell me the rest of the story. And then I think it's time you told the police."

Martha glanced at all her ingredients laid out on the counter, sniffed the chipotle-basted smoked turkey in the oven, and tapped the hardening candy with a fingernail. "I have fourteen people coming to dinner. I just can't get involved with the cops right now."

"If you won't talk to Lieutenant Torrence, you're going to need to tell me what *exactly* happened in the past. Because I feel like I'm working a giant jigsaw puzzle with only the outside pieces available. And maybe the cat batted away some of the pieces in the middle."

I flashed a friendly smile and then shut up. On the way over, as I'd practiced what I would say to her, I'd made myself a promise—I would say what I had to and then fall quiet. Biding my time and biting my tongue didn't come to me naturally, but I'd become convinced that this was the only way to encourage her to talk. It felt like a ten-minute stretch of silence, and I had to squeeze my fingernails into my palms to keep from bailing her out.

Finally she spoke. "You have to understand that this happened long before the MeToo movement. There was no one to turn to. He had all the cards. He was the executive chef and the owner of the restaurant where I worked. He'd written a cookbook that had shot off the shelves and even hit the *LA Times* best-seller list. All the foodies in Seattle were vying for a reservation at his restaurant. He even had a short-lived TV show, and he was named one of the most eligible, desirable, and adorable bachelors on the West Coast."

"This guy was a fancy chef on a TV show?" I asked, touching Marcel's face in the paper. My voice betrayed the disbelief I was feeling. He looked like a washed-up biker, not a celebrity chef.

She only nodded.

"There was no one you could talk to? No one who might have noticed he wasn't quite what he seemed?" I had to push back my impatience, let her tell the story in her own time.

She shook her head emphatically. "Even the other kitchen workers wouldn't have believed me. There were women salivating to go out with him, and well, look at me." She gestured at herself from head to toe—tattoos, ponytail, jeans. "I'm neither elegant nor eloquent. And besides, he told me that he would ruin me if I opened my mouth. And I absolutely believed him. And I believed that I was the only one he had abused."

Of course my mind jumped instantly to wondering what exactly he had done. But her lips pinched together as if to say that's all she'd reveal about the matter.

"And I also believed I was oh-so-lucky to be on his team, regardless of how he treated me." Her gaze met mine. "And honestly, I was in a way. I learned so much. He was brilliant in the kitchen. Brilliant."

She fell silent again, fingering the crimped edge of the newspaper. Could he really have changed enough that Martha wouldn't have recognized him? And what about him; had he seen her? Had he not realized she was working in Key West at this venue?

I had a million questions about what had actually occurred, but I didn't think the details mattered so much as the effect it had had on her.

"And so how did you get out from under that situation?" I asked, pinching myself mentally for the awkward phrasing.

"I knew I had to leave. Disappear. But me leaving wouldn't have bothered him a bit. He would have told the world I was flighty and unreliable. And then he could have replaced me with one of the other up-and-coming female chefs who wanted to work with the master."

"Sounds so frustrating," I said. "You must have been furious."

She nodded her head emphatically. "Heartsick and angry. I wanted to make him suffer for what he'd done, and the only thing I could come up with was food poisoning. So the last afternoon before I ran away, while the rest of the staff was eating their family meal, I stirred a laxative into every sauce and every salad dressing. It was odorless and tasteless, so all it did was make every liquid a little bit thicker than normal. But more than half of the customers who came in that night became ill. It was a huge scandal that rocked his reputation. A friend in the kitchen called me later and told me he interrogated every single staff person the next day. And then he started on the vendors. He was livid, enraged. Somebody must have seen me in the kitchen, or maybe suspected me when they remembered I didn't eat with the rest of the staff. And they snitched. Then it all made sense to him and he blamed me for ruining him. But he had no way to punish me—I was gone. Poof. Vanished."

"And that turned out to be the very night the food critic was visiting with her dining companions?"

She nodded again. "For me, bent on revenge, the timing couldn't have been better. For him, it couldn't have been worse. My friend told me not to come back anywhere near his restaurant. She believed he was angry enough that he might really hurt me." She looked straight at me. "So you see, he may have felt he had reason to damage me in any way he could."

"The police may come question you before tomorrow," I said. "I have no control over that. But if they don't, you will go to the station in the morning and make a report? You need to tell them what you told me so they can clear you as a suspect."

"I promise that I will."

"What happened after you left his restaurant?"

"If you took a look at my work history, you saw there was a big gap after I left his place because I had no references. I didn't even want to say I'd worked in his restaurant for fear they'd contact him. I couldn't risk that. On the other hand, I was never going to get promoted past line cook without references; it didn't matter how good my food was or how innovative my ideas were. I was out of a job and starting from scratch. And I felt so incredibly guilty and ashamed. But I had no way to fix any of it. So there was no point staying in Seattle. I traveled for a while and I drank more than I should have and finally ended up here. You know what they say about the people in this town, right?"

"Yeah, hold the state of Florida upside down and shake it, and all the loose nuts fall down to Key West." We both laughed.

"Do you mind telling me a little more about him? What was he like as a man and a chef?"

She sighed heavily. "When I started out, women were not thought of as chefs. We were cooks and prep staff. We had to work twice as hard to prove ourselves as competent in the kitchen. And it was a given that the atmosphere would be like a locker room. I could take all that. I wanted to be there. It was what came after that that I couldn't take. He shouldn't have had the right to assume he could mess with the bodies—and minds—of the women in his kitchen. I don't care what a genius he was. But if you wanted to stay there, you went along with it."

I frowned, wondering where Marcel fell on the continuum of harassment, and how much it really mattered. It was her story, and her life that had veered off the course she'd set for herself.

"You may be wondering whether his sins boiled down to a little butt patting or ogling. But it was more than that, I promise you. He was on another level altogether. He wanted to hurt me and humiliate me. It wasn't something I could live with any longer." She patted her face with a dish towel. "I was afraid of him, honestly. And I felt so ashamed about what had gone on between us. But also, what I'd done to retaliate. I ruined him. And because his restaurant tanked, all the people who worked for him lost their jobs too."

She was trembling as she talked, and I thought I could see how hard it had been to hold that secret.

"I'm sorry you had to go through that. And really sorry that you had no one to talk with. But I'm very glad you've landed on your feet here."

For the first time since I'd come in, she smiled.

"Do you have any idea why his wife died? Or what happened to him? Or even why he was in town?"

"I truly don't know. I can only say that after Audrey died, I began to wonder if this was some kind of payback. If he'd sent someone to sneak into my kitchen and plant something that made her ill." She picked up a tiny hammer and began to crack the habanero candy into jagged chunks.

"You mean you thought he was paying you back by poisoning someone in your kitchen? To make the death look as though it was your doing? But why choose his wife as the victim? Unless he was trying to get rid of her anyway."

"I have not one clue," she said, sinking onto a barstool.

"Knowing what you know about him, could there be any other reason that Marcel was in Key West?"

She thought this over. "Remember how you were asking yesterday about trends? And I mentioned saffron and culinary gold?"

I nodded. "In fact, I was reading about some of that stuff in one of your magazines." I pointed to the magazine on the rack across the room.

"I wouldn't be surprised to learn that he was involved in distributing that kind of thing."

That didn't sound like cause for murder to me. "Who do you think could have killed him? Are you sure you didn't recognize the other people on that tour?"

Martha's head dropped to her hands. "I am so sure. I didn't even recognize *him*, even though that face has haunted me for years. But why on god's green earth would he have been on a small-town tasting tour with a crazy woman if he was in the middle of something illegal, something big enough to have gotten him killed?"

"Think about it," I said. "And think about what your history has to do with what happened this week. The cops are going to be very interested in that."

Honestly, if I'd been a cop, I would have insisted on hearing a lot more from Martha.

Chapter
Twenty-Two

*The nifty thing about being omnivores is that
we can take nourishment from an endless vari-
ety of flora and fauna and easily adapt to a
changing world—crop failures, droughts, herd
migrations, restaurant closings, and the like.*
—Jeffrey Steingarten, *The Man
Who Ate Everything*

After leaving Martha's kitchen, I drove north on
Eaton Street for a straight shot to my houseboat.
But it occurred to me that the Metropolitan Community Church website had noted that JanMarie
Weatherhead was helping to prepare their Thanksgiving dinner, a feast that would be distributed to
shut-ins and the elderly later this afternoon. Might
she have overheard a conversation the other day that
could shed some light on either of these deaths? It
was not far out of my way, and it couldn't hurt to
ask.

The church was located just north of White
Street on Petronia, in a residential neighborhood
that tourists didn't often see unless their conch tour
train driver took a detour. This morning, the front

doors were thrown wide open, and I could hear a buzz of conversation coming from inside and smell the ubiquitous scent of roasting turkey.

After calling hello and getting no answer, I went inside, following the wonderful smells. The kitchen was located down the hall, light-years from the fancy setup at Isle Cook Key West. A middle-aged woman with short graying hair whom I recognized from the food tour looked up from the industrial stove where she was mashing sticks of butter into a giant pot of potatoes. A steaming bowl of stuffing redolent of celery, onions, and powdered sage sat on the counter next to the refrigerator. And next to that was an enormous green bean casserole, the fried onions toasted to a perfect crispy layer on top. No caramelized jalapeño relish or cornbread financiers would come out of this kitchen—this was the kind of holiday menu my grandfather would have preferred.

"Happy Thanksgiving," she said in a bright voice. "If you're here to help deliver the meals, please take the stuffing and go on back to the coffee room where they're setting up. As soon as I get the potatoes ready and Woody finishes carving the bird, we'll be ready to go."

I felt sheepish about arriving under false pretenses and interrupting their busy day. "You're Jan-Marie Weatherhead, right?" I asked. "We sort of met on the seafood tour last week."

The expression on her face grew instantly serious. "That was so tragic," she said.

I slid the article about Marcel out of my pocket, unfolded it, and showed it to her. "It's gotten worse. Now the dead woman's husband has been killed. I was hoping you'd have a few minutes to chat about what you might have noticed that morning."

She wiped her hands on her apron and took the clipping to read it more carefully.

"Did you know any either of them?" I asked.

She handed the paper back. "No."

"How about the other guy on the tour with us?"

She returned to the potatoes, pausing to grind in a few rounds of pepper. "You mean Zane. I sort of know him. He made a big splash when he opened his restaurant a couple years ago. I belong to a dinner club and we rotate choosing where to eat each Friday. They weren't thrilled when I chose his place up the Keys. No one wants to drive home in the dark with a couple glasses of wine under their belt. You can bet the sheriff's department is looking for that." She chuckled. "So I became the designated driver. And also took lots of ribbing about his menu—charred this and beurre blanc that. Honestly, we should have stayed on Stock Island and ordered pizza. I believe Zane has been working at Matt's on Stock Island since his restaurant went under."

"Looking back, did you get any sense that Marcel and Zane knew each other? Or whether Marcel knew Analise or Martha?" I was floundering in theories about the two deaths, none of which really added up.

She wiped her wrist across her forehead, leaving a trail of flour like the tail of a shooting star. "I thought Audrey sounded super-forced—a little manic-y, you know? And Marcel seemed to be trying his best to tamp her down. Meanwhile, Zane watched all of this very, very carefully. I got the sense he was focused on Marcel. Of course, I was watching all of them, too." She laughed. "It was equal-opportunity observation. At one point, I swear he was watching me watching Marcel."

I hadn't noticed the watching details—I'd been too focused on my own work and distracted by the intensity of Audrey. But if what JanMarie had seen was accurate, either Zane was annoyed by Marcel and his too-bright wife or Zane knew Marcel. Or could it have been that Zane was Audrey's boyfriend? Honestly, I hadn't noticed any sparks between them—and I was tuned in to these things.

JanMarie scraped the finished potatoes into a big serving dish and started back down the hall to the fellowship room. I followed with the stuffing and placed the bowl on the long table as instructed. A horde of cheerfully chatting volunteers picked up Styrofoam carryout trays and began to move down the line, filling each one with turkey, gravy, stuffing, potatoes, and green beans. A small older woman with curly white hair sitting at the end of the table placed a dinner roll in each finished tray with a satisfied flourish. The dinner rolls looked like something from the supermarket, nothing fancy like Martha's rosemary brown-butter masterpieces. But I suspected all of this food would be very welcome to the guests who received it.

"I'd love to do a little piece on your Cooking with Love program for our magazine," I said. Could this be one of the bigger stories that Palamina was hoping for—who on this island fed the needy and the homeless? And what did they fix? "Not today, of course."

"That would be fun," JanMarie said. "We're here every Saturday with different volunteer cooks in charge of the meal. They're very good at choosing recipes based on what's been donated and what will serve a crowd. We don't make anything fancy, just good old-fashioned rib-sticking meals."

She gave me her phone number and email, and I promised to be in touch. Outside on the sidewalk, I checked my phone to see if I'd missed a text or email from Nathan. Nothing. Where in the world could he be?

I drove back to Houseboat Row but felt too darn anxious to sit around by myself, worrying about all the possible dangers facing my guy. I considered taking the drive out to the next island north, Stock Island, where Zane was now working at Matt's Stock Island restaurant. I fed the cats an extra Thanksgiving treat, hopped back on my scooter, and drove north.

Stock Island has been having a bit of a resurgence, as land and rents are less expensive than anything that can be found in Key West. As a result, though the first streets off Route 1 have an industrial feel, the area further off the highway appears on the verge of thriving, as workshops and showrooms and restaurants have begun to relocate here. I wound through some of the streets until I reached the Atlantic side waterfront, where Matt's Kitchen was located in the complex of a new resort on the harbor. The hotel had a modern, industrial decor that felt warmer and more inviting than it sounded. The restaurant included a large outdoor area with fire pits and dog-friendly tables, and inside, a rustic bar featuring tall, wooden communal tables. WRITE DRUNK, EDIT SOBER was written in huge type on the floor. Hemingway, no doubt.

"Are you meeting someone?" the hostess asked. It often seemed that restaurants could not comprehend a single woman asking for a table to dine alone. Particularly, I guessed, on a big holiday.

"I need to speak with Zane Ryan for just a few moments. I'm a food writer at *Key Zest* and wanted to talk to him about—well—food."

She looked dubious. "I'm certain he's busy. This is not a great time. They are crazed in the kitchen, neck-deep in Brussels sprouts and bacon." She glanced at the iPhone that rested on the hostess stand. "Our first Thanksgiving seating starts serving at noon."

"Five minutes?" I asked.

She clacked across the wood floor in her platform heels and disappeared through the door next to the kitchen's open window. Within a few minutes, she was back. "He says he can give you a minute."

I followed her into the kitchen, which was filled with spotless stainless-steel surfaces and appliances and busy workers in white coats. She gestured at Zane, who stood by an enormous double sink. He was dressed in chef's whites, and his face looked gloomy and tired. I needed to think and talk fast.

"So sorry to bother you during rush, but my impossible boss has me on a ridiculous deadline. I won't keep you long. And please, keep chopping." I grinned, motioned at the bin of vegetables in front of him, and began to rattle through my introduction.

"I'm doing a piece on up-and-coming chefs and restaurants. You've probably noticed that some visitors to Key West are not interested anymore in accepting the same old fried fish on their plates. I'd heard that you were thinking of opening a pop-up restaurant out here on Stock Island. It will be very welcome. And I'd love to do a story on it. My angle would be following you as you build the concept from the ground up. Is that something you'd be interested in?"

The suspicious look on his face faded a little. "I'm planning to call it the Hidden Kitchen." He glanced around as if to be sure others weren't listening in. "To start with, I'll do dinners on my day off, which happens to be Monday, a day when a lot of restaurants in town are closed. So I'm hoping that will bring people in—even if it's desperation at first."

"What style of food will you prepare?"

He laughed and began to chop the pile of Brussels sprouts in half. "Whatever I feel like cooking. That's my idea of how to keep things fresh; it's always chef's choice at the Hidden Kitchen. So you don't come in and order this or that, you eat what I'm making. Like Mom when you were growing up, only the food will be a lot better. No gluey potatoes or overcooked, gray beef. I'll be able to experiment with recipes and ingredients that would never go over in a restaurant like this." Suddenly a flicker of recognition came over his face.

"You were on the food tour where that lady died."

I nodded. "It was awful. Did you know her?"

"No, I did not." He frowned. "And though I may go to hell for speaking ill of the dead, she was a major pain. She never stopped talking, so it was hard to enjoy the day."

"She was a little annoying," I said. "Why did you decide to take the tour?"

"I'm always scanning for ideas—what's working, what's falling flat . . . To be brutally honest, I didn't learn too much that day. I'm hoping to get an 'in crowd' vibe going, so people will want to come because they don't want to be left out. You don't get that vibe by serving plain steamed shrimp, or doctored-up macaroni, or key lime pie." He paused to scrape his sprouts into a large bowl. "Everyone's still got a little bit of the gangly high school kid deep inside them, the kid who wants to belong, don't you think?"

A man in a tall chef's hat called across the kitchen. "Ryan! Bacon! Now!"

Zane scowled and rolled his eyes.

"OK if I follow up by email?" I asked, and then jotted his address in my phone once he'd reluctantly nodded.

I left the resort and drove home, thinking about what his personality was like—he was a planner, a take-charge guy with a lot of energy. He was not the kind of man who would be happy prepping vegetables in a resort hotel, taking orders barked out by a bossy chef. But somehow I got the sense he had the patience to bide his time as well.

Chapter Twenty-Three

Now if you'll excuse me, I'm going to go baste the turkey and hide the kitchen knives.
— Mrs. Pascal, *The House of Yes*

Once home, I whipped two pints of organic cream to peaks with a splash of almond extract. I ate a spoonful to stave off my hunger. By the time I took a quick shower and dressed in slimming black leggings and a flowered orange swing top that brought out the reddish glints in my hair in honor of Thanksgiving, I was running late.

When I reached my mother's house, Palamina had already arrived. She was helping in the kitchen, arranging the crudités with fish dip and crackers on a large ceramic platter. She wore one of Sam's oversized aprons, her cheeks were pink, and her blonde hair had frizzed as the humidity in the room rose. She looked happier than I'd seen her in many months.

"You made it!" Mom said. "Happy Thanksgiving. You look so cute. Where's Nathan?"

"I was hoping he beat me here. I've texted him all morning and haven't heard a peep." It was hard to keep the worry out of my voice.

"He's probably napping like Miss Gloria."

"Your roommate is so sweet," Palamina said. "To be perfectly honest, I never understood why you were living with an eighty-year-old woman. But I get it now that I've met her. She's adorable. And so is your mom."

My mother pecked her on the cheek and came over to give me a hug. "I'm sure he's going to show. If he was up all night again, no wonder he wanted to sleep in." She dropped her voice. "Did you read the story about the man they found in the dumpster? Do you suppose that's the story he was working on?"

I shrugged. "No idea. I tried to ask him last night and got nothing." I wanted to tell her about my conversation with Martha this morning, and also the phone call from Miss Gloria's jailbird friend, but it was downright rude to stand here whispering in front of my boss.

"What can I do?" I asked, after sliding the whipped cream into the refrigerator. The doorbell rang, and out in the living room I heard Sam greeting my father, stepmother, and Rory.

"Maybe best to help them get settled?" my mother asked, looking anxious. "Take a couple of bottles of champagne with you. We may need some extra lubrication."

"I'm so impressed that you and your husband are hosting your ex for Thanksgiving," said Palamina to my mom. "It's very modern, like a TV sitcom featuring a blended family solving their problems by cooking together."

"Oh lord, I hope not; that sounds unwatchable," I said as I exited the kitchen, the door swinging closed behind me. I was relieved to see that Lorenzo had come in right behind my father's family. He could help me grease the skids of the conversation, and if that didn't work, exchange eye rolls with me. And gossip later.

I introduced Sam to everyone, and stood back while Allison and my father chatted politely about how lovely the Truman Annex neighborhood was and how grateful they were to be invited to dinner. Sam took drink orders and urged everyone to move to the back porch for cocktail hour.

"What did you guys do today?" I asked, looking at Rory, who'd spread out on a lounge chair.

"He talked us into a little outing on one of the Danger boats," said Allison. "I've never been snorkeling, and I'm not much of a sailor, it turns out." She laughed. "Your father said he's never seen me in that shade of green."

"But we guys loved it," my father said, patting Rory's shoulder. "Although I was surprised the water was so chilly. Even with a shorty wetsuit, I only lasted half an hour."

"I don't swim unless it's bath tub temperature," said Lorenzo, wagging a finger. "My blood's gotten thin living down here."

"I wonder how many of your customers will come looking for you tonight and be disappointed?" Allison asked. "It seems as though the town is quite busy. And Hayley said you've developed quite a following?"

He nodded modestly. "People often return for second and third readings after they begin to understand how useful a little guidance and support can be."

I could see my father bursting to say something that would no doubt be rude. Fortunately, Palamina's entrance onto the deck carrying the tray of vegetables and fish dip distracted him from voicing his opinion. I introduced her around, and then, as Sam served champagne and cranberry cocktails, I took a minute to slip into the bathroom to check for messages.

Nothing. I texted Steve Torrence under the pretext of wishing him happy Thanksgiving. Which I meant, of course. But I also asked him if he'd seen Nathan. Or heard from him, or had any explanation about why he wasn't at my mother's place right now. I could feel my anxiety level surging again, so I ducked out of the powder room and into the kitchen to offer help to my mother and keep myself busy.

Mom was mashing potatoes with butter, cream, and a handful of snipped chives from Miss Gloria's houseboat herb garden. "Could you pull the bird out of the oven and tent it with foil?" she asked. She ticked off the remaining jobs on her fingers. "I'll put the potatoes in the oven to stay warm. In about half an hour, Sam will slice the turkey, I'll make the gravy, and we'll reheat the pasta and the beans. What am I forgetting?"

"Breathing," I said. "That's what you always tell me." I slid the turkey onto the stovetop and put the yellow oven mitts aside. "Let's go have a glass of wine and enjoy the company." I grabbed a plate of hot-pepper jelly cheese puffs that she'd pulled from the bottom oven, and she followed with sausage balls and we marched out to the deck.

As I passed the hors d'oeuvres around, Sam topped off drinks. He was taking his role as chief lubricator very seriously.

"Where's Nathan?" my father asked.

"He should be here any minute," I said, swallowing a big glug of champagne. "It's getting chilly out here; should we move into the living room?" I bustled around, picking up plates and glasses and ignoring sympathetic looks from Allison.

Once settled on the flowered couches inside, Allison said to Palamina, "Tell us about your magazine. Hayley is so thrilled to be working for you."

Palamina described *Key Zest*'s mission—to provide interesting commentary on local issues for local people, along with information for tourists that reflects the realities of island life, but also special people and places. And local problems. "We certainly don't want to drive people away, but we want to present a more nuanced picture than the Chamber of Commerce might, for example." She grinned and nodded to Sam, who was offering to freshen her cocktail.

"What kinds of unusual pieces are you considering?" my father asked.

"Hayley and I talked about her tackling trends in the food world." She looked briefly in my direction. "I did a little research after you left the office on the most expensive culinary ingredients. One of them was gold. Can you imagine? Putting metal flakes in your food? All that glitters is not gold," she added, slurring the *s* on *glitters*.

"She has me worried about our wedding cake," I said with a laugh. "It will be frosted with buttercream and decorated with flowers. Not a sparkle to be found."

"I'm certain your cake will be divine," Allison said. "Speaking of local problems, did you all read about the man they found in that dumpster last night? Did you know him?"

My first instinct was to tell everything I knew. Luckily, Lorenzo shook his head and answered. "The name isn't familiar. I suspect he was a tourist. People who frequent a place like that often find more trouble than they may have imagined. Though no one deserves an end like that."

"I despise the idea of women working there," said Palamina. "We should do an exposé on that place." She glanced at me, but I only shrugged. Nathan would have a cow if I got involved in investigating troubled businesses and police matters. And she was beginning to sound more than a little tipsy.

Miss Gloria emerged from her nap in the bedroom upstairs, blinking like a mole in a sudden shaft of sunlight. Allison sprang up and ran over to greet her with a big hug, and they began to gab.

"I'm going to see if Mom needs a hand," I said to no one in particular, standing up and melting away.

My mother was stationed at the stove, stirring a bubbling pan of gravy. Sam had finished slicing the turkey and was arranging it on a bright-yellow ceramic platter, white meat at one end, dark at the other. He'd had the idea of carving the bird in the kitchen so as not to flaunt his status as head of the family—*this* family, anyway—in front of my father.

"How long should we wait?" Sam asked, glancing at me. "It's already six thirty and we told them dinner would be at six."

A difficult conundrum for my mother, as she prized being an excellent hostess. The hors d'oeuvres trays were empty, and the group sipping cranberry cocktails in the living room was getting restless. And worst of all, she was known for her fluffy, perfectly seasoned potatoes. Tonight, her mashed potatoes were on the edge of turning to glue—a terrible sin for a Thanksgiving dinner.

"Nathan will be here any minute; he said we should go ahead." He hadn't said that—in fact, he hadn't answered my last three texts at all. But I was afraid my mother wouldn't start the meal without him, and that would make me even more anxious—and her along with me. Not to mention ruining the dinner. "And some people out there need something besides alcohol in their stomachs. Like my boss."

I helped them ferry all the dishes out to the sideboard in the dining room—the turkey, gravy, Sam's cornbread stuffing, pumpkin biscuits, pasta with sage and roasted squash, green beans almandine, and an enormous salad topped with walnuts, dried cherries, mango, and goat cheese. Then my mother invited everyone to grab a plate and fill it.

"It would be nice to have a blessing," my mother said, looking at my father first—he made a horrified grimace—and then Sam.

"I'm the senior citizen," Miss Gloria said. "May I? I have so much to be grateful for." She smoothed the napkin on her lap, smiled, and bowed her head. "Three years ago I was living alone on a small houseboat, my sons hounding me to move north. And then along came Hayley Snow, who has become a daughter to me, and brought with her a delightful and precious family. I'm so grateful to God and the Universe for that. And grateful for the opportunity to live on this island, in this country, in this world. Remind us always to give back more than we receive. Amen."

"That was lovely," Allison said. And Lorenzo reached over to cover my roommate's hand with his, his eyes shimmering with tears.

When we'd finished eating, Sam, my mother, and I got up to clear the table and move the desserts into the prime viewing space on the sideboard. In the lull before tackling dessert, my mother poured coffee and Sam offered brandy.

"This dinner has been outstanding," my father said as he moved along the dessert buffet. "Thank you for including us. And I'm grateful for your hospitality and for the maple pumpkin pie." He grinned at me, then piled a mountain of whipped cream onto his slice and slid a pecan bar next to that.

Allison turned to Lorenzo. "I'm so curious about how your brain works when you're doing a reading. Are you watching your customer's body language for cues about what they'd like to hear from you?"

"Not at all," he said. "I know some people think the whole thing is a hoax. That we fortune-tellers read people by listening to what questions they are asking, looking for wedding rings, and so on. And I suppose there are bad eggs in this business, like every other venture. For me, the message comes through in many ways, but my cards are the medium. They fine-tune it for me. But the truth is, I can read people by holding one of their shoes."

I could see my father's eyes practically rolling out of his head. Even Allison, who was both warmer and more polite than my father, seemed to be struggling with Lorenzo's description. She was a scientist, and scientists weren't that open to reading the future through a set of multicolored cards.

"Will you read my cards?" Rory asked.

Lorenzo glanced at my father and then Allison, as if to ask her permission. She shrugged.

"Think of a question you want answers for," Lorenzo said to my stepbrother.

"How will I do on the SATs?" he said quickly.

We all chuckled, and my father said, "I think that answer is more likely to come as a result of how much you're willing to study, and whether you'll go to bed early the night before." Obviously this had been a sore point between them.

"Never mind, then. How about Detective Bransford?" Rory asked. "Can you read his fortune when he isn't even here and you don't have a shoe?"

"That's not really fair to ask," I said, with a wink in Lorenzo's direction.

"To play a parlor game, you should be in the room," my father said.

As I was opening my mouth to protest his rudeness, Lorenzo smiled at me and said, "It's OK, my friend, I understand skeptics. I've faced them all my life." He looked directly at Rory. "My readings happen after the querent—that's the person who is seeking the answers—adds his or her energy by shuffling the cards. So, for example, if Hayley draws the cards"—he pushed the deck across the table—"we might be able to read Nathan through her, and through their relationship."

Everyone looked at me, but I felt frozen.

"Go ahead," said my mother. "Isn't it always better to know?"

I nodded my OK, and Lorenzo said, "Let's see what is revealed." He bowed his head and did his prereading centering that always looked to me like a prayer, and then asked me to divide the deck into three piles and choose one of them. From the pile I chose, he turned over three cards—the Devil, the Empress, and the Eight of Pentacles.

He studied the cards and then glanced quickly at me. "The Devil is one of the Major Arcana, and those cards carry more weight. This is a dark, heavy card with a lot going on underneath the surface. It has to do with being bound up in our attachment to the material world, feeling compressed and contained. It's a Capricorn card."

"Nathan's definitely a Capricorn," I said.

"He may face a dark force," Lorenzo added.

"That's no surprise, being a police officer," my mother inserted. "And Nathan's a very cautious man. That's one way he and Hayley differ, and it makes them a good match. And I can say that because I'm a little impulsive too. So she comes by it absolutely naturally."

She was babbling the way I always did when I felt nervous.

"Do you usually worry when your customer draws this card?" Allison asked.

"Not if the card is reversed," he said. "That would mean liberation from feeling bound up, imprisoned."

But the card had not been in the reversed position. After this first card in Lorenzo's reading, I was beginning to feel cold tendrils of fear snaking up from the pit of dread in my stomach and encircling my heart and squeezing, squeezing. To make things worse, I could see the worry in his eyes, too.

"What else?" I asked. If he could really sense trouble, my mother was right, I'd rather know about it than be taken by surprise.

He tapped the second card, the Eight of Pentacles, reversed. "This has to do with evaluating a situation, possibly a time of diligence and focus. And perhaps realizing there is not enough." He cocked his head to one side, appearing puzzled, but continued on to the third card after I shrugged.

"The Empress is often a woman's card. It has to do with nourishment, getting enough of something, fertility, abundance. In this case, the Empress is reversed, so the querent is not comfortable, not getting what he needs." He touched the card, which showed a queenlike figure with a crown, a scepter, and a voluminous white robe dotted with red flowers. My friend seemed even more puzzled. "Could he be concerned about food?"

I looked at my mother, and we both burst out laughing. "He eats to live, rather than living to eat," I said, feeling better immediately. "Nathan leaves the food obsession to the Snow family. And we tackle it with gusto." Sometimes Lorenzo got signals crossed when there were too many people in the room.

"Can we offer anyone a ride home?" my father asked as he got to his feet, his hand on Allison's back. "I hate to break up the party, but tomorrow's a big day."

"Do you mind dropping off Miss Gloria and Lorenzo?" I asked. "I'm going to help with dishes and stick around in case Nathan comes by for leftovers."

Chapter
Twenty-Four

Amina opened her refrigerator. A collection of takeout boxes slumped together like old men in bad weather.

—Mira Jacob, *The Sleepwalker's Guide to Dancing*

After we'd all exchanged hugs and our friends and my father's family had trooped out into the perfect Key West night, I returned to the kitchen, where Sam and my mother had begun to tackle the mountain of dirty dishes.

"We can do this," Sam said. "We have a good system and we're almost finished."

"I'd rather stay busy. I can't imagine going home to bed to just worry." I scraped the debris on the plates into the trash while Sam rinsed them and loaded the dishwasher. Meanwhile, my mother covered the leftovers and put them in the fridge.

"I'll pack some up for you and Miss Gloria. A little something to snack on tomorrow before the wedding. Or for later if Nathan gets hungry. Or you can freeze them."

"I'd say that all went very well," said Sam, sinking into one of the kitchen chairs and reaching for a pecan bar.

"Except for the no-show," I said, picking up a snickerdoodle and then putting it back down. I kept hoping for the friendly ding of my mother's doorbell. Even a text message saying Nathan was exhausted and going directly home to crash would have been welcome. "I don't get it," I said, perching on the chair across from Sam. "It's Thanksgiving. Couldn't he manage to tap out one line to say he wasn't coming?"

"If he's in the middle of a stakeout or something, he isn't going to be texting," said Sam firmly. "He has to pay attention every minute he's on the job. And he did warn us this was a crazy week, right?"

"He didn't give you any idea about what he was working on?" my mother asked, her brow furrowing. "Lorenzo said something about food. Could the case have anything to do with food?"

I hadn't thought so. But then the smuggling ring that Martha Hubbard mentioned, which I in turn had mentioned to Steve Torrence, flashed into my mind. I explained what little I knew to my parents. "The only thing is, if the stakes were high enough, I suppose he could be involved. If the bad guys were ruthless and they needed their top dogs, they'd call on Nathan. If more people were in danger, he'd for sure be in the middle of it."

I felt sick to my stomach with worry, and it must have shown on my face.

"Have you learned anything more about the man who died? Or his wife?" Sam asked. "Is this part of what Nathan is working on?"

"I don't know if there's a direct connection." I told them about visiting JanMarie and Zane earlier in the day, where I had learned exactly nothing. And then, because I trusted them completely and I could feel a wave of panic growing about Nathan, I told them about Martha's history with Marcel.

"He sounds like an awful man," my mother said.

Sam nodded. "Sounds like he would believe he had a reason to get back at her, hurt her in some way—if he realized that she was the one who'd torpedoed his restaurant," Sam said. "But can you picture Martha being responsible for either of those deaths?"

"No, I really can't imagine that at all." And then I remembered the conversation I'd had with the Naples food critic. "Apparently Marcel was a hot ticket on a fast track to celebrity chef. I wonder if I could find a copy of his cookbook? Maybe there'd be old photos that could give us a clue about who he hung out with back in those days?"

I was on the phone Googling Marcel's cookbook before I finished speaking. Every link I checked indicated that it was out of print and unavailable. And it had been published long enough ago that there wasn't a "look inside" feature available on Amazon that might have shown me what I was looking for. If I even knew what that was. And then it occurred to me to call Suzanne Orchard, the owner of the Key

West Island Bookstore that carried many older used books, including a stash of cookbooks. Luckily for me, even on Thanksgiving, she picked up on the first ring.

In a breathless rush, I explained that Nathan was missing and that I was afraid his absence was connected to the two deaths on the island earlier this week. And that I needed to get my hands on a copy of this old cookbook. "I know I'm not making sense, but I'm desperate."

"It doesn't sound familiar at all. So I'm pretty sure I don't have it. I don't even remember seeing it, but let me check with Paul." Paul was her husband, another local chef.

In a few minutes, she came back on the line. "He doesn't know the cookbook, but he's pretty sure he's seen this Marcel on a YouTube video."

"I don't think YouTube had been invented when this guy had his restaurant," I said.

"Maybe not, but that doesn't mean that someone couldn't transcribe and post older film clips. It's done all the time with musicians."

I thanked her, hung up, and typed Marcel's name into the YouTube search bar.

"I've got it," I called out to my mother and Sam.

They came over to the couch and flanked me on either side to watch. The film was grainy and the sound faded in and out, but I recognized Marcel behind the counter and in front of the stove. He had a very attractive assistant with long hair and deep cleavage who had apparently prepared the ingredients for the chef. As he cooked, a complicated recipe for duck pâté *en croûte*, he rewarded her by pretending to peer down her shirt and slap her on the rear end. She giggled and protested, but he reminded her he was the brilliant chef.

"He's utterly obnoxious and disgusting," my mother said.

"But totally in character," Sam said, "when you think about Martha's experience with him."

We watched all the way to the end, after the cooking part of the show had finished, but the film kept rolling. The videographer had caught the tail end with Marcel reaming out his assistant for allowing his pastry dough to get too warm to roll out perfectly.

"He's an awful bully," my mother said.

And the film ended with a snippet of another man arguing with Marcel about whether a retake was in order. I hit the pause button and moved it back to replay.

"I swear, that was Zane. The other man from our food tour. If Marcel knew Zane, Martha maybe knew him, too." I felt sick to my stomach and even more frightened.

"If all the people on the food tour knew each other, wouldn't you have noticed?"

"You'd think," I said. "But Martha was hardly there. And Audrey pretty much sucked the air from the room. And I was working, taking notes. I wonder if I should call Zane directly, ask him what the H–E–double L is going on?"

"No," said Sam, at the same time my mother said, "Let's put another call in to Steve Torrence."

Reluctantly, I called my friend again. He didn't pick up, so I left a second message, this time adding the bit about recognizing a younger version of Zane in Marcel's cooking show, trying not to sound hysterical. "Three of the people on that food tour knew each other years ago. There has to be a connection to the murders. I just don't know what it is." Then I turned back to Mom and Sam and held my arms out as if to say, *What now?*

My mom took one of my hands and squeezed. "There's nothing else to do here, and honestly I think you should get home and get some rest so you look your very best tomorrow," said my mother. "We don't want gray circles under your eyes in all the wedding photos." She stroked my hair, which brought me back to being comforted as a child. "I feel in my bones that everything will be fine, and you know my bones are always right," she added.

I smiled, but my chest felt tight and heavy. "I'll call you if I hear something."

But then an alert flashed on my phone's screen from the Monroe County Sheriff's Office: SHERIFF'S DEPARTMENT AND KEY WEST POLICE SEEK LEADS IN MURDER.

I clicked over to their page. POLICE REPORTED A BODY FOUND IN THE DUMPSTER BEHIND THE BUOYS' CLUB ESTABLISHMENT WEDNESDAY NIGHT. SOURCES STATED THAT THE VICTIM WAS OF WIRY BUILD, WITH A BEARD, AND THE APPEARANCE OF GLITTER IN HIS

HAIR AND POCKETS. MURDERER REMAINS AT LARGE
AND IS LIKELY TO BE ARMED AND DANGEROUS. ANY-
ONE WITH INFORMATION ON THE DEATH SHOULD
CONTACT . . .

Glitter? That would have been common during
the Fantasy Fest week leading up to Halloween.
Though during that festival, arrests for public nudity
and drunkenness were more the norm than murder.
There had been one terrible murder a few years ago
involving fairy wings and glitter. And Palamina had
seemed obsessed with the idea of gold in food. What if
Zane and Marcel were working together in some kind
of foodie smuggling operation? I remembered the
check marks I'd seen on Nathan's food tour information brochure. And the magazine at Martha's shop.

This line of thinking was beginning to make me
literally nauseous, fearing for Nathan's safety. I
punched in his cell number again, but it went directly
to voicemail as it had all afternoon. My panic was
swelling, making me feel as if I might choke.

"Honey, you have to breathe," my mother said,
reading the distress on my face. I followed her lead,
sucking in some air and pushing it out. "You haven't
heard one word from him? Is it possible that you
overlooked a text?"

I shook my head and handed over my phone so
they could read the grisly report about the dead man
found in the dumpster.

"Not since last night."

"Have you talked with any of his colleagues?"
Sam asked, while studying my phone.

I tried to breathe again, and to push my shoulders away from my ears, to not let the terror that was knocking on the door overwhelm me. It was as if all the scary moments from the past few years—and there had been too many of them—were rushing into my brain. Those memories gathered and circled like mean girls, chanting, "And you thought we were bad . . ."

"Steve Torrence told me that Nathan would stay safe. He knows what he's doing and his fellow officers would not let him get into trouble. I think he even said not to worry if Nathan doesn't make it to the rehearsal at the beach in the morning. He said that he has the easiest part in the ceremony—all he has to do is walk down the path and stand at the altar looking madly in love. And if he gets lost along the way, Steve will nudge him in the right direction. *He doesn't have your complicated family to worry about*; that's what he said verbatim," I told them.

"Sounds like he knew something big was in the works," my mother said. "Maybe you should call the person on duty tonight. Ask what's happening with the murder."

"I'm a civilian; they won't talk to me about an active case. I could call the police department, but tell them what?" I asked after I'd taken back my phone. "My fiancé didn't show up for supper?" Then I thought of Danielle, whose cop boyfriend was at her family's Thanksgiving dinner. I dialed her number and explained that Nathan was missing and had not contacted me.

"It's probably nothing," I said in a wobbly voice, "but we're so worried. Do you think your sweetheart might have heard anything?"

"Oh Hayley, of course you're worried. I'll ask him," she said. "He's only a patrol officer and obviously he's off today. And he's had a couple of beers. But I'll ask. Maybe he knows something. Call you back in a few."

Several minutes later, her name lit up my screen. "There's some kind of sting going on. It's big, and many of the high-level guys in the police department are involved. That's all he knows. Or all he can say. How did it go with Palamina?"

I laughed. "Ha. She got soused and ate more than I've seen her eat the whole time we've known her. I have a sneaking suspicion that she wants us to do an exposé on the KWPD."

"She must have been loopy to suggest that," Danielle said. "Try not to fret about Nathan. I swear if I hear one more word, I'll text you instantly."

I thanked her, hung up, and explained what she'd said to Mom and Sam.

"Call the department and insist they patch you through to Steve Torrence," my mother suggested softly. "He won't give you the brush-off if the call comes from them."

"It's Thanksgiving night. And I've called twice already."

"It's Nathan," said Sam.

Chapter
Twenty-Five

Besides, she could smell a scandal like other folk smell rotten eggs.
          —Ann Cleeves, *Red Bones*

After making yet one more unanswered call, this time to Torrence via the dispatcher at the police department, I started home. I took the back shortcut toward Santiago's Bodega instead of riding through town, which would be bustling with drunken tourists by now. This way, I could skirt the edges of the new park and come out on Truman, which would funnel me directly home.

There were more lights in the Shipyard condominium complex than I was used to seeing. Probably guests or owners who'd escaped to Key West for the long weekend. As I rode, my mind spun. I felt both furious with Nathan and sick with worry about him not showing up.

As I rounded the corner toward the Bahama Village, I wondered again what the town was going to do with those abandoned brick buildings. At least the park area around the new amphitheater was beginning to look like actual green space. I slowed down and pulled over to the side of the road to check for messages that I might have missed. Nothing from Torrence, which was fair enough, even though it wasn't like him. He would know that I was edging toward hysteria. On the other hand, it was Thanksgiving—time to be with either the family you were born with or the one you chose. The scared and hopeless part of me worried that I was neither to Nathan. Instead of zipping past the spooky area containing the older brick buildings and the previous missile site, I stopped for a moment to peer down Angela Street.

I swore I could feel a tingle of danger. I suspected that my mind was suffering a miniature meltdown under the influence of Lorenzo's scary cards and Nathan's absence. Where could he be? And why wasn't anyone calling me back? Out of the corner of my eye, I spotted a car that looked very much like Nathan's rental. I backed the scooter up and drove down the street to get a closer look.

Stopping several car lengths behind the silver SUV, I pulled the scooter over and hopped off. This street ran between a block of older Bahama Village homes and the rear edge of the Shipyard condominiums in the Truman Annex. I couldn't imagine what Nathan would be doing here. With my fingers poised to dial 911, I crept around the car, checking the doors. Locked. Using the flashlight app on my phone, I peered down toward the floorboards in the front and back seats, dreading, dreading, dreading what I might find. I once again saw Ziggy's dog bed and the big fleecy bone in the back seat. Nothing else. But then I heard ringing, a vintage telephone ring like the one Nathan had downloaded. The area under the driver's seat flashed with light each time the ring sounded. Nathan never forgot his phone.

Only one of the homes on the right side of the street was lit up, and through the front picture window I saw an older couple watching television. I was feeling desperate and frantic enough to march up the sidewalk and tap on their door.

"Happy Thanksgiving," I said when the man answered. He had dark skin and gray hair and wore gray pants and a white shirt. He peered at me and then around either side of me, as if puzzled and trying to place me.

"Can I help you?"

I nearly burst into tears. "My fiancé is missing and we are supposed to get married tomorrow. He's a Key West Police Department detective, and for some reason his car is parked out here. I was so worried because he hasn't answered his phone all day, and now I see it under the driver's side seat. But there's no sign of him."

With a shaking finger, I pointed to the silver car. "You haven't by any chance seen a man get out of this car and walk around the neighborhood? He's tall with broad shoulders and usually wears a blazer and jeans. Ridiculously handsome."

Now I started to snuffle.

The man insisted that I come inside. Their home smelled of turkey and bacon and pumpkin pie, like half the homes in the country tonight. "This girl has lost her fiancé," he said to his wife. "She wonders if we've seen anyone in that silver Buick parked outside?"

The woman struggled out of her recliner and came over, looking concerned. "You look so sad. Can we get you a little glass of something, a coffee, or a piece of pie?"

"Oh no thank you," I said with a wobbly smile. "I am very full of pie already."

I explained again what Nathan looked like and pointed out their window to his car.

"Now that we're talking about it," the man said, "I did see a fellow when I was taking out the garbage. But that was yesterday I think, last evening. Not today at all."

"No," the woman said. "That must have been last night. I'd said we'd better empty it early because of Thanksgiving dinner and the turkey carcass and all, remember? We had the grease from the bacon and all the potato peelings and the cans, and it would have been overflowing onto the floor, remember? Tonight's trash is still in the kitchen."

I gently interrupted her before she could describe every item they'd discarded.

"Did it seem that he was looking for someone or something? Was there anyone with him?"

"He had a small flashlight," the man said, "so I wrote it off to a dog walker. Although come to think of it, he did not have a dog. Not with him, anyway. And he was moving quickly, like an athlete, going in that direction." He pointed south, the way I had driven in.

"Can we do something for you?" the woman asked, her eyes full of concern.

"I wonder if . . . Would you mind calling the police and mentioning that there's an abandoned car on the street and maybe say you saw a suspicious man? At least that way we'll get some officers here in this neighborhood. I'm going to drive around and look for my fiancé."

I thanked them, got back on my scooter, and headed the wrong way down the one-way street in the direction the man had pointed. I noticed a funny smell in the air, something burning. Maybe one of our island visitors had decided Thanksgiving wouldn't feel right without a fire in the fireplace. Most people didn't have fireplaces in Key West, and even if they did, it was usually too warm to build a fire unless you jacked your air-conditioning up, and what sense did that make?

I turned toward the abandoned buildings and drove slowly, peering from one side of the street to the other, looking for any sign of Nathan. As I drew closer to the first building, the odor got stronger. It wasn't cigarette smoke or marijuana, but the stink of burning clothing and wood and something bitter, like smoldering hair and hay and rotten apples. Nothing that I should be smelling here tonight.

Then I noticed a narrow plume of carbon-colored smoke snaking out of one of the broken windows high up. It reminded me of the tarot card I hated most. The tower shown on that card, with flames licking out of the windows and horrifying figures falling to their death, meant change was coming. Not necessarily disaster. The memory of Lorenzo telling me many times over the past few years that the Tower card should not be taken literally flashed to mind. But this was a fire, a real fire, a fire where there shouldn't be one. My brain zinged with a new jolt of fear, and my heart began to pound nearly out of my chest. I stopped the scooter, pulled out my phone, and dialed 911.

While I was waiting for help to arrive, I left my scooter parked by the side of the road and began to creep around the perimeter of the complex. I couldn't get close to the building, as the doors were blocked by a tall white fence. Even if I'd had the strength to hoist myself over the fence, the doors were boarded up with pieces of plywood. I was feeling as frightened as I'd ever felt, and horribly vulnerable. Spotting a two-by-four lying in the grass, I picked it up and kept moving, staying to the shadows. On the far side of the building, the fence petered out. Thick, black smoke poured out of the windows above a door covered with plywood. I ran over and touched the plywood, which felt warm. A bad sign if anyone was inside.

Choking on the fumes, I pulled my shirt high to protect my nose from the acrid stink and banged on the plywood with my two-by-four and yelled. "Nathan! Nathan, are in you there? The fire department is coming! Can you get yourself to this door?

I'm here. I'll help you." The last bit came out incomprehensible as I'd started to sob, my voice clogged with fear and hoarse from smoke. I heard heavy breathing and saw movement to my right. Without thinking, I swung hard—the wood-chopping move that Leigh had taught me at the gym.

I heard a terrible crunch, then "Oof," "Dammit," and the thud of a body hitting the ground. I took a quick peek to be sure I hadn't clobbered Nathan, then bolted for the street.

Moments later, the area was swarming with fire engines and police cars. With all the historic wooden structures and a history of blazing disasters that wiped out entire sections of town, Key West doesn't fool around with fire. Firefighters in their heavy tan-colored suits and big hats and masks began to unspool the hoses from their trucks. Their shouts echoed in the darkness. They surged over the white fence, and I heard the splintering of the plywood covering the nearest door.

A young cop came up behind me, grabbed my elbow, and pulled me away from the building. "Did you call this in, miss?" he asked sternly. "It's not safe to be this close."

"I've knocked a man out," I squawked, pointing in the direction of the form in the tall grass and holding up my piece of wood. Then I told him about noticing the smoky smell and finding Nathan's car parked down the road, and how he'd been MIA for probably twenty-four hours and totally missed Thanksgiving dinner with my family. By the time I started on the wedding date being tomorrow, I was blubbering, and he was searching madly for tissues and any words that might staunch the hysteria. "If he's in there, we'll find him." He spoke into his radio, summarizing what I'd told him, only without the drama. Two firefighters jogged up to the man I'd hit and carried him off on a stretcher.

More smoke swirled out of the building, and the firemen tugged pulsing hoses inside. I tried to edge closer but the young police officer pushed me back.

"Officer down!" came a muffled call from inside the building.

I knew in my heart that it was Nathan. More firefighters carrying a second stretcher rushed into the building. What seemed like forever later, they carried someone out, about the size and heft of Nathan. His face was black with soot and his clothes were bloody. A medic ran up to slide an oxygen mask over his face, while a second man applied pressure to what appeared to be a wound in his right leg.

"Please," I implored the officer who was holding me back. Neighbors from the streets nearby had begun to gather to watch the unfolding drama. "That's Detective Bransford. We're supposed to get married tomorrow."

"Stay here," he said, "I'll check this out." He jogged toward the knot of medics surrounding the stretcher.

Minutes later, he returned. "He has some injuries, but he'll be fine."

What could that optimism be based on? They loaded Nathan into the waiting ambulance and roared away.

"Meet them at the hospital," the cop said. "Do you need a lift? They didn't want to wait."

And that scared me even worse. I choked out my thanks and waved him off. Instead of heading north, I sped back over to my mother's house, lurched the scooter onto their lawn, and pounded on the door.

"Nathan is hurt badly," I shouted when they answered, wrapped in matching pink and blue terry bathrobes. "Can you take me to the hospital? I'm afraid I'll crash my scooter if I drive myself."

My mother gasped and pulled me into a tight squeeze.

"Of course," said Sam. "Let us throw on our clothes."

Chapter
Twenty-Six

Although most people talked of hunger as a matter of the stomach, what Asha recalled was the taste—a foul thing that burrowed into your tongue and was sometimes still there when you swallowed, decades later.

—Katherine Boo,
Beyond the Beautiful Forever

Steve Torrence was waiting outside the emergency room. He grabbed both of my hands and kissed me on the cheek. I didn't know whether this meant tragic news or good. "I came as soon as I heard. He's in surgery right now. I'm sorry they couldn't wait for you to see him. Honestly, there wasn't much to see." He tried for a laugh.

But I gripped his hands and squeezed back the waterworks that threatened to take me over. "What happened? What kind of surgery?"

"He was shot in one leg; the tibia might be broken in the other. And his face looked a little battered. We won't know the extent of the damage until the doctors can get a closer look."

"But what happened? Why was he in that building?" Sam asked.

"I'll find out," Torrence said. "Wait here. I will be back as soon as we know something more."

An hour later, a nurse bustled up with Steve in her wake and informed us that Nathan was almost out of treatment—they hadn't needed to perform surgery after all. He had been assigned to a patient room and would be transferred there soon. She narrowed her eyes at our group, and I knew what was coming. But Steve nudged her a few feet away before she could get the words out and whispered an urgent plea.

"Hayley . . . Her parents . . . married . . ." He came back over. "Let's go up before they change their minds."

We took the elevator to the top floor and Steve ushered us to the end of the hallway, where a fierce, uniformed officer was pacing outside the door. "Family," Steve explained as we sailed into Nathan's room.

I perched on the edge of the empty bed, shivering. "This place is so cold," my mother said, circling an arm around my back and rubbing. "Are they trying to freeze their patients out?" she asked of no one in particular. I leaned into her warmth.

"Does your father know you're here?" Steve asked.

"No." I hadn't seen the point of telling the other side of my family what was going on—they would hear tomorrow and might as well get some sleep.

Ditto Miss Gloria, who slept like the dead and was unlikely to notice I was missing until morning.

"I'm so sorry I couldn't return your texts and calls," Steve said. "I had the ringer off because we were waiting outside the Buoys' Club thinking our man would come out shortly. We'd planted one of our guys inside to try to make a deal with him. We believe he killed his partner Wednesday night."

"Marcel?" I asked.

Steve nodded.

There was a clattering noise out in the hallway and Nathan was rolled in on a gurney, his face as pale as the sheets wrapped around him. But he was alive. His eyes flickered open. He looked groggy, his green eyes dull and murky. But he smiled when he saw me. Then he spotted my mother and whispered hoarsely, "So sorry about Thanksgiving dinner. I'm not usually that rude."

She laughed, and I pushed the tears back and straightened my shoulders, feeling bad that I'd spent any time being mad at him. We moved away from the bed while the orderlies transferred him, the nurse fussing with his IV and connecting the monitor that squatted by his bedside.

"This will measure his blood pressure, pulse, oxygen saturation, and so on," she explained when she saw us watching. She adjusted his johnny coat and tucked extra pillows under each leg, one of which was in a boot, the other bandaged from knee to groin. He groaned with pain. "He's got a fracture of the fibula on the left. And a gunshot wound on the right above the knee. Fortunately, it passed through the flesh without doing much damage."

When she was finished, she waggled a finger at us. "I'll give you ten minutes, and then we want everyone out so he can rest."

"What in the world happened?" my mother asked once the staff cleared out.

"We can talk tomorrow if you'd rather," said Steve.

"I'm busy tomorrow," Nathan said, winking at me.

A nod to our wedding, which would have to be postponed. Bummer, but I'd rather have him alive and still my fiancé.

"I was following him—"

"Which him is that?" Steve asked.

"Marcel's partner, Zane Ryan. Though if I had a partner like that, I'd rather work alone."

"Partners in what?" Sam asked. "Hayley was thinking it was something to do with culinary ingredients?"

"That was their cover," Nathan said. "Culinary gold and Indian saffron and such. But those were being used to disguise the drugs. Cocaine and heroin."

"So you were following," I prompted. "And what?"

"I lost track of him completely when the light turned red on Duval and the post-Thanksgiving hordes pushed across the street. If I'd had my police vehicle, I could have hit the lights and siren." He frowned and plucked at the top sheet. "I drove into the Bahama Village, thinking where would I store stolen goods if I had them? I figured the abandoned buildings where you found me would be perfect, if there was a way in. So I parked on Angela and walked over." He shifted his position and grimaced as the monitor beeped and chirred. "Could I get a sip of water?"

"Of course," said my mother and I at the same time. She filled a white Styrofoam cup with ice and water and handed the cup to me. Nathan sipped and nodded his thanks.

"Since I was undercover and driving a rental, I didn't have the police radio or the scanner."

"You told me your brakes were bad and that's why it was in the shop," I said. "I can't believe you'd take a risk like that—chasing him without backup. And no phone, either."

"It fell between the seats and I was in a hurry," Nathan said, looking sheepish.

Steve Torrence looked sheepish too. "We had half the department combing the island and all the way up to Big Pine for the last twenty-four hours looking for this guy," said Steve. "And you found him, right under our noses."

He sighed and nodded for another sip of water.

"It was easy enough to get over the fence around those old buildings. And there were plenty of hand-holds in the bricks. Not so easy after you've been shot."

I winced as he reached for the bandaged leg.

"I was halfway in that window when he whacked the other leg with something and I fell inside. Both legs hurt like hell. After that, things get a little foggy. He tied me up and gagged me." He shuddered and smoothed the sheet over his chest. "Honestly, I didn't see myself getting out of there alive. And I felt terrible about that in many ways—mostly to do with you. But sometimes you have to be realistic." He reached for my hand, grimacing at the movement or the thought—I didn't know which.

I hated hearing how close I'd come to losing him.

"And then he set fire to something. I clearly couldn't drag myself out of there."

I sucked in a big breath of air, thinking about the serendipity of noticing that smoke. What if I'd gone home on the other route and not thought about avoiding the drunken crowds on Duval Street? What if I hadn't seen his car parked on a nearby street and realized something was off? He would have been burnt to a crisp in that fire. I shook my head to try to clear those images out of my mind.

The nurse bustled into the room and clucked her tongue. "No more chatting for you tonight, mister. You need your beauty rest." Steve and my parents got up and headed toward the door.

"I'd like to stay the night with him," I said, gearing up for a tussle.

"And I'd rather you come by first thing in the morning with a large Cuban coffee, and possibly even a doughnut." Nathan flashed a big grin and kissed the tips of my fingers. "Then I can spend the rest of our life together thanking you properly for your premonition."

Chapter Twenty-Seven

*It is a gesture of love, my dear. The tender flak-
iness, the soft crumb, the delicate sweetness.
These are the things that speak to the heart.*
—Krista Davis, *Color Me Murder*

When I arrived at the hospital Friday morning,
Nathan looked light years better than he had
the night before. His face had lost the bluish hue
that had scared me half to death, he'd shaved, and he
was dressed in his own blue plaid flannel shirt over a
pair of hospital scrub pants.

"I loved you in that johnny coat," I said, kissing
him softly, "but I love you even more looking a little
healthier."

On the way over, I had given myself a stern talking to—I would not regret the lost wedding, I would
be only grateful that my Nathan was alive. The ceremony on the beach and the party with the Hemingway cats were small potatoes in the big picture of
what I hoped would be our long life together.

I perched on the side of the bed and stroked his
face where a big red bruise was forming above his
right eye. He grabbed my forearms and pulled me

closer. His familiar scent was mixed with the smell of industrial soap and something medicinal.

"I love you, too," he said, and I could have sworn that tears were shimmering in his green eyes. "I'm ready to get hitched today. I don't want to wait one minute more."

I gulped. When had it ever been any girl's dream to get married in a hospital room? But I was certain that it had been done before, and what the heck, the outcome would be the same. And it would make a great story for our descendants, should we have any.

"I'll call Steve Torrence and see when he can get over here," I said, my voice as chipper as I could make it. "We can fit another ten to fifteen people in this room—at least the out-of-towners and family, if they all stand sideways."

"I'm not marrying my best girl in a hospital, johnny coat or no johnny coat. I'm blowing out of here. And then we'll do it right."

I tried to picture him in a wheelchair or even on crutches making his way down the sandy path to the water at Fort Zachary Taylor beach. Even strong, determined Nathan would have difficulty managing that with two bad legs.

"Honestly, I don't mind at all tying the knot right here in the hospital," I said. "I want to see you get well, and I think we should follow doctor's orders. I almost lost you once, and I don't—"

But he'd already rung the nurses' station and announced that he wished to be discharged. When the woman on the other end of the line started to argue, he hung up and rang the call button furiously. As he began to throw back the covers and swing his legs out of bed, his face crumpled in pain. He smoothed that expression away before I could begin to protest in earnest.

"You shouldn't be going anywhere," I said, "let alone to the beach."

He began to chant:

Would you marry me here or there?
Would you marry me anywhere?
Would you marry me on the beach?
Would a houseboat be out of reach?

I wondered just how much morphine they'd given him this morning. "Shhhh," I said, patting his shoulder, "we'll figure it all out when you're feeling better and are up and around. Right now the doctor said you need to rest."

"The houseboat would be perfect," he announced, ignoring my attempts to coax him back into bed. "There's plenty of food—I'm certain your mother and her minions made sure of that. They can bring it over to the docks. All the people we love will be there. It's a beautiful day in paradise." He gestured to the morning sun streaming through the slats of the blinds and pooling on the hospital floor.

Then he scrambled for his phone on the bedside table and punched in a number. "Steve Torrence, please." He winked at me while he was on hold for a minute, beginning to hum "Going to the Chapel." I could not believe he even knew the tune.

"Hello! Feeling great," he answered to Torrence's query. "Hayley and I want to get married. Today. This afternoon. At Houseboat Row. Can you make it?"

I could barely hear Torrence's tinny argument in the background.

"Can you make it or not, man? Or do we have to track down a justice of the peace?" Nathan waited. "Four o'clock is perfect. Can you send over a couple of our biggest guys to the hospital to spring me out of here and help get me cleaned up? Hayley needs to go do her bride stuff and I look like hell."

Once he'd hung up with Torrence, he called my mother and explained the plan. He turned back to me after my mother had agreed to phone the guests, get the food delivered, and ice the champagne.

"I'm not waiting one more day for this," he said, cupping my cheeks in his palms. "Do you understand? You're too precious to me."

I felt hot tears slide down my face as I nodded my agreement.

"Four o'clock, then. Now go do whatever you women think women need to do before they get married. For good this time."

* * *

Later that day, after I finished showering and had emerged onto the deck in my bathrobe with a towel wrapped around my head, my heart wobbled with gratitude and excitement. Someone, probably my mother and stepmother and Connie and Miss Gloria, had set up all our decorations so they lined the finger leading to our boat. There were white balloons and swooping white ribbons and bows, and exactly the tropical flowers I'd chosen for the beach arranged at the posts along the dock. A banner had been hung, connecting Miss Gloria's houseboat to the wreck that belonged to Nathan and me. CONGRATULATIONS HAYLEY AND NATHAN! WE LOVE YOU!

My mother came up behind me and put her arms around my waist. "Pretty, right?"

"How did you do this so quickly?"

"We had it ready and waiting at our place. Sam ran it over here and we put it up. Done! Pouf! I'm thinking we seclude ourselves in the laundry room before Nathan arrives so he doesn't see your dress." She looked over at me, and I nodded my OK. "The dock will serve as the aisle. As long as your father doesn't hog the space, the three of us will fit just fine. And if he does hog the space, I'll hip-check him into the bight." She winked. "The musicians can set up on your new boat so they're out of the way of the crowd. Meanwhile, my hair wizard, Freya, is here to do your hair and makeup."

When my hair was dried, the curls subdued and woven with small white flowers and topped with a delicate, waist-length veil that had been worn by both my grandmother and my mother, I stepped into the dress I'd finally chosen after multiple trips to shops in Miami. My mother zipped up the back as Connie adjusted the spaghetti straps.

"You look gorgeous, sweetheart," said Miss Gloria from her perch on the couch. "Like Audrey Hepburn. Just don't get your heel caught in the decking and pitch into the drink."

I laughed. "Thanks for getting that image stuck in my brain."

* * *

By three thirty, the food had been set up on Miss Gloria's deck and the guests had begun to stream in, sipping champagne and mojitos while they waited for the ceremony to start. Just before four, I watched from the laundry room window with my parents as three of Nathan's burly police department friends and Steve helped Nathan out of the black SUV that pulled in close to the entrance of Tarpon Pier. One officer handed him the crutches that had been stashed in the back seat. Torrence straightened the knot of Nathan's blue striped tie and smoothed his hair. It was a moment too sweet for words.

"Ready?" I heard him ask. Nathan nodded curtly, but then grinned. And I saw him wince with pain as he began to walk—or stump was more like it—the length of the dock. A trumpet and two violins, courtesy of Connie's husband's friends, began to play Pachelbel's "Canon in D." My stomach lurched so hard I had a little trouble breathing.

"Deep breath in," said my mom.

"Deep breath out, too," said my dad, and then he looked at her with a tender smile that gave me a tiny window into what their relationship might have been like at the beginning. Staying married took commitment and a little luck and family support and lots and lots of tending, which they had been too young and too overwhelmed to manage back then.

Connie's baby came toddling down the dock wearing her pale-yellow flower girl dress that picked up accents from Connie's. When they reached the laundry building, Ray gave her a tiny basket of rose petals.

"Remember what we did yesterday?" he asked. "We will walk toward the people and you throw the flowers." Claire looked back at Connie, as if to ask permission.

"Go ahead, baby girl," Connie said. "I'm coming right behind you, just like we practiced." Claire broke into a heartbreaking smile and began to throw fistfuls of petals.

Next to me, my father in his neatly pressed khaki trousers and blue blazer had a glaze of tears in his eyes. "I remember when you were that small," he said. "You never stopped chattering."

"So nothing's changed much," I said, grinning.

"I'm sorry I missed any time with you at all growing up. Thanks to your mother, you've turned out to be the best person I could have imagined."

I stood on my toes to kiss him on the cheek, too choked up to say more than thanks. Then Erik Powell and Christy Haussler from Steve Torrence's church began to sing the most beautiful wedding duet I'd ever heard—"Whither Thou Goest" from the Book of Ruth.

"And thy people will be my people love . . ."

Erik's voice soared to an impossibly high note, and I reminded myself that this day could not have been more special if I'd planned it exactly this way. And wasn't that a lesson for the future, too?

For one brief moment, I wondered what the wedding day had felt like for Audrey and Marcel, before things went so badly sour. Regardless of the trappings of dress and food and venue, I hoped they felt a little sliver of the joy and hope that I was feeling now. I could have sworn that they had looked happy during the food tour, though Marcel had made it sound as if their marriage had been mostly unhappy when I talked to him later. Which was achingly sad. Maybe he'd gotten so caught up in his drugs and his criminal activities that he'd forgotten the good parts. Maybe he'd been so disappointed in the turn his career had taken that he didn't see his wife at all.

At last it was time for my parents to walk me up the wooden finger all the way to Miss Gloria's houseboat, where Nathan balanced on his crutches next to our dear friend Steve. When we reached them, my parents kissed and hugged me, my father shook Nathan's hand, and then they moved aside, leaving the two of us. Steve looked around at our family and friends. I glanced around too, seeing all the people I'd grown to know and love on this island, and others who'd traveled long distances to support us.

"We are gathered here—rather unexpectedly"— Torrence continued with a big grin—"to celebrate the union of Hayley Catherine Snow and Nathan Andrew Bransford. I've gotten to know both of these people well, so I think I understand the basis of their relationship. Hayley grounds Nathan by sharing the good things in her world—her friends, her family, her food." He paused and smoothed his mustache. "And Nathan provides his sturdy and steady presence."

"And don't forget," shouted out Miss Gloria, "he's a hunka hunka burnin' love!"

Our guests broke into hysterical laughter, and Nathan turned the color of a bougainvillea bush in full bloom.

"By now you've all heard about the events of last night," Steve continued when the chaos died down, "and how Hayley noticed the smoke from the fire where Nathan was trapped. This is a very good sign for their relationship and their future as a married couple, because Hayley sensed that something was wrong. And that led her to noticing the smoke and calling the police department. There is a deep connection between the two of them, and knowing them both, I can say confidently that it goes both ways. And so I charge you:

"Nathan and Hayley, treat yourselves and each other with respect, and remind yourselves often of what brought you together. Give the highest priority to the tenderness, gentleness, and kindness that your relationship deserves. When frustration, difficulty, and fear assail your relationship—as they threaten all relationships at one time or another—remember to focus on what is right between you, not only the part which seems wrong. And when you are troubled, remember to call on God."

The rest of the ceremony whooshed by in a blur of joy and tears—I did, he did, I would, he would, I had a ring, he didn't. Finally Torrence called for a kiss and our friends and family cheered and I knew I'd never been happier.

Chapter
Twenty-Eight

First we eat, then we do everything else.
—M.F.K. Fisher

At the end of the ceremony, Ziggy Stardust, in a bedraggled white bow, streaked across the deck through Steve Torrence's legs and onto the Renharts' boat. With our two cats in hot pursuit, he scattered Mrs. Renhart's three elderly pets like bowling pins. He'd already fallen into the pecking order of our pier, and my tiger Evinrude was still king of the dock. And somehow he'd managed to communicate to Nathan's dog that Sparky was second in command.

The musicians shifted into playing dance tunes, joined by the cheerful keyboard sounds of Allison Millwood, and the caterers began to circulate with trays of champagne and mojitos. The drinks were followed by mini crab cakes, and steamed pink shrimp with two kinds of sauce, one sweet mango, one tomato-based and fiery with horseradish. Sam had supplied his specialty, another one of my favorite foods—his famous cornmeal-crusted empanadas filled with spicy beef, which were served with bowls of pale-green guacamole, sour cream, and hot red salsa. And to suit Nathan's taste, the waiters also passed thick slices of pink roast beef on Cuban bread toasts with horseradish and mustard—and not a shred of greenery.

Finally, as the dusk fell and the fairy lights on the boats began to twinkle more brightly, Nathan and I cut the wedding cake. Then my mother's catering assistants, Irena and Maria, brought out an enormous tray of shimmering Cuban flan. "Remember how you asked us last winter to make this for your wedding?" Irena asked. "You helped so much when our brother was murdered, we wanted to do something special for you in return."

As the flan and cake were dished out and distributed, a familiar figure struggled up the dock. I recognized Martha Hubbard; she was balancing a heavy tray covered with cheesecloth. Sam took the tray and Martha gave me a big hug.

"I wanted to bring you something delicious to thank you for all you did for me. And celebrate your wedding."

"You're very welcome," I said. "Thanks so much for thinking of us." I didn't have the heart to ask if she'd brought her special mini key lime pies. Because it might be forever before I could tackle *anything* key lime. Unfortunately, based on the shape of the little jars under the cheesecloth, that's what her offering looked like.

"Ta-da," she said, pulling the cloth off the tray. "Heavenly strawberries-and-cream trifle, made with lime-kissed sponge cake and Florida berries. I knew you'd never go for key lime pie."

I burst out laughing. "You couldn't have chosen better. I wouldn't have wanted to hurt your feelings, but key lime is not going to be on my menu anytime soon." I gave her another big hug. "We'd love it if you'd stay for a while."

Miss Gloria and my mother each took one of her elbows and drew her into the celebration. "And besides," Miss Gloria said, "we want to hear about your old pal Marcel."

"Tell us more about what happened," I said, sitting on the deck next to Nathan and squeezing his hand. "You really didn't recognize him while we were in your kitchen on the tour? And what about Zane?"

"Am I allowed to talk about this?" she asked Steve.

"Yes," he said. "You gave your formal statement at the station earlier."

"I barely saw your group that morning," she said, nodding in Analise's direction. "I had so much to do to get ready for the Thanksgiving class. And besides, I'm not sure I would have known Marcel anyway. He'd lost a lot of weight since I'd worked for him, and he certainly didn't dress like a middle-aged hipster back in those days. And the beard was new, too.

"But last night when Hayley texted me about how the cops found a packet of glitter in the pockets of the dead man, that jogged something in my brain.

Marcel was always on the lookout for weird ingredients. Culinary gold was something he had experimented with, especially in spotlight cocktails. He loved to see our customers' eyes bulge when the servers delivered them something way out of the ordinary."

"Culinary gold?" My father looked puzzled. "Why in the world would you use a metal in something people are going to eat?"

"There's a fierce competition among chefs these days to one-up each other," Martha explained. "Some end up feeling that if they want to make a name for themselves in the top echelon of restaurants, serving consistently excellent food isn't enough anymore. The menu has to include recipes with an extra sparkle or truly exotic ingredients to get noticed by some of the influential critics. Even the amateur critics on Yelp and review sites like that have caught this fancy-food fever."

"I guess I didn't get that gene," said my father.

Martha chuckled. "If you think culinary gold is weird, I've seen worse. Things like coffee beans that have been pooped out by civet cats, gelatinous bird's nests, and saffron hand-harvested by young women in India. Some chefs insist they only buy from companies that hire virgins because that changes the flavor to something more pure."

My father looked horrified.

"So chefs use ingredients like that to burnish their reputations with snooty foodies?" Allison asked. "I doubt my family would ever eat such a meal."

"Trust me, we wouldn't," my father muttered.

"The gold is big in cocktails and cake decorations and all kinds of fancy stuff," I said. "Even a couple of the cake decorators in town wanted to know if we'd like the glittery look on our wedding cake. But I don't think these two guys were interested in appealing to an audience of home cooks. They wanted to reach big-name chefs who were striving to showcase their imagination and demonstrate how they could push the boundaries of what's considered great food."

"And after the celebrity chefs come out with something new, chefs in the smaller restaurants often copy what seems to be all the rage," Analise added. "They want to know what a Thomas Keller or a Bobby Flay or a Mario Batali is making."

"Unless the MeToo movement takes them down," said Martha. "Then they aren't making anything." She snuck a glance at me. "Marcel Chaudoir had a similar kind of hubris. With his star long burned out, he had taken a series of dead-end jobs as a line cook. Then he started talking with Zane Ryan about this new business where they wouldn't have to work as hard and they could make a lot more money."

"Figures they'd need to be chefs to know what to steal and who to sell it to," I said. "And Zane Ryan getting involved in the smuggling enterprise makes sense, too. His own restaurant had failed, and he was working as a sous-chef out on Stock Island. His boss was certainly not treating him like a celebrity. I suspect he'd soured on becoming financially successful in restaurants even though he was telling me about his plans for the future—fancy recipes all the way."

"Give me meatloaf and mashed potatoes," said Torrence. "Nothing fancy, and definitely nothing that would come out of an animal's behind or glow in the dark."

My new husband blanched. "Please don't ever serve me something like that."

"She never would," said Miss Gloria. "She understands exactly what kind of man you are. But no law says you can't learn to cook too and serve her once in a while. My Frank got very good at cooking."

I'd never have the heart to tell her that her recipes were bad enough that it was in her dear husband's self-interest to take up the mantle of cook in their family.

Nathan squeezed my hand before letting it go again. "I wouldn't have the guts to compete with this woman, or her mother. My mother-in-law," he corrected himself, grinning at my mother. She beamed right back at him.

"So Marcel came to town to talk about distribution of the stuff Zane had collected?" my mother asked. "Were the products actually illegal?"

Torrence nodded. "Some of it, yes, and some not. But the main thing is they had moved on to dealing drugs and using the foodstuff as cover. We suspect that Audrey had gotten wind of this and begun to worry about Marcel. And then he went a little crazy after she died. And that's what we think the fight in the parking lot was about. Maybe Marcel had even decided he was going to turn Zane in to the police. Possibly he thought Zane had killed his wife. Zane saw him unraveling and believed he was going to the authorities. He didn't plan to kill Marcel, but he had to act to save himself."

"But how did Marcel end up dead? And was his death related to his wife's?" Sam asked. "Who killed her?"

"According to Marcel, when Audrey got wind of the fact that he was flying to Key West, she insisted on coming along with him as a mini vacation," Torrence said. "Audrey's sister had reported that she had just started on the MAO inhibitor and was feeling remarkably better after a long stretch of depression. And manic enough to ignore any professional advice about diet and side effects. She also refused to take the lithium that's supposed to act as a stabilizer." He glanced over at my psychologist friend, Eric Altman, who was sitting on deck with Miss Gloria and his partner, Bill.

Eric nodded.

"Zane did not like the idea of Marcel's wife getting involved—she was a loose cannon and could easily have said more than she should, giving the whole enterprise away," said Torrence. "He began to feel that he needed to watch them both carefully."

"So he attended the seafood tour to keep an eye on them?" Analise asked.

"Exactly," Torrence said.

"And then," Martha said, "Marcel recognized who I was, because of course my name was plastered all over the literature, both for our kitchen's events and Analise's tour. Seeing me successful probably raised old feelings of rage. And as Officer Torrence said, after Audrey died, he went a little crazy. Maybe he even imagined that I had killed his wife as the final act in some long-delayed revenge. Maybe he snuck into the store later and spiked my Ol' Sour. I don't think he meant to kill anyone, only to pay me back."

"Are you saying the salt killed Audrey? I'm confused," said my mother.

"No," said Nathan. "Her death was a result of her antidepressant interacting fatally with all the food and beer she shouldn't have been consuming. Sadly, she had a massive stroke."

"Then Zane saw Marcel meet with Hayley after Audrey died," said Torrence. "He panicked about what Marcel might have revealed in his grief-stricken state. He warned him to stay out of trouble and not talk to anyone about anything."

"Which explains why Marcel was so cool to me when I contacted him a second time," I said. "Zane had warned him away."

Torrence said, "He claims, and the courts will decide whether to believe him, that Marcel pulled a knife on him in the parking lot of the Buoys' Club when they were fighting. He clobbered him in the head with a two-by-four, allegedly in self-defense, but Marcel keeled over dead. So he disposed of the body in the dumpster and fled."

"Must have been right after all that happened on Wednesday night," my new husband said, "that I drove by those old brick buildings, thinking where would I stash things if I was a smuggler. Zane saw me sniffing around and shot me in the leg. As I was kicking my way into the window, trying to get away, he whacked my other leg with a two-by-four. I fell inside the building and he trussed me up like a turkey. He had twenty-four hours to stew over how much trouble he was in: he'd left in his wake one dead man, one injured, a kidnapped cop, and a big load of stolen merchandise and drugs. Last night, I believe he set fire to the building to get rid of the whole mess, including me. But I don't know what happened to cause that late and final panic."

He wasn't going to be thrilled to hear that my questions in Matt's Stock Island restaurant might have been the reason for Zane's panic. But on the other hand, we'd just finished pledging our honesty to one another. "What happened was me," I said, biting my lip.

"I stopped over at the restaurant where he was working Thanksgiving morning. His shift didn't end until seven, so he had the whole day to get worried and decide he wasn't going to get out of this scheme unscathed without disposing of the stolen property. And you." I turned to Steve Torrence. "When did the cops realize that Nathan was in trouble?"

Torrence said, "Not as fast as we might have wanted, because he disappeared so quickly and completely. So it took us a little while to realize he was gone, not home taking a nap as he should have been. It's not that big of an island, and we were doing a search of all the places they might have taken him. But the truth is, if you hadn't gotten there when you did and noticed the smoke, we might have been too late."

Nathan reached for my hand again and kissed the knuckles. "I'd like to know how you tracked me down. Because in another half an hour, I'd have been toast."

I shuddered at the thought. It was not going to be easy to be a cop's wife. I'd have to learn how to manage the anxiety of knowing any day I could lose him. And somehow I'd have to come to terms with the truth: it wasn't my job to save him from the bad guys he chased. It was my job to be there for him after he saved people from those bad guys. I pushed those thoughts away.

"As we said, Eric was the one who realized that Audrey might have been on a new antidepressant. But I kept wondering why Marcel wouldn't have known this. His story about not knowing his wife was on the new drug just didn't hang together. I know I'm barely, barely married"—I reached to stroke the back of Nathan's head—"and that things can go south quickly in a relationship if you don't tend it. So maybe it's possible that you could live with someone day to day and not be aware of what medications they were taking, but it seemed unlikely."

"Being married takes work," my mom said, glancing at my father. "Life gets stressful and hectic and you stop paying attention. And then trouble comes calling."

"So the antidepressant story didn't hang together. What else?" Nathan asked. "I'm always amazed at how your mind works."

"Well." I took a breath and a sip of champagne. "I admit to stalking you a little because I was so worried." I chuckled when he glowered. "Soon after I noticed your car on the street next to the club, I saw Marcel come out of the Buoys' Club. What would a recent widower be doing in a strip club? I know people have different reactions to grief, but this seemed extreme. Something else had to be going on."

"Surely you didn't believe I was visiting that place for a bachelor's last hurrah?" Nathan asked, a look of mock horror on his face.

I squirmed and then smiled. "It crossed my mind, but only for the briefest moment."

I paused for a minute to sort out what else had alerted me to the smoke in that building. I thought about the cards Lorenzo had read for me earlier this week, and how he had warned me to pay attention to my instincts because they were almost always solid. And I knew the cards he'd read at the Thanksgiving table were telling me plainly that Nathan was in trouble. I explained all that to Nathan and the others. "I know you don't necessarily believe in this stuff, but I do," I said to Nathan, and then winked at Lorenzo. "He was reading your cards through what I chose."

"I'm sorry to have scared you," Lorenzo piped up. "The cards are the cards. But it wasn't only the reading that helped you find Nathan," he added. "You've really developed your intuition since I've known you. You were tuning in to the vibrations around you, whether you knew exactly what they meant or not."

He ignored the rolling eyes of my new husband.

Husband, yikes! That would take some getting used to. "By the way, what about that hardened criminal who got out of jail and was coming for you?" I asked Nathan. "Was he involved in this scheme?"

"Which one?" he asked after a long pause. "I've put dozens away." He grinned as if it was all a big joke. "Where did you hear about that, anyway?"

"Odom," Miss Gloria piped up. "My friend. He's a well-informed resident of the Stock Island jail."

Nathan glowered.

My mother clapped her hands and motioned for the band to swing into dance music. "You'll have the rest of your lives to dissect all of this."

My father grabbed my hands to dance, then passed me off to Eric, who passed me off to Bill, and then Steve.

All of my friends and relations continued to eat and dance and laugh and drink until close to ten, when Nathan's energy began to flag in earnest. But the party had come together so quickly that we hadn't had the chance to talk about where we'd spend the night.

"We should get out of here and let Nathan get some rest," said Sam. "Miss Gloria is going to stay with us."

"But only till Monday!" she said. "I definitely need to be here to watch over the new contractor. And the new husband, too."

"Do you want us to take Ziggy off your hands for the weekend as well?" my mother asked.

"Definitely not," I said, pointing to Nathan's little dog, who was curled up on my lounge chair with the two resident cats. "He's part of the family."

Recipes

Chef Martha's Sponger Key Lime Pie (courtesy of Martha Hubbard)

½ cup Ol' Sour (see below)
½ cup key lime juice
2 (14-ounce) cans sweetened condensed milk
3 egg yolks
1 teaspoon salt
Cuban crackers

Put all ingredients in a bowl and mix well. Divide into small canning jars. Serve with crumbled Cuban crackers on top.

Ol' Sour

1 quart key lime juice
1½ tablespoon table salt

Mix key lime juice and salt. Let sit at room temperature for two weeks, disturbing daily for first week.

Smoked Fish Dip

8 ounces smoked trout or other fish
4 ounces cream cheese, softened
8 ounces sour cream
3 scallions, cleaned and minced
Heaping ¼ teaspoon Old Bay Seasoning
¼ lemon

In one bowl, flake the fish.

In another bowl, combine the cream cheese, sour cream, scallions, seasoning, and lemon. Mix well.

Fold in the fish.

Serve with crackers or chips, or with celery sticks and cucumber slices, or stuffed into endive leaves. For another variation, leave out the scallions and Old Bay and replace with 1 tablespoon horseradish and 2 tablespoons chopped fresh dill.

Mojïto Cookies

These cookies are a lovely pale green and would be excellent as a spring dessert or as part of a Christmas cookie platter. You can make the icing or not, as you prefer. But Hayley's tasters loved the frosting with its subtle rum flavoring!

For the cookies:

Zest of 1 lime (about 1½ teaspoons)
1 bunch fresh mint, enough for one tablespoon
    chopped (or more to taste)
½ cup butter, at room temperature
½ cup white sugar
1 teaspoon vanilla extract
1 egg
2 cups all-purpose flour
½ teaspoon baking powder (low-sodium works fine)
Pinch salt

For the rum lime glaze:

½ cup powdered sugar
1–2 teaspoons fresh lime juice
1 teaspoon light rum

Zest the lime, reserving the fruit for the icing. Wash and dry the mint and chop it into small pieces in a food processor. Cream the butter and sugar together until fluffy. Add the vanilla, egg, lime zest, and mint and mix well. Stir the flour, baking powder, and salt together, and then add this to the butter/sugar and mix on low speed only until combined. On a sheet of parchment paper, shape the dough into a log, cover with the parchment, and refrigerate two hours or more.

Preheat oven to 375 degrees. Place a second sheet of parchment on a baking sheet. Slice chilled dough into ¼-inch slices and transfer to prepared sheet. Bake 10 to 12 minutes, or until bottoms and edges are a light golden brown.

Mix the powdered sugar with the lime juice and rum and beat until smooth. Ice the cookies once they are cool. (You can adjust the amounts of lime versus rum to please your palate. And add more sugar if it seems too runny.)

Pecan Pie Bars

The recipe is not very difficult and it makes a lot—so it's great for a party. But be warned, it's very, very sweet! So cut your bars small.

3 cups flour
½ cup sugar
¼ teaspoon salt
1 cup cold unsalted butter

For the topping:

4 eggs
1½ cups light corn syrup
1½ cups sugar (I decided to use ½ cup brown sugar and 1 cup white)
3 tablespoons unsalted butter, melted
1½ teaspoons vanilla extract
¼ teaspoon salt
2½ cups pecans, lightly broken into pieces

Put the flour, sugar, and salt in your food processor. Cut the cold butter into small chunks, and with the machine running, feed them into the dry ingredients. This should all begin to hold together a little like pie crust.

Cover an 11 × 15–inch sheet pan with parchment paper so the paper hangs off the sides. (The paper will stick better if you grease the pan, then lay the parchment on top.) Dump the shortbread mixture into the pan and spread it evenly. Bake this for 20 minutes at 350 degrees.

While the crust bakes, whip the eggs in your food processor and then add the other ingredients up to the nuts. Fold in the broken pecans. When the short-bread crust has baked, remove the pan from the oven and pour in the filling, taking care to spread the pecans evenly over the top. Bake for 25 to 30 minutes until nothing jiggles.

Let the pan of bars cool completely before lifting the bars out of the pan with the parchment overhang. Place them on a large cutting board and divide them into individual squares. Store in the refrigerator or freeze them for your party!

Sam's Cornbread Sausage Stuffing

Sam contributed this recipe to the big Thanksgiving dinner—he credits it to his grandmother.

1 pound bulk sausage
4 tablespoons butter
1 large onion, chopped
2–3 sticks celery, finely chopped
Fresh sage leaves (optional)
8 ounces mushrooms, baby bella or whatever you like, sliced
1 recipe cornbread (make this a day ahead)
2–3 cups cubed whole-grain bread (stale is good!)
Butter for greasing
Chicken broth

Fry the sausage until well done, breaking it into small pieces as it cooks. Drain the sausage well on a plate covered with paper towels. Wipe the frying pan clean and melt the butter.

Add onion and celery and sauté in the butter several minutes until soft. If you have some fresh sage leaves, you may cut those into slivers and add them at the end.

Add the sliced mushrooms and cook until they give up their liquid.

Crumble the cornbread and mix it with the cubed bread.

Stir the sausage, vegetables, and butter into the bread mixture, and turn this into a buttered dish. Moisten with chicken broth until it reaches the consistency you prefer. Bake for 30 minutes at 350 degrees.

Butternut Squash Pasta with Leeks and Fried Sage

This makes a good no-meat main dish, or it can be served with the Thanksgiving feast for your vegetarian guests.

1 medium butternut squash
3 large garlic cloves, unpeeled
3 tablespoons olive oil, divided
1 cup chicken broth, divided
3 medium or 2 large leeks, cleaned and finely
    chopped
1 cup grated Parmigiano-Reggiano cheese, divided
1-pound good-quality rotini or penne pasta
8–12 fresh sage leaves, stems discarded
2 tablespoons vegetable oil
Grated Parmigiano-Reggiano to serve on the side

Cut the squash open, seed it, and cut it into slices. Place these on a baking pan with the garlic, drizzle with half the olive oil, and toss to coat. Bake at 350 for 20 minutes until soft and just beginning to turn golden. Cool and peel, then process the vegetables in a food processor until smooth along with ½ cup chicken broth. Keep this warm.

While the squash is baking, sauté leeks in remaining olive oil until soft and lightly browned, 8 to 10 minutes. Add the prepared squash to the pan and simmer over low heat, about 2 minutes. Stir in ½ cup cheese and season with salt and pepper to taste.

Cook rotini in a pot of boiling water until al dente.

While the pasta is cooking, heat the vegetable oil in an 8- to 9-inch skillet over high heat until it shimmers. Add the sage leaves and fry until crisp but still green, under 30 seconds. Transfer to paper towels to drain. Crumble these into smaller pieces, reserving a few whole leaves for decoration.

Drain the pasta and add it to the squash mixture and the crumbled sage leaves in a large bowl, thinning with warm chicken broth if it's too thick. Decorate with a few of the fried sage leaves and serve with remaining grated cheese.

Hayley Snow's Holiday Pumpkin Pie

Hayley uses maple syrup and chai spice to jazz up her pumpkin pie and help it stand out from the flocks of pies served at Thanksgiving. You can substitute cinnamon if you don't have chai spice.

For the crust:

1½ cups flour
Scant tablespoon sugar
Pinch of salt
6 tablespoons unsalted butter
2 tablespoons chilled cream cheese
3 tablespoons water

Mix the dry ingredients together in a food processor. Add the butter and cream cheese and pulse until you have small crumbles. Don't overdo this. Add the water 1 tablespoon at a time until the crust barely holds together. (You will think you haven't added enough, but you did!)

Dump the dough onto a piece of waxed paper or plastic wrap, and gather it together, then press into a disk. Refrigerate for an hour or more. (This is a good time to make the filling.)

Roll the crust out between two sheets of waxed paper, trying not to overwork it. Peel off the top piece of paper and lower the crust into your 9-inch pan. Bake for about 40 minutes until the crust seems done, just browning around the edges and golden all over.

For the filling:

1 15-ounce can organic pumpkin
½ cup good-quality maple syrup
⅓ cup brown sugar
1¼ cup evaporated milk
1 teaspoon chai spice or plain cinnamon
2 tablespoons flour
3 eggs

Whip the pumpkin with the two sweeteners, the milk, and the spice, and taste to see if it's sweet enough for your crowd. Add a little more if needed. Then beat in the flour and eggs until the filling is smooth.

Carefully pour this mixture into the hot pie crust. (This is the hardest part of the recipe.) You should have the pie pan on a sheet pan in case of spills or drips. Bake at 350 for 30 minutes, then check to see if the crust is too brown. If it is, fold some thin strips of aluminum foil to cover the crust. Bake until set, that is, barely jiggly, probably 50–60 minutes.

Cool to room temperature and either serve as is or refrigerate overnight. Serve with freshly made whipped cream. Hayley likes a teaspoon of vanilla and a dash of maple syrup in hers!

Decadent Lobster Macaroni and Cheese

There is nothing low calorie or health conscious about this dish, but it is delicious and good for special celebrations. I don't know how close my rendition is to the one that Hayley eats at Bagatelle, but it's pretty darn good. If you want, you can add garlic or shallots to the roux, as Hayley did. I decided to leave those out and let the cheeses and the lobster stand alone.

4 cups shredded cheese (I used 2 cups Gruyère, about 1½ cups white cheddar, and ½ cup Havarti; you can mix and match according to what's in your fridge and which are your favorites—but avoid preshredded)
4 tablespoons unsalted butter, divided
3 tablespoons flour
2 cups whole milk
4 ounces cream cheese, cut into chunks
Several splashes of Tabasco sauce, to taste
2 or 3 slices good-quality bread for bread crumbs
1 pound good-quality short pasta, such as ziti
Meat from the claws and tails of 2 lobsters

Grate the cheeses and set them aside. Melt 3 tablespoons of butter in a large pan over low heat, and stir in the flour to make a roux. Gradually add the milk, stirring constantly until everything is absorbed and the white sauce is beginning to thicken. Stir in the grated cheese, cream cheese, and Tabasco. Whisk until smooth.

Toast the bread, break it into crumbs, add a tablespoon of melted butter, and set aside.

Cook the pasta in boiling water, but for 2 minutes shorter than the package tells you.

Tear or cut the lobster meat into bite-size chunks, and whisk this into the cheese mixture. Stir the white cheese sauce into the pasta. Pour this into a well-greased 9 × 13–inch pan.

Top with the buttered breadcrumbs. Bake at 350 for half an hour until everything is piping hot and the top is starting to brown.

Strawberries and Lime Sponge Cake Wedding Trifle

Martha Hubbard brings this dessert to serve at Hayley and Nathan's wedding reception. She layers the ingredients in individual-sized mason jars, but you could also serve slices of the cake garnished with whipped cream and strawberries. It would also be nice with raspberries or peaches, depending on what's in season.

For the strawberry layer:

2 cups hulled and halved or quartered strawberries
Sprinkle of sugar

For the whipped cream layer:

2 cups whipping cream
2 tablespoons powdered sugar
1 teaspoon vanilla extract

For the cake:

6 large eggs, separated
½ teaspoon cream of tartar
1½ cups sugar, divided
2 teaspoons grated lime rind
¼ cup lime juice
¼ cup water

1¼ cup flour
¼ teaspoon salt

Preheat oven to 325 degrees.

Sprinkle the strawberries with sugar and set aside.

Whip the cream until stiff with the powdered sugar and vanilla. Put this in the refrigerator while you make the cake.

In a large bowl, combine the egg whites with the cream of tartar and beat with an electric mixer until they hold soft peaks. (You can test this by slowly withdrawing the beaters from the eggs. Soft peaks should stand up with the slightest droop at the top.) Next, gradually add ½ cup of the sugar, beating until whites are stiff but not dry.

In another large bowl, place the separated yolks. Beat them with unwashed beaters until thick. Add the remaining sugar, 1 tablespoon at a time, beating until the yolks are very thick and ivory colored.

To the beaten yolks, add the grated lime rind, lime juice, and water, beating until just blended. Beat in the flour and salt at a very low speed. Add the beaten egg whites to this mixture, and fold them in with a rubber spatula—gently.

Turn the cake batter into an ungreased 10-inch tube pan. Cut through the batter several times with a knife to break up any air bubbles and then smooth the top.

Bake at 325 degrees for 50 minutes to an hour. The top of the cake will appear golden and the cake should spring back when lightly touched.

Invert on a wire rack to cool. Loosen cake from the sides of the pan with a spatula. Set on a serving plate.

When the cake is completely cool, cut it into bite-size squares. In small mason jars, alternate squares of cake with strawberries and whipped cream. Refrigerate until it's time to serve.

Acknowledgments

I owe a million thanks to the real Martha Hubbard and Analise Smith for allowing me to use their names in this book, and for feeding me material that helped coax the story to life. As always, murders and criminal behavior are strictly fictional, even if the people and Key West places are real. Thanks also to Eden and Bill Brown for agreeing to become cameos in the book. They have retired from Isle Cook Key West, but Martha Hubbard and Daniel McCurdy will continue and expand their vision.

Thanks as always to my other very real and very wonderful Key West friends, Steve Torrence, Renee Spencer and Chris Fogarty, Leigh Pujado, Ron Augustine aka Lorenzo, Eric and his adorable dogs Chester and Barkley, and Erik, Christie, JanMarie, and Allison from the MCC church. Thanks to Ruth McCarty, Tracy Green, and Tim Hallinan for helping me come up with the Buoys' Club.

Thank you to the folks at Crooked Lane Books for their fabulous editing, artwork, production, and general support of the Key West mysteries. I'm also grateful to my wonderful agent, Paige Wheeler.

Enormous gratitude is due as always to Christine Falcone and Angelo Pompano, who read multiple very rough drafts and helped me shape that mess into a book.

I consider myself so lucky to be part of the mystery writers and readers community. Special thanks are due to my friends and talented writers, the Jungle Red Writers, Hallie Ephron, Hank Ryan, Julia Spencer-Fleming, Rhys Bowen, Deborah Crombie, and Jenn McKinlay. They are my family! Thanks to all my readers—I love you guys—and to bookstores and libraries who carry these books out into the world. And finally, thanks to my precious family at home, especially John.

Read an excerpt from

THE KEY LIME CRIME

the next

KEY WEST FOOD CRITIC MYSTERY

by LUCY BURDETTE

available now in hardcover from
Crooked Lane Books

CROOKED
LANE

NEW YORK

Chapter One

To whom does our island belong? I found myself wondering that as I sat on my scooter in the rain, late for my pricy-but-absolutely-necessary-for-a-person-who-eats-for-a-living personal trainer, attempting to cross a massive traffic jam on Eaton Street. Underneath the beads and the beer and the outdoor burgers and music on Duval Street where the tourists found their "happy place," there was a struggle for ownership. I'd seen this on Instagram and Facebook when I posted something especially beautiful about our little knob of coral. Outsiders craved a piece of paradise as much as the locals—the insiders—wanted them gone.

This week between Christmas and New Year's, Key West was bursting at the seams. Even my general practitioner had confessed he wouldn't leave his condo complex unless going to work; he'd never seen the island this busy. People wouldn't stop for anyone—on a bicycle, walking, on a scooter, in a car. Old folks, children, chickens, residents, visitors—we were all in the cross hairs of holiday-crazed motorists. Already since Monday there had been five accidents, including two couples airlifted to a Miami trauma center, outcomes unknown.

And that pointed to one of the drawbacks of living on a small island and getting sick, with the way to mainland being a four-hour drive to Miami. You could get by fine visiting local doctors with a garden-variety cold or to get a few stitches or an eye exam, but detach a retina or bash your head on the pavement, and you had an expensive helicopter trip to Miami ahead of you.

Because of the congestion, I seemed to be running late for everything. Adding to the chaos of the holiday season, key lime pie aficionado David Sloan had persuaded the city to host his key lime extravaganza and contest this busy week, rather than waiting for the slower summer months, I couldn't avoid the additional madness because my bosses had assigned me to cover the event. Every pie purveyor in Key West (and there were a ton of them) was determined to claim the key lime spotlight—and win the coveted Key Lime Key to the City. My bosses at *Key Zest* magazine wanted me to get a jump on other foodie journalists by reporting on as many pies as possible before the contest even began, along with writing an article about Sloan's contest, not to mention my regularly featured restaurant roundup, this time a review of fast but delicious island options. Call me Hayley Snow, food critic and frantic foodie fanatic.

I dashed through a slight break in the traffic and whizzed across Frances Street, nearly slamming into a golf cart loaded with tourists.

"Even in Key West on vacation, a stop sign is not a suggestion," I hollered.

They waved their beer cans and hooted with laughter.

"Chill, baby," the driver yelled back. "Anger isn't an aphrodisiac."

Idiots.

Several blocks later I noticed blue lights in my rearview mirror. I pulled over to the curb. It had to be Nathan. My new husband, a Key West police detective, was not usually a prankster. But we'd had a little kerfuffle this morning—about nothing important, really—and he'd stormed off mad. He must finally be getting over his annoyance with me and lightening up. I took off my helmet, fluffed my sure-to-be-wayward auburn curls, blotted the skin under my eyes where my mascara had no doubt smudged because I was always in a hurry, and smiled warmly.

But it wasn't Nathan who emerged from the cruiser; it was two police officers I did not know, one tall and lanky with a shaved head, the other shorter, with the smallest smirk on his face. He stood about ten feet away from the tall man and watched him approach my scooter.

"Did you mean for *me* to stop?" I asked, feeling confused and annoyed. I tipped my head back to look him in the eyes—he had to be at least a foot taller than me.

"Yes. Were you aware that you ran through that stop sign without even looking? Do you have a medical reason to be in a hurry?"

How should a person answer a question like that if she isn't nine months pregnant, clutching her contracting belly, or staunching an obvious blood flow? Maybe *Give me the freaking ticket and let's get on with it*?

Nathan would be furious.

"No. I've got nothing. I'm late for the gym. That's the best I can do." I shrugged my shoulders and grinned, trying to communicate that I was admitting to being in the wrong, that I promised never to do this again, and that I hoped we could settle on a warning.

He did not smile in return. "I like going to the gym, too, but this is a matter of safety—your safety and the safety of the people you might have hypothetically mowed down."

That made me mad. And since I hadn't slept well in weeks, it was hard to tamp down a rising head of steam. "What about those lunatics in a golf cart who blew right through the stop sign on Southard and almost laid me out? I assure you, that was not hypothetical."

"I didn't see them run a stop sign, I saw you," he said, his lips and chin setting like hardening cement.

"You didn't see them? Maybe that's your problem right there," I said, sorry almost as soon as the words came out of my mouth.

The cop watching my officer frowned and nodded, his hands now on his hips, near the equipment on his belt.

"License and registration," the rookie cop said.

Chapter Two

"*You can train someone to use a knife, but it's hard to train someone who doesn't have heart,*" the chef Masayoshi Takayama wrote in an email.

— Julia Moskin, "Where the World's Chefs Want to Eat," *The New York Times*, February 25, 2019

On the way back home from the gym, I wrestled with whether to confess the cop stop incident. I decided I had to tell Nathan about the citation, police-speak for ticket, because he'd find out sooner or later. Worst of all would be if the brand-new officer chose to show him the video of our transaction before he'd heard anything about it. As the partying tourist had suggested, anger in general, and angry arguments with the police in particular, were not an aphrodisiac. Nathan abhorred uncooperative citizens who thought they knew better about everything. Best to get ahead of the situation and admit I'd made an error in judgment. And beg him not to look at the damning video.

I zipped over First Street, crossed Route 1, and lurched into the parking lot for Houseboat Row. Seemed like everyone in our little blended family was irritable lately. Even my octogenarian roommate Miss Gloria's usual cheeriness was sagging. Probably the adrenaline that had carried us through Nathan's on-the-job injury and dramatic rescue and slow recovery and the wedding and multiple visiting family members had evaporated, leaving us tired and sore and crabby. The renovations on our houseboat next door to Miss Gloria's place were not yet completed. Our contractor, Chris, had taken the week off to enjoy his family—and who could complain about that? But with Nathan installed in Miss Gloria's adorable houseboat along with two ladies, two cats, one hyperactive dog, and one small bathroom, our home felt tiny and cramped. Like too many rats jammed into a cage, we were beginning to turn on each other.

No one was sleeping well. I knew Nathan was suffering from the aftermath of his injuries, though damned if he'd say so. Evinrude, my gray tiger cat, was incensed about being upstaged by Nathan's dog. And I felt crowded by my brand-new husband. Considering that I'd been married only three weeks, this seemed like an unfortunate time to lose the glow.

As I reached the finger of dock that led to our houseboat, my phone burred. Nathan's name came up on the screen.

"I'm sorry," I said, before he could get a word in edgewise.

"Me too." He chuckled. "Of course, I was calling to apologize if I was a heel in any way, but I had another matter to discuss with you as well. My mother's coming to town."

"That's fabulous!" I said. His mom had declined to attend our wedding, real reasons unknown. I was pretty sure they related to her disappointment over Nathan's divorce and her reluctance to embrace a second daughter-in-law when she'd adored wife number one.

"I am so looking forward to meeting her," I added, though the idea of his mom in Key West scared the pants off me. "Let's get it on the calendar so we don't book anything else that might conflict with her visit. What kinds of things does she like to do? Do you think she'd be interested in a food tour or a cooking class? I can start looking for what's happening in the next couple weeks at the Tennessee Williams and the Waterfront Playhouse and—"

He broke in. "Tomorrow. That's when she's coming."

"Tomorrow?" I gulped. "Where will she be staying?"

"I'm hoping with us."

I could feel my inner harridan rising up, ready to shriek. *Deep breath, Hayley.* "Hmm," I said. "I would adore hosting her, but I can't imagine how that's going to work exactly. Would she find sleeping on the couch acceptable? Or I could sleep on the couch, but that leaves you sleeping with your mom. He-he." No return chuckle from Nathan. "I could call around, see if there might be a room in any of the bed-and-breakfasts in Old Town." Which there wouldn't be—during the week between Christmas and New Year's, even the dodgiest lodging options were full. "Maybe my mother knows someone."

"Sorry about the notice," he said. "She only called this morning. And I couldn't say no."

"Of course not," I said. "She's your mother; apology accepted. We'll figure something out."

"But what were *you* apologizing for?" he asked.

So I had to explain my stop sign transgression and the ensuing citation, babbling longer than I probably should have. "Okay, I did run the stop sign, but I'm certain I looked both ways, and honestly he was more grim than he needed to be. If he had smiled even a little tiny bit, this never would have gone as far as it did. I'm not exactly the kind of criminal they're looking for, right?"

"If you broke the law, they had every reason to stop you. I can review the video of the incident and see if the rookie did something wrong, but it's a little early to be pulling strings—"

"Please don't pull the video. How about those guys giving me the benefit of the doubt? Shouldn't the more experienced cop have known who I was? Everyone knows you just got married, right?"

"So, what, the police department is supposed to let every cute girl with a smart mouth off the hook because she might be my wife?"

"Not funny," I said.

"I don't think it is funny," he said. "Look at it this way. New cops have to learn to follow procedure in every way. If he lets you off for a traffic citation because you're married to me, next time does he let another cop's family member go scot-free after a felony assault? Entitlement can creep in before anyone notices, and then the rot starts in the department."

I couldn't argue with his reasoning. With cops in the news in all kinds of trouble, he took training the new guys very seriously. He wanted them to do their jobs with compassion, gravitas, and the right amount of discipline. And humanity, too. I loved and admired him for that.

"Besides," he added, "this stop may very well have saved your life." I could hear someone rapping impatiently at his door, and his desk phone was ringing, too. "Look," he said. "I'm going to spend the night at my apartment tonight, to pack up my kitchen. I'd love to have you join me, but maybe with my mother coming, we should all get a good night's sleep?"

"Problem solved," I said brightly. "Your mother can stay at the apartment."

"The movers are coming tomorrow to pick up the furniture and put it in storage. So no bed, no couch, no table, nothing." He sighed. "Listen, it's going to be a late night, and if I expect to have any time off at all while my mother is here, I've got to dig in. Four of our incoming reinforcements for New Year's Eve have already canceled, and none of our regulars want to fill in. And why should they? We've had the schedule made out for weeks."

"That sounds so stressful," I said, remembering Miss Gloria's wisdom about calming an agitated husband—show that you understand and appreciate him, even if at that very moment, you don't. "Call me later?"

I hung up and went inside to stretch out on my bed next to my cat. He circled around and wedged himself in the little curve between my neck and the pillow. I had a whirling mixture of feelings— irritation with Nathan for bailing out, embarrassment that I was failing this first test of our relationship. And sadness, too. This evening, I would miss his warmth and the soft sounds of him breathing in the night, and his good-morning kiss. And the way he smiled at me early in the day, before he'd donned his cop armor to face the world, when he wore an expression that said he was the luckiest guy alive.

I flapped my arms and legs like a snow angel. On the other hand, the bed felt gloriously roomy—it wasn't intended for two people full-time, one of them a muscular six-footer. And I hadn't heard Evinrude purr like this in days. Face it, we'd both be relieved to have a night alone. If there was a Guinness world record for shortest marriage ever, I was deeply afraid Nathan and I were in contention.

I buried my face in the cat's striped fur and tried to channel his calm. Purr . . . breath in . . . purr . . .

breath out. After a few minutes, I got up and went out to the kitchen and living area, imagining I was seeing it for the first time as Mrs. Bransford would. The windows were fogged from salt spray, the grout around the sink was trending gray, the flooring at the edges of the kitchen where linoleum met paneling was faded and starting to curl.

It's not that Miss Gloria and I were dirty people, but we weren't the obsessive deep-cleaning types either. The houseboat was funky; that's what Mrs. Bransford would see. And she wouldn't be looking around with eyes rosy from the idea of having added a beloved daughter-in-law to her family. She'd already had her beloved daughter-in-law, and it wasn't me. For whatever reason, Mrs. Bransford had adored Nathan's first wife, and she probably always would. I felt as though nothing I could do to curry her favor would ever be enough—and I hadn't even met the woman.

Twenty phone calls later to all the bed-and-breakfasts I could imagine she might find palatable, I decided the couch was the only choice. My mother called when I was on hands and knees in the bathroom, scrubbing the baseboard behind the toilet.

"What's wrong?" my mother said. "I hear something in your voice."

Which under ordinary circumstances might have annoyed me, because what girl wants her mother sensing her every mood? But she was right in this case—something was wrong, and I needed support. I told her about the police stop and the little argument with Nathan. "He's going to spend tonight at his place to finish his packing. Or so he says," I couldn't help adding. "But that's okay, that's all good; what's more stressful is that his mother is arriving tomorrow. Spur-of-the-moment plans. And I'm late for the opening salvo of this silly key lime extravaganza." I could hear my voice breaking, and I was sure she could too.

"How long is she staying?" my mother asked.

"I didn't even ask. Once he mentioned that he hoped she would stay with us, I kind of lost track of the details because I was so busy freaking out. The place looks cleaner than it ever has, but it's not going to get any bigger no matter how much I scrub. I wondered if Nathan and I could sleep on our boat next door on a blow-up mattress, but we're still in the wall-studs stage with no bathroom and no electricity." The longer I talked, the more desperate I felt.

"That problem is easily solved," she said. "She'll stay with us. We have a perfectly lovely guest room with a private bath—both of which I offered to you and Nathan, remember?—and it will be perfect. You can spend all the time you want over here, and bring her to your place for delicious treats and local color, and when you've had enough, you deliver her back to us."

"This is your busiest—"

"Don't even start on how Sam and I don't have time to entertain a stranger. Almost all the parties

I'm catering this week are low-key. I have most of the prep work done already. I insist. We'll go about our business, and it will be so much fun to get to know her!"

It seemed a little like cheating, foisting her off on my mother. But on the other hand, I felt a heavy weight lifting, as though someone had been holding a boot to my neck and I could breathe again.